RESCUED
BY A
Highlander

KEIRA
MONTCLAIR

Cover Design and Interior format by The Killion Group
http://thekilliongroupinc.com

Thank you.

ALSO AVAILABLE FROM KEIRA MONTCLAIR

CHAPTER ONE

Scotland, the 1200s

Warm fluid meandered down her cheek into the cracked corner of her mouth. Madeline MacDonald caught the blood with her tongue, and the saltiness invaded her senses. She forced herself to stand tall and unflinching as she watched her stepbrother's hand swing in a wide arc before it connected with her other cheek. Steeling herself not to cry out in pain, she stared into his eyes, trying to gauge his mood. Experience had taught her that if she cried out, he enjoyed it more, and the beating would last longer.

The chamber was silent except for the distant sound of a slow, piercing drip off in the distance. Blood pounded through her heart in fear. Her instinct was to run, but she knew there was no escaping Kenneth. Her hand trembled as she reached up to wipe the blood from her face. The touch of her own fingers sent pain rippling through her body, but still she made no sound. Her breathing became faster, more frantic. She needed to stay in control. Closing her eyes, she willed her heart to slow, but to no avail. How long would this beating last? Each time she toughened a bit, so he wouldn't be able to break her so easily today.

A perverse pleasure washed over her stepbrother's face. He was cruel, uncaring man—a fact she had learned all too well since her parents' death two years ago.

He leaned in close to her, grabbing her by the throat. "You will marry him. Do you hear me, bitch? You will not ruin all my plans. You will marry Niles Comming in less than a fortnight. Agreed, Madeline?" Kenneth MacDonald's spittle just missed her face.

In a quick turnabout, he released her and began pacing the chamber. "I could force you. I don't need your approval. I know just the priest to bring here. He would never deny me." Kenneth's head bobbed as he continued to walk back and forth in front of her. "But you have the following of half the clan. I cannot afford any revolt from my guards or the servants. You will do my bidding so as not to upset your clan. Understood?"

Madeline reached down to her core for the effort she needed to shake her head. She would never marry the Comming—the man who had raped her—no matter how her stepbrother threatened her.

"You dare to refuse me again?" Kenneth bellowed.

Yes, just as I have before. I will endure the beatings. They could never be as bad as the humiliation and pain she had endured at the hands of their neighboring laird.

Madeline willed her body to relax. Bones were less likely to break if she was calm. But Kenneth's fist aimed straight for her belly, sending visceral pain exploding through her body. She lost her footing and slammed into the cold stone floor. As her stepbrother's foot shot out toward her middle, she attempted to curl into a ball, but her reflexes were too slow. The pain that shot through her body made the world around her fade to darkness.

Sitting at the dais of the MacDonald keep, Laird Alexander Grant found himself staring at the filth coating the rushes on the floor of the great hall. The place had definitely deteriorated since his last visit. He glanced at his brother, Brodie, as their host, Kenneth MacDonald, barked orders.

"Get us ale, you lazy wench," Kenneth bellowed to a maid as he swatted her behind to motivate her.

"Aye, my laird," she mumbled, hurrying toward the kitchen.

"My apologies, Laird Grant. My stepsister usually handles everything in the kitchens, but she is ill at present. See how lazy the wenches are when she is no' around? My servants are no' worth the food I give them." Kenneth clambered onto the bench at his table, sweeping crumbs and debris onto the floor around them.

Alex checked his annoyance before he spoke. "Laird MacDonald, we do no' mean to be a bother. We will be on our way as soon as we discuss our concerns with you. We are dealing with more and more small attacks and thievery on our lands. There must be new reivers. Have you seen the same here?"

"Nay, no one dares to bother us. My guards are too strong. Reivers, you say?" Kenneth turned his head away as he spoke.

Alex caught a subtle shift in his host's eyes. He assessed his neighboring laird carefully before he spoke. "We have not caught up with them, but rest assured that we will. Summer is the time to call on neighbors, in any case, and it was time for us to visit."

"I cannot help you with your problem. You are welcome to stay the night before you are on your way," Kenneth said.

Brodie spoke quickly, "Nay, there is no need. A drink will be much appreciated before we take our leave. We have much ground to cover before we return to our lands."

Alex's vision wandered around the dirty hall. There were no beautiful tapestries here, and no chairs with cushions. The stench of sour food permeated his nostrils. His sister, Brenna, kept everything spotless in his keep. His hall spoke of the rich Grant clan history. He was proud of the weapons on display, of the craftsmanship evident in the high-back chairs and tables. After seeing this disaster, he would be sure to thank his sister more often for her hard work. Unlike this laird, Alex believed in treating all his clan well. Even the man's dogs stayed far away from him.

Instinct took over as he turned back to face his host. "Nay, Brodie, I will accept the laird's offer. I would like a good night's rest before we continue. Tell the guards we stay one night."

Brodie glared at him, clearly wishing to be away from this place. Alex knew his decision to stay did not make sense, but something was not right here. He could hear his father's words clearly in his mind: *Follow your instincts, son, they will never let you down.*

His instincts told him to stay.

⁓

Madeline attempted to open her eyes. One must've been swollen shut, as it didn't move. She could see well enough to realize she was in her chamber. It was not the beautiful chamber she had resided in while her parents were alive, but the spare, cold chamber her stepbrother had moved her into after their death. Attempting to roll, she groaned as her bruises hit hard wood and sharp pain seared through her midsection. The pallet was no longer filled with soft feathers—he had taken her every comfort. Instantly, her maid, Alice, filled her line of vision.

"Maddie, oh, Maddie, are you all right, my dear?" Alice asked.

Her feeble attempt to follow Alice's nervous movements failed. "Alice, please stay still, my head is pounding enough."

"Oh, Mac and I have been beside ourselves with worry. You may have at least one broken rib, and your eye is swollen shut. Can you see? Tell me he did not blind you. Please, Maddie."

"Alice," Maddie croaked, "I am fine. Mayhap some water, please?"

"Of course." Alice brought a cup to her lips to help her drink. "What shall we do? He will kill you eventually. Would you not be better with Niles Comming? He cannot be as bad as Kenneth. Say yes, please! Agree to the wedding. I cannot bear to lose you. I promised your dear mother I would take care of you."

Painful memories of the large, cruel body of Niles Comming forced their way into her mind. "Nay, I will not marry him. I must find my way to a convent. I will never be able to bear any man's touch." Maddie's eyes closed as she finished the last of the water.

Brodie followed Alex through the corridor to the two chambers they had been given for the night.

"Alex, you must be out of your head. Why stay in this filthy place? I would rather sleep under the stars with our men."

"I don't know why, but something is no' right. We stay. Get some sleep." Alex nodded toward Brodie's door down the corridor before stepping into his own chamber.

After spying the thin straw mattress on the pallet, he sighed. Why was he here? He peered around the chamber. Dust covered almost every surface. Though he removed his sword, he set it next to his bed in case of an attack in the night. He wrinkled his nose at the smell of the stale rushes on the floor. A small knock on the door interrupted his thoughts, and a dark haired woman crept into the room when he bade her to enter.

She curtsied to Alex. "My laird sent me to be at your service this night." She leaned toward him, offering him a view of her ample bosom.

Alex stared at the woman. She had soft curves, and he hadn't been with a woman in a sennight. He should probably accept the gift.

But he could not. The fear in her eyes was too much for him. What a cruel man her laird must be.

"Lass, I will tell your laird that you served me well, but I find I am too tired to see to it."

"Please, I will do anything you ask, but do no' send me back now."

Alex searched her face and found it to be truthful. The lass had chewed her lip hard enough to draw blood.

"See to my brother, lass. I will not send you back to your laird."

"Thank you, thank you." She spun on her heel and rushed out the door.

Alex sat on the pallet, stirring up a cloud of dust. What was wrong with him lately? He used to pay frequent visits to certain women in his village, but he had yet to meet any woman who sparked anything beyond lust. And lust was easily sated. In truth, he wanted a relationship like his parents had enjoyed. They had adored each other. Of late, he was less interested in the meaningless dalliance he used to seek out.

Now that he had lost his father not long ago and officially became laird of his clan, he was too busy to think about finding a partner. He had been betrothed once, but it had left him cold. The woman had not been one of his choosing, so the breakup certainly had not upset him. Maybe he was not meant to be a husband or a father. His father had told him he was born to lead. Would that be enough?

Alex found himself walking toward the door. He entered the corridor and looked in both directions. The parapet, he needed to find the parapet. That was what he needed this night. He knew the cool night air would help clear his head. If he opened enough doors, he was certain he would find the right one.

He headed down the corridor, shaking his head at the giggling sounds he heard from within his brother's chamber. The next chamber was empty. He moved on to the door after that and opened it quietly.

Just as he was about to close it, he froze. The room was dark, but the candle from the corridor lit the side of a woman's face asleep on the bed. Following his instincts once more, he took two more steps into the room, found a nearby candle, and closed the door behind him.

She was asleep on her side. Her gentle curves were visible through the thin blanket that covered her to her chin. He wanted to step closer, but did not dare, lest he wake her. As he inhaled her lavender scent, a strange sense of peace entered him. Her hair fell in soft golden waves over her shoulders. Who was she? Was this the laird's stepsister?

His eyes fell on her full pink lips and he was hard instantly. He ran his eyes down her body again. She had to be the most beautiful woman he had ever seen. He returned his gaze to her face and took note of her porcelain skin and her small pert nose. Her long lashes rested on high cheekbones. But what he noticed next caused his erection to leave him in an instant.

She had been beaten. He stepped closer and brought the candle close enough for him to see the dried blood and swollen bruises on the other side of her face. She was the vision of an angel, and someone had beaten her. Anger raced through his veins, followed fast by protectiveness. He could see some discolorations on the soft, exposed skin of her neck. He reached down, wanting to touch her and comfort her. Wanting to protect her from whoever had done this.

Her eyes flew open, and he was instantly lost in an ocean of blue. Realizing how she would probably interpret his sudden presence in her room, he expected a scream. Instead, she pulled away from him, groaned in pain and whispered, "Nay."

Not wanting to confuse or frighten her, he turned and fled. He found the door to the parapet at the end of the corridor and raced up the stairs.

But neither the view nor the night air brought him any peace. Who was the beautiful woman? And who had hurt her?

He would find out.

CHAPTER TWO

Alex hadn't been able to sleep much. The few times he had been able to doze, a blonde angel had called to him in his dreams, but he had never managed to reach her. He raked his hand over his face as he paced in the great hall, thinking of the beautiful woman he had seen last night. Had he dreamed it? Who would beat a woman so? He had never seen his father raise a hand to his mother, and he had been raised to protect—not hurt—the fairer sex.

Brodie's voice interrupted his thoughts. "We need to get away from here. The keep was never like this when the previous MacDonald laird was in charge."

Alex pulled up short and stared at his younger brother. Should he tell him? He shook his head. Tell him what? He had found an angel who had been grossly beaten? What could two of them do about it, anyway? They only had a few of their own guards outside, and they were in a strange man's keep, surrounded by the laird's own guardsmen. Before he had time to give it more thought, the laird entered from outside.

Alex spoke bluntly. "Laird, you made mention of a stepsister. Is she of age to be married?" He had to ask to settle his mind. After all, who else could it be? He had mentioned his stepsister being ill, and the angel had been shut into a bedroom above the great hall.

"Madeline? Madeline is long in the tooth, unfortunately. She is to wed my neighbor, Niles Comming. Good riddance to her. The Comming will know how to get her to behave. He will take her strong mind and crush it quick, which is as it should be. Her father spoiled her and I cannot wait to get her wed. She is naught but trouble to me."

Alex noticed the servants kept their eyes focused on the floor as their laird spoke. One finally dared to peek at Kenneth behind his back, her eyes seething. Was MacDonald lying about his stepsister? Even if she were as much of a shrew as he claimed, who would give one of their own kin to Niles Comming? The man had a horrific reputation in the Highlands. He was cruel to every woman unfortunate enough to make his acquaintance. Alex pressed the issue further, unable to stop himself.

"Is she fair-haired?" he asked.

"What interest is it to you?" Kenneth asked with narrowed eyes. "You will never set eyes on her. She stays in her chamber unless I allow her out. Don't push me, Laird Grant. Be on your way. I have much business to attend to." And with that, Kenneth turned on his heel and left.

Alex glanced at his brother. It had to be Madeline he had seen, but what could he do about it? Before he could ponder his choices, his brother forced his hand.

"'Tis time to take our leave, brother," Brodie ground out.

Madeline opened one eye and realized it was past dawn. She needed to get out of bed. Pushing herself up on one side, she searched the room. The vision of a dark stranger surfaced in her mind.

"Alice? Alice?" Maddie's anxiety grew at the thought of a strange man being in her room.

"Maddie, I am here. What is it?" Alice asked.

"A man...there was a man right here, someone I did not recognize." Maddie turned her head slowly to allow her one good eye to search the chamber.

"Nay, there is no stranger here. No one has entered your chamber this morn." Alice grabbed Maddie's hand to rub it in comfort.

Madeline crumpled back in her bed. She was exhausted. Could she truly have imagined him? His scent was ingrained in her mind. Horse and pine and something else she didn't recognize.

Perhaps she was going daft from being shut in this room too often. Her eyes closed and she slept.

Madeline dreamed of a large, handsome stranger much like the one she'd thought she'd seen. He reached for her and caressed her cheek. He tried to tell her something, but she could not understand his words. His arms reached for her and pulled her into a warm, comforting embrace.

Wrapping her arms around the strange man, Maddie rested her head on his chest and sighed, letting his warm breath caress her forehead. His gentle touch eased her mind. She was finally safe again—something she had not imagined she'd ever feel with such a big, strong man.

But who was this mystery man?

Alex and Brodie made their way to the stables to retrieve their horses. Alex nodded at the stable master.

"Good day to you, Laird Grant. The name is Mac. Any other way I can be of service to you?" Mac asked as he led his horse to him.

"Nay, Mac." Alex reached for Midnight. He could tell his favorite horse had been treated well by the exuberant way Midnight greeted him.

"Nice piece of horse flesh, Laird."

"Aye, he is. Have you been here long?" Alex raised an eyebrow at the stable master. Perhaps this man could tell him more about his angel. He had to ask.

"Started with the old laird, James MacDonald," Mac said. He lowered his voice. "Naught like the new laird."

Alex stared at the stable master. The man did not seem overly loyal to his master. How much would he be willing to say?

Alex decided to take a chance. "There be a young, yellow-haired lass here?"

"Aye, the old laird's daughter, Madeline." His eyes crinkled in the corners, clearly demonstrating his fondness for the lass. "Sweetest lass in the Highlands, e'en if she was born part English. Her maid be my wife. She came here when the laird brought the English lass, Elizabeth, here to wed. There were none kinder than James and Elizabeth MacDonald, and none fairer than their daughter."

"My sister, Brenna, mentioned her. She remembers Elizabeth visiting our keep long ago with her daughter." Alex ran his hand down Midnight's coat, appreciating how carefully Mac had brushed his horse.

"Is that so?" Mac would have said more, but he was silenced by his laird's sharp entrance.

"Mind your tongue, Mac." Kenneth appeared in their view on his horse. "'Tis time for you to be on your way, Grant. I will not say it again." He turned and brought his crop down hard on his horse's flank and sped away.

Mac whispered, "Things are not the same, sadly."

Alex and Brodie rode out, followed by their guards. A sick feeling in Alex's gut told him he was making a mistake. How could he leave the lass behind? He was a Scottish laird, head of his clan. His people looked to him to do what was right. That should include protecting the innocent.

They also depended on him to protect his clan and their possessions. One of the reasons he was on this journey was to find out who the new marauders were—and stop them. Kidnapping a woman from a neighboring clan would only cause more trouble. He could not endanger his family or his people that way. His father had ensured he knew his obligations. Chasing a beautiful lass was reckless and dangerous. He simply couldn't do it.

Yet he could not erase the blue-eyed beauty from his mind. Mac had said her name was Madeline. Though he knew not how to intervene, he could not let her marry the Comming.

Alex would not allow it. Madeline was his.

A few days later, the Grant brothers began the journey back to their keep. Alex had no more information than he had when he had left, except that he did not trust the MacDonald laird.

After finding a clearing, he motioned to his men to make camp for the night. Several went off in the hopes of finding some fresh meat to roast. Alex stood in the center of the clearing and kneaded the muscles in his neck, attempting to relieve the tension there.

"Brodie, build a fire and I'll find us something to eat." He wandered off into the wilderness with his dagger in hand.

A short time later, he and several men returned with enough rabbits to roast for dinner. Alex tossed one to Brodie to skin.

"They are not much, but they will have to do."

Brodie peered at him. "Alex, something is in your head. What is it?"

Alex motioned for his brother to follow him away from the clearing, not wanting his guardsmen to know his private thoughts.

"Brodie, do you remember the MacDonald lass?"

Brodie smiled. "Aye, the dark-haired one you sent me?"

"Nay!" Alex shouted. "No' her. The laird's stepsister."

"I ne'er saw her. How could I remember her?" Brodie asked.

"Well, I did."

Brodie whistled. "Och, 'tis why you asked those questions about a yellow-haired lass. Why did you no' mention this before?"

"Mayhap because I could not believe my own eyes. She is every bit as fair as the stable master said."

"Brother, if she is still on your mind, that tells me more than aught else you could say." Brodie's face broke out in a big grin. "A lass has finally caught your eye?"

"She caught more than my eye. I opened her chamber door by mistake. She had been beaten."

Brodie's face registered the same shock Alex had endured upon seeing the bruised side of the lass's face. "Beaten? Who would dare beat the laird's stepsister?"

Alex raised one eyebrow as he peered at his brother.

"No' the laird? You think he would beat a woman so?"

"Did you no' notice how he was with the servant girls, Brodie? He hit them. The lass I sent to you lived in fear of him. He must be cruel. He ordered us out because I questioned him about his stepsister. There is something wrong there. I cannot get her from my mind." Alex grabbed at some brush in frustration, collecting the dry materials in his arm before returning to the clearing. It could be used for another fire so they could eat.

"Is that why you have been riding so hard? Trying to banish her from your mind? But what can you do? She is his stepsister, and besides, he claims she is betrothed to another." Brodie fanned the fire, giving his brother a hard look.

"I am tired enough tonight to sleep. We will think on it on the morrow." They finished cooking their meat and ate in silence, but Alex's mind raced with thoughts and worries. He threw the remainder of the rabbit bones over his shoulder and strode to his horse. As he tugged on his extra plaid, two pieces of parchment fluttered to the ground. He bent down to retrieve them. A sick feeling swirled through his gut as he opened one.

Laird Grant,

Laird MacDonald has been beating his stepsister Madeline whenever he sees fit. We fear for her life. Is not right to beat a woman so. She is only eight and ten summers. Afore her death, our lady Elizabeth bade us to call to you for help if we were in need. She sed you were an honorable man. Ples help us.

Mac Dumfrey

Alex read the note and then handed it to his brother.

After he finished reading, Brodie glanced at his brother with one eyebrow raised, "What's on the other?"

Alex answered with his jaw clenched. "A map. Our plans are changing."

CHAPTER THREE

Madeline eased her legs to the side of the bed and sat up slowly.

"How long have I been here, Alice?" she asked her maid, unable to hide a grimace of pain.

"Three days, and you still do not have the strength you need to be getting out of bed!" Alice grumbled as she rounded the bed to help her.

Madeline groaned as she rose to her feet. "I need a warm bath to ease my aches."

After sending a girl for hot water, Alice helped her remove her night rail. Maddie forced back tears as the maid removed the binding from around her ribs and gently probed her multiple bruises. As soon as the girl came with the water, Alice filled the tub with it and sent the other servant away.

"I thought they might have been broken, Madeline, but perhaps they are just bruised," she said once they were alone again. "Even so, bruising a woman's ribs is beyond madness. You need to get away from him," Alice cried out as she helped Madeline into the tub.

"And where will I go?" Maddie sighed as the warmth enveloped her body.

"I know you mean to escape to a convent, lass, but have you thought to ask him to allow you to join one?" Alice's voice softened as she swept Maddie's hair back from her face.

"No. For I know what his answer would be. Kenneth means to marry me to Niles Comming to strengthen his bonds to the man. But I will not do it." Maddie cringed at the thought of what her life would be as the Comming's wife. "I could not suffer through even one night by his side after what he did to me."

Alice's voice grew quiet as she carefully washed her mistress's back. "I fear for your life. In fact, Mac and I asked the laddie you have been schooling to pen a letter for us. Laird Grant and his brother stopped here the other day. Mac hid it in the laird's things before he left."

"You did what?" Madeline cried, lifting herself from the tub and promptly falling back into it as pain lanced through her. "How could you do such a thing, Alice? Kenneth will beat you when he finds out. And who is Laird Grant?"

"Your mother gave me Laird Grant's name before she died. We were to contact him if we ever found ourselves in any trouble. We did not realize he had passed on until his sons came to the keep. Your father believed the old laird to be an honorable man. Do you not remember visiting them when you were a child? You loved to spend time with the old laird's daughters, Brenna and Jennifer. Wee Jennie was just a babe when we were there. The Lord looked down on us by sending the new laird to our keep. That is what I believe. The Grants are good people."

"Aye, I do remember them," she said with a small smile. "Brenna was sweet. It was so nice to have a friend my age. And Jennie was so wee and cute, and she followed her brothers everywhere. But why would you involve them? I don't want anyone getting hurt."

"Someone needs to come to your aid, lass. Mac and I cannot fight Kenneth ourselves, much as we love you. I just pray the laird finds the missive and puts a dagger through Kenneth's cold heart."

"What an awful thing to say," Maddie said, dipping a bit deeper into the warm water of the bath. "I hate Kenneth, but I do not wish him dead. He cannot help his nature. They say his mother was a mean-spirited woman. Mayhap 'tis not his fault he has ended up the same way."

"That does not make it right. He could have chosen to be different. He should have learned the ways of your precious mother. He was around her enough." Alice plaited Madeline's long golden tresses while she finished soaking. Maddie leaned her head back toward Alice, enjoying the soothing ritual.

"And if not, he could learn from your kindness, Maddie. Everyone knows you would never knowingly hurt anyone. But it seems the more kindness you show, the meaner he gets."

"I shall find a way out of this without hurting anyone. Besides, where would I go if I managed to escape Kenneth?" Maddie's voice dropped as she stared into the water. "I have no other kin. Finding an abbey that will accept me is my only alternative to his plans."

Alice's voice trembled as she spoke. "I do not know what to tell you, lass. You know that Kenneth and the Comming will force you to do their bidding if you stay here. Between the two of them, their power is too mighty for us to resist. The Lord needs to help you either to a convent or a more powerful lord's keep. No good will come from you staying. The danger is too great for your fine-boned constitution."

Alice sighed as she brushed the stray curls back from Maddie's face. "You belong with a strong, gentle man and many bairns at your feet. You know you are happiest around the wee ones, and if you join a convent, you will never have a family of your own. But you belong with a good man, Maddie, not the Comming. I hope the Grant laird heeds our message."

Maddie placed her elbow on the side of the tub and leaned her head on her hand. Every night her mother had told her a story at bedtime. She would rub Maddie's back as she spun fantastical stories about fairies and dragons. But the stories changed over time; in the last year of her life, Maddie's mother had always told her stories about a blonde-haired knight who would come to claim her as his bride. Sometimes the story would simply be about the knight arriving to meet her and her family. Other times, he would rescue her from terrible situations.

She sighed as she thought of her troubles. Was her current situation bad enough to warrant being rescued by her knight in shining armor? Oh, how she hoped it was.

"Do you know I have been having dreams?" Maddie asked as she raised her gaze to the only woman she trusted.

"About what, child?"

"A dark-haired man, a stranger. He comes to me and comforts me. He seems familiar, but I have never seen him before. He makes me feel as safe as my da did. But he is not fair like him, and he is much larger." Maddie ran her finger through the water as she thought.

"In my dreams, he touches me. He is so gentle. I think he loves me. But I know it could never come true."

"Why is that, lass?"

A single tear gathered in the corner of Madeline's eye. "Because I could never allow another man to touch me."

Alex and Brodie sat together on a log in a clearing a wee bit away from their men. The peaceful silence of the dawn and Highland forest surrounded them. Crisp morning air always cleared Alex's head. He rubbed the rough stubble on his face as he listened to the rustling of critters through the trees.

"If we ride most of the day, we should make the MacDonald keep by nightfall," he said, "and we can search for the hidden entrance on the map. We shall enter the tunnel a couple of hours after dark. I only hope the tunnel is still functional. If the previous laird is the only one who knew of it, it could be difficult going."

"Most castles have secret tunnels built into them."

"True, but 'tis unusual for them to be secret from the laird himself." Alex stood up, striding over to a patch of mint leaves and grabbing a few to chew on.

Brodie didn't answer right away. He crossed his arms in front of his chest before he spoke. "Alex, are you sure this is what you want to do? You know it could cause a war if MacDonald believes 'tis us."

"Aye, I understand your concern, but I cannot walk away. I saw the bruising around her eye and on her throat."

"Mayhap she fell."

"The missive from the stable master says the laird beats her. How can I walk away from an innocent lass? Someone has to help her."

"Is this what da would have done?" Brodie stared into his eyes.

Alex didn't look away. "Aye, without a doubt. You know our father would not walk away from such a thing. Do you no' remember the night he and our mother sat and talked to the three of us about women and how they should be treated? Our brother knew how serious da was. Robbie ne'er made a joke through the entire conversation. 'Tis near impossible for him."

Brodie chuckled as he looked up at the clear blue sky. "Aye, I do remember. Never have I seen Robbie so serious."

"He knew how important it was to them both for us to take our leadership of Clan Grant seriously."

"You mean your leadership?"

"Nay, da said we are all leaders for the clan, no' just me as laird." Alex rubbed the sleep from his eyes, deep in thought. "Had you seen her, you would not be able to walk away. 'Twas only the fear of starting a clan war that made me leave the keep without her. I could not deliberately start a clash."

"Then why deliberately start a clash now?" Brodie asked with a raised eyebrow. "What has changed?"

"A plea from someone privy to the old laird's business. Clearly, the MacDonald trusted his stable master. If she were my daughter, I would hope someone would help her."

Alex decided to conceal the strongest reason he was going back, because it held no logic at all. A pair of ocean blue eyes had haunted his sleep last night and he would do anything to stop the fear that had gripped them.

His brother sauntered over to his horse, swung his leg up and mounted in less than a second. "Aye, let's do it."

CHAPTER FOUR

Madeline slowly trudged up the hill, returning to the keep after her lessons with the wee ones. How she loved her time with the children. They were always so sunny and bright, always so willing to work hard. She envied them their innocence.

From her vantage point, the keep had the same strong appearance it had always possessed, but nothing was the same once she stepped inside. The powerful stone walls now kept her imprisoned—not protected. She gazed out over the outside walls, wishing her knight were out there somewhere. The sun dropped against the horizon.

Alice had tried to keep her in her chamber, but it dampened her mood to stay in there alone. She needed the young ones to keep her going. Truth was, she did hope for many of her own bairns, but to carry a bairn, she would need to get close to a man. She thought of the few men she remembered from the Grant keep. While she recalled how Brenna and Jennie had loved their brothers, Maddie had never had a good relationship with any men except for her father and Mac, Alice's husband.

If only her parents were still with her. Under their protection, none of this would have happened, but they had been gone two summers. She missed them so much. How she wished she could talk to her mother again just once. Her father had been so kind and gentle. She missed the long afternoons they would spend riding horses and how her mother used to lull her to sleep by brushing her hair before bedtime. Every day had been wonderful back then, but now many of her days were nightmares. She had nowhere to turn, no one to trust but Alice and Mac.

No sense looking back, Madeline thought. She slowed her pace, trying to ease the pain from her bruised ribs. As she reached the keep, she held her breath and glanced around, hoping to avoid Kenneth. She had not seen him since the last beating. Earlier in the day, she had gone to the kitchens to go over the menus with the cook, hoping good food and drink would appease her brother for a time.

She stepped inside the door without seeing him, but before she could feel any relief, she turned toward her chamber and immediately slammed into him.

"Ah, Maddie, how are you feeling today? Better?" Kenneth asked with a grin on his face. "Must be time for another one of our talks, or have you changed your mind about the Comming?" Kenneth leaned in toward her, coldness deep in his eyes.

"Nay, Kenneth, I have not changed my mind. I will not wed him."

Kenneth grabbed her arm and pulled. "You will do as I say, Madeline, and if I have to beat you until you cannot walk, I will," he ground out, pinching and twisting the tender skin on the inside of her upper arm. Madeline bowed her head to draw the strength not to scream. All had gone quiet in the great hall, and warriors and servants alike had turned their heads away, not wanting to witness the cruelty Kenneth was inflicting on their beloved Madeline.

"Do not go far tonight, Madeline, I think we need to talk again." Kenneth's lips curved into a smile as he roughly let her go. "As always, I look forward to it!"

Madeline turned and proceeded toward the stairs, making sure to pause and greet each servant she passed. He could beat her all he wanted. She would not do his bidding. When she reached her room, she slipped quietly inside and lowered herself to the bed.

Only then did she let the tears flow.

What recourse did she have, after all? Her parents had taught her to respect her elders. But try as she might, she could not please Kenneth. His harsh treatment of her had started way before the Comming had asked for her hand. She did not understand it.

Her father had never raised his hand to any woman. Why was Kenneth so vicious? Was it the usual way of the world? Did most men treat women callously? After all, the Comming was no better than Kenneth, and she had noticed peasants slapping their wives on occasion. Thoughts of her knight in armor danced through her head. But would such a man beat her into submission as well?

Mayhap her mother and father had protected her from the cruelties of the real world. If that were true, she wasn't certain she wanted to be part of that world. At least she would be protected from such ugliness if she joined a convent, and according to her mother, orphaned children abounded in such places. Perhaps she could care for them as her life's vocation. Their innocence and trust needed to be protected.

She needed a plan. Somehow, she had to get away.

Help me, Papa, help me.

According to the map, the secret passageway started in a cave in the woods and led deep into the MacDonald keep. Alex and Brodie tied their horses in a small clearing not far from the place indicated on the map. They had left his guards a distance away to watch for anyone's approach. They crept quietly through the trees, surveying the area for signs of the entrance, speaking little as they searched diligently through the forest. Alex crinkled the map in his hand, uncertain how far they were from the MacDonald castle, and stared into the dark night lit only by a wee moon visible through the trees. The black soot he wore on his face for protection itched, but he refrained from rubbing it off.

"Here, Alex!" Brodie called out.

As Alex reached his brother, Brodie started to tear at overgrown branches and vines. "I think this is it."

"This map had best be accurate," Alex said as he climbed through the brambles and peered into the darkness. He and his brother yanked on the old wooden door. Rusted hinges creaked as they tugged. The door finally gave way and they crept inside, lighting a torch to see what they could discover about the passageway. After they removed massive amounts of cobwebs, a tunnel beckoned in the dark off to the left. Alex's heart pounded fast in his chest. The sounds of running critters echoed throughout the cavern. As they carefully made their way, intent on their mission, neither of them spoke. Bristles of the unknown crept up the back of Alex's neck, forcing a shudder. But visions of the bruises on Madeline's porcelain skin propelled him onward.

When they reached a split in the tunnel, Alex checked the map under the torchlight. Following the fork to the left, they inched along until they were close enough to pick up sounds from inside the castle. But while they could distinguish voices, they could not make out any words. Alex motioned for Brodie to stop.

Madeline relaxed in her chamber, trying to rest even though she knew it was only a matter of time before Kenneth came looking for her. No matter how many times he hurt her, she vowed to remain strong.

"Do not get up, lass," Alice said as she patted Madeline's shoulder. "That nasty man is looking for you again. I think we can keep him away for a few more days if you stay abed." A knock sounded on the door. Egan, Kenneth's second in command, yelled out, "Bring me the lass!"

"Stay there, Madeline, I will send him away," Alice whispered.

Madeline climbed out of bed and grabbed Alice's hands. "It is no use. I will go with him. Kenneth's rage only increases if he's made to wait."

"But you will be stronger in a few days. Don't go with him yet. Who knows what he will do to you this time?" Alice sounded almost frantic.

"I am coming, Egan." Madeline turned and lifted her chin. "I will be fine, Alice. I must do as my stepbrother bids me."

Madeline followed the hulking brute down the dark hallway and the stairway that led to Kenneth's command room off the great hall. Egan shoved the door open when they arrived. Sidestepping the disgusting man, she strode into the room, her shoulders back and her head held high. Her eyes met her stepbrother's with conviction. She would not give him the pleasure of seeing her fear.

Kenneth stood behind a large table covered with various tools. She had been whipped before, but she had never seen some of those tools. Long ones, short ones, pokers, dirty ones, tools that turned her stomach just to look at them. She had no idea how they were to be used. Raising her gaze to meet her stepbrother's, she saw the rage and the madness boiling inside him. Madeline sucked in her breath as she stared down at the table once more.

"Well, what say you, Maddie? Are you ready to marry the Comming?" he asked as he picked up a horsewhip from the table.

Maddie thought very hard before answering. She had never told him about the rape. Mayhap if she did, he would allow her to stay. But Kenneth never had any interest in her feelings or her happiness. He seemed to care for nothing and no one. His horses all had marks on their flanks from frequent whippings. He kicked any dog that got in his way. And he had no more regard for people than he did for animals.

He had not always been this way. Their father had been able to control him. But no one had been able to reach him since her parents' death. His twisted actions were escalating. She was sure Kenneth would not offer her any compassion, regardless of circumstances. Telling him about the Comming would only give him another reason to humiliate her. Nay, she would not allow Kenneth that pleasure. Sweat broke out on her forehead as Kenneth caressed the horsewhip. But she refused to cower before him. She would remain strong. "Nay, Kenneth, I will not marry him," she said, daring to lock eyes with him.

Kenneth's grin grew as he peered over the table. "We will see how long it will take for you to change your mind. The Comming will be here in a few days with a priest, and you *will* marry him. You will not leave this room until you agree. 'Tis up to you how much pain you withstand. Egan, get another guardsman in here immediately."

Egan left the room quickly. Kenneth smirked at her, probably hoping she would beg for mercy once they were alone together, but she refused to relent. When Egan returned with another guard named Iain, the men immediately moved to either side of Maddie. Their nearness made her tremble with fear. She could handle the beatings, but what else did Kenneth have planned for her? Her stomach turned as she thought of the many possibilities.

Why did he do this to her? Madeline closed her eyes to draw strength from within. A quiet prayer echoed through her bones. *Please, God, let it be quick.* Truth was, she didn't know how much more she could endure. Her mind retained its strength and quickness, but her pain tolerance had been overloaded of late. A brief vision of the man from her dreams—her knight— entered her thoughts, but it left quickly, chased away by the sound of a metallic clink in front of her. Her eyes flew open.

Kenneth picked up a long tool with a sharp point and arranged it so that the end was sitting in the fire. He picked up the horsewhip and said to Iain and Egan, "Hold her tight." Then he stepped behind her and tore the back of her gown so that it fell below her waist. As he snapped the whip on the floor twice, Madeline felt her legs start to give way. When he raised his arm to bring the first stroke of the whip across her back, Maddie glanced over her shoulder in time to see his smile.

Alex and Brodie held completely still. Alex thought he heard the swish of a whip, but it was difficult to discern where the sound originated. He listened again, then followed the secret passageway in the correct direction. As they approached the source of the sound, they could hear the whip connecting with flesh, but naught else.

Brodie whispered, "It cannot be a lass, or we would hear screaming or sobbing."

Alex crept forward and motioned for Brodie to be silent. A slice of light peeked out near the stones on the left. Inching across the floor silently, he made his way close enough to take stock of the situation inside the chamber. His whole body tensed as he realized what was happening. Madeline was facing him, he thought restrained by two men, though it was difficult to tell through the small opening. Her head was down, so Alex couldn't see her expression, but he had a partial view of Kenneth standing behind her with a whip in his hand.

Alex stilled as his whole world went into slow motion. Kenneth raised the whip over his head with a sneer. He swore he saw the bastard smile as the whip tore into his stepsister's flesh. She made no sound at the contact. Kenneth set the whip down and grabbed her by the hair, "Do you agree, Maddie?"

Slowly, Maddie opened her eyes. Her lashes fluttered, revealing the blue eyes that had been haunting Alex's dreams. He had trouble focusing. Tears trickled down her face, and her blonde hair curled from the sweat on her brow. She never made a sound, but as her chin came up, fire sparked in her eyes. "Nay," she said.

It took every ounce of control Alex possessed to prevent him from doing something foolish. He turned to Brodie, who glanced at him and mouthed, "Is it her?" Alex nodded and searched the tunnel for a doorway.

At the same time, two guards rushed into the chamber yelling,

"Laird, there's trouble! Fire in the cottages!"

Kenneth turned to Maddie and said, "We will finish this later." Glancing at Egan and Iain, he said, "Leave her." And with that, they rushed into the great hall and out the doors into the courtyard.

Maddie reached for the table for support. She wanted to scream as fire tore through her back where the whip had connected with her tender flesh. She needed to get away and soon. How much more could she endure? Her gaze ran over the tools on the table. This could have been much, much worse. Before she turned to leave, she ran her arm across the table, flinging the various paraphernalia onto the floor.

Her head jerked up in surprise as a man rushed through a hidden door in the wall and caught her by the arms. Maddie shoved against him and whimpered, "Nay!" But she wasn't strong enough to fight the muscular arms that gripped hers.

"Leave me be, please! Who are you? Go away." Maddie stared into steel gray eyes, shaking her head in denial. She knew her will was dissolving, but she had to fight this new threat. Where had he come from? Who was he? But then she realized she recognized him from her dreams. She had seen his kind face there.

He lifted her into his arms and carried her back into the tunnel. She pushed against his chest, but her hands met rock. Tears fell as she realized she had once again been overpowered by a man. This man seemed different, but that did not make the situation any more welcome.

As she continued to squirm, he said to her, "Madeline, I am Alexander Grant from Dulnain Valley. I will not hurt you. Mac asked for my help. My brother and I will keep you safe. Trust me!"

His eyes reached into her soul, begging her to heed his words. Trust him? A man other than her father? Other than Mac? Was such a thing possible? But this was the man from her dreams... She realized her fingers were digging into his shoulders, so she forced herself to relax.

Madeline searched his face, but she could not see through the dirt on his face and the darkness of the tunnel. He had a strong chiseled jaw, long, dark hair, and an intense gaze. Her arm wrapped around his neck and brushed the soft locks. When she touched the skin on his neck, she jerked her hand away as if it had been burned.

So this was Brenna's brother? He stirred strange feelings in her belly. He was talking to her, but she couldn't understand him. Her head leaned against his shoulder. She was having trouble focusing. All she could feel was the pain in her back and a pair of strong arms supporting her. They continued down a dark corridor, but she knew not where they were headed. She decided to trust him. At least for now.

Resting her head against him, she asked, "Are you my knight? No, you cannot be. You are not blonde." He smelled familiar, of pine, horse and leather, not at all like the stench that came from her stepbrother's guards. The man radiated heat, so she wrapped both her arms around his neck and closed her eyes, his breath warm against her forehead. "I will come with you, Laird Grant, but only for a bit," she whispered against his chest.

Alex pulled Maddie tightly to him. He looked down at her angelic face and immediately lost track of his thoughts, distracted by her full pink lips as she sighed. How would they taste?

What was happening to him? Why couldn't he just focus on the task at hand? She let out another little sigh and reached up to run her fingers through his hair. Alex brushed a quick kiss on her forehead and forced himself to keep moving.

At the end of the tunnel, Brodie went ahead to make sure all was safe. As soon as he got the clear sign, Alex carried a sleeping Madeline to his horse. Whether she was asleep or passed out from pain, he did not know. He set her on her side on the ground as they readied the horses and she never once moved.

When he picked her up, she awoke briefly and said, "Where are you taking me?"

"Away, my lady, to a safe place," Brodie answered. He nodded at Alex, a grin on his face, "I'll carry her while I ride. She is a bonnie lass."

Alex gave his brother a hard look.

"She rides with me," he growled.

CHAPTER FIVE

Alex and Brodie caught up with the guardsmen and rode furiously for several hours. Madeline slept with an occasional squirm in the saddle. Alex kept her leaning on her side to protect her wounded back. She was dead to the world. Her pain tolerance had to be incredibly high. He had pulled the back of her gown up to protect her skin, but blood had seeped through the rough material. His mother would never have allowed such tender skin to be clothed with coarse threads. She belonged in only the finest garments.

Maddie's ability to sleep while riding with open wounds told him how exhausted she must be. He had no idea how many lashes she had endured, but even one was too many. How could her own kin treat her in such a heartless manner? Alex's jaw clenched every time he thought of Kenneth MacDonald.

He glanced at her face as she slumbered. Bruises, whippings, what more had she been forced to endure from her own stepbrother? Clearly, the man did not respect his own kin. She looked so innocent, so bonnie. He vaguely remembered the MacDonald family visiting them a number of years ago. His wee sister, Jennie, had clung to Madeline. Alex recalled a thin, quiet girl with yellow hair. The endless legs and the pale golden hair were the same, but much had changed in between. Gone was the awkwardness of the young girl he remembered—the softness brushing against him now was all woman. Her curves felt wonderful in his arms, as if she belonged there.

They rode off the path into the forest, seeking a stream. It was still dark, but it was time to wake Madeline and cleanse her wounds. The horses needed watering and he hoped to eat something before they continued their journey to his keep. He did not think they were being followed, and they were now far away from the regular path.

After they halted, Brodie got off his horse and reached for Madeline. She awoke with a start, and after a quick glance around, fear crept into her eyes. "Put me down," she snapped at Brodie.

"As you wish, my lady," Brodie replied as he lowered her to the ground.

"Where am I?" she asked, staring up at Alex and Brodie and their guardsman, who had gathered around the clearing.

Alex motioned for Brodie to back away. "We are but half a day away from your stepbrother's keep. You do not remember last night?"

Maddie shook her head. "I recall going to see my stepbrother." She winced as she turned away from Alex. "My back!" she exclaimed. She stared at him as her memory filled in the missing pieces. "You took me into a tunnel off Kenneth's chamber. Who are you?"

"As I told you last night, my lady, I am Laird Alexander Grant and this is my brother, Brodie. We received a missive from your stable master saying your life was in danger. We are trying to help you escape your stepbrother."

Maddie shook her head in disbelief. "Truth? I am away from my stepbrother? You will not return me to him?"

"Nay, he will never touch you again. I promise you that, my lady." Alex reached up to brush a leaf from her hair. He wanted to do more, to wrap his arms around her and hold her tight, but he was sure she would bolt if he did such a thing. Caution ruled her every movement, and for good reason.

She bowed her head slightly toward him. "Forgive my manners, Laird Grant. I thank you for rescuing me from my stepbrother's hands. I don't know if he would have stopped this time. But where are you taking me?"

"I think it best to return to our keep for the moment. My sister, Brenna, is a healer, and she can help you with your injuries. 'Tis all we need to decide for now," Alex stated. "I think it best we wash your wounds so they do not fester, my lady. There is a stream nearby you may use."

She nodded, so Alex led her to the stream. "You have much

dried blood on your back. Do you wish my assistance? You have my word that I will act honorably."

The lady stepped away from him, staring at him with eyes so blue they almost took his breath away. "Nay. I thank you, but I can manage. If you will allow me some privacy, please? Send your men in the other direction?" Madeline stood by the water with her chin held high.

The lady did have spirit, which he admired. Most lasses in her situation would be sobbing uncontrollably.

"If you need anything, my lady, please ask. I will not be far. Here is a sliver of soap you may use." Alex turned and walked back to the clearing where the others waited. He kept his back toward the river—and insisted that the others do the same—but he still heard Madeline's pained gasp as she entered the water.

Maddie removed her dirty gown and stepped into the stream. The water was brisk but bearable. She lowered herself slowly into the water, crying out a little from the way it burned the angry, raw skin. She finally managed to get her upper body in the water, but her thin chemise still clung to her back. After several attempts to free it from her wounds, she realized it was probably stuck. If she didn't get it cleaned soon, she feared it would fester.

Tears gathered in her lashes, but she held strong. She really didn't know any of these men. Should she really put this much trust in them?

They certainly were handsome, especially the one called Alexander. When she'd first seen him, she'd thought he was the man in her dreams, but now she wasn't so sure. Was he named after their king? Somehow, that seemed appropriate. Whenever he glanced her way, she felt unnerved. Her father had kept her sheltered and protected, so she was unaccustomed to strangers, but she still felt it was not normal to feel this unsettled by an attractive man's gaze. It wasn't just his face, but his size—Alex was a large, powerful man. Yet she knew—without quite understanding *why* she knew—that he was an honorable man.

There was too much information for her to think about presently. Truth be known, she was glad to be away from her stepbrother, but Alice would worry about her. Mac had sent Laird Grant a missive. She only hoped her maid would guess she was with the Grant brothers.

"Laird," she called out. "How long will it be until we will arrive at your keep?"

Alex appeared at the edge of the stream, his presence taking her off-guard again. She stared at him until she recalled where she was at the moment. "Turn around, please! I am only in my shift," Maddie shouted.

"Your pardon, my lady," Alex said as he obliged. "We have a day or two travel ahead yet."

Madeline sighed with resignation. She looked at the tall highlander, his back to her. She wished there was another woman to call upon for help, but she had no choice except to trust him in this, too.

"Laird Grant, I need help getting the fabric out of my wounds. Will you assist me?"

"Of course, but you may prefer to turn your back to me. I will need to doff my plaid. I only have an extra tunic with me, and cannot soak all of my clothes." She watched Alex strip off his boots and quickly turned before he tossed aside his plaid. There was a splash as he hit the water, and then she could sense him surfacing directly behind her. She trembled beneath the water.

"Lass, I will try my best no' to hurt you," he said softly. As he pulled on the material, she winced. "I am afraid this will hurt a bit," he whispered.

Maddie braced herself and said, "Go ahead. Be done with it."

Alex worked carefully to free the material from the dried blood. His hands were so gentle, Madeline could not stop herself from sneaking a peek at the tall laird from over her shoulder. He was even more handsome now that he had washed the black soot off his face. He had the broadest shoulders she had ever seen, and his torso was all muscle. She unconsciously licked her lips as her eyes caressed his bronzed skin.

When he caught her staring, she blushed and snapped her head back around. He continued to work carefully on her back, his warm breath washing across her neck. She jumped as he freed part of the cloth from her lash marks. Suddenly it occurred to her that he might think she had done something horrible to warrant such treatment from her own kin.

"My stepbrother is demanding that I marry Niles Comming,"

she offered quietly.

"And this was his way of forcing you?" Alex asked. "Niles Comming is known for treating women poorly. While you should not normally refuse your laird, you were wise to say nay." When he finished pulling the chemise free, he said, "Hand me the bit of soap, lass, and I will wash your back."

Madeline handed him the soap and bit her lip as she waited for the pain. But his touch was so gentle, his ministrations only burned a bit. He washed her entire back, and she melted beneath his touch. A soft moan escaped her lips.

His gruff voice pulled her back to reality. "I think 'tis done, lass. I will leave you to finish now."

"Thank you, Laird," Maddie said as he turned away.

She finished bathing as quickly as possible and returned to the bank. Holding the ruined gown in her hands, she sighed. Another gown ruined, but it was the best she had for now. She managed to tie the back enough to make it decent.

Maddie returned to the clearing with her wet, ripped gown. She tugged on the sides in an attempt to prevent it from clinging to her, but she caught most of the men staring at her, including Alex and his brother. Alex made a barking noise and his guardsmen all turned away. She blushed and bowed her head, realizing what they must think of her threadbare clothing. When she returned her gaze to Alex, she noticed his face had turned dark and his lips were pressed into a grim line. He abruptly stepped away from her and busied himself with his horse. What had she done to make him so angry? She noticed the laird's brother was looking away from her, too, his attention focused on the rabbit he was roasting over the fire. What was wrong with them?

"Come have something to eat, lass." Brodie waved her to the log next to him.

Madeline balanced herself on the far end of the log and reached for some of the meat Brodie tore off for her. She did not wish to offend him, but she could not sit next to him. Her stomach growled at the sight of the roasted meat. She bit into it, blushing as juice trickled down her chin. The tasty morsel was better than anything she had eaten in a sennight. The heat of the fire washed over her, warming her wet gown. She shivered as she thought of her circumstances.

Alex dropped down next to her on the log. Instant sweat beaded on her forehead as his scent reached her nostrils, and a swarm of butterflies fluttered in her belly. Why did he have to sit right next to her? She didn't want him so close, but how could she remove herself without being rude? If he reached his hand out, he could grab her or hit her. She swallowed a lump in her throat, forcing her eyes away from him.

She was familiar with the anxiety that overcame her when men were near, but this strange feeling in her stomach, this extra pounding in her veins—this was all new to her. Why was he different? Abruptly she stood. She grabbed another piece of meat to cover her awkwardness as she wandered over to a log on the other side of the fire. Her brow furrowed as Brodie glanced at his brother, a teasing grin curving his lips.

"I do not bite, lass," Alex said as he tore into a piece of rabbit meat.

"At least not you, lass," Brodie added with a chuckle as Alex continued to rip through his food.

"Forgive me, Laird, but the smoke bothered me," Madeline said, lowering her eyes. She needed to change the subject quickly. "When do we move on?"

"Right now," Alex stated as he jumped up. "Brodie, take care of the fire and get ready to move. We cannot wait around in case MacDonald has sent men after us."

"Mayhap I should ride with Brodie this time, Laird. I do not wish to be a burden to you." Maddie glanced from one brother to the other, sweat breaking out on her face again as she thought of having to be so close to one of them. At least Brodie did not appear to be angry with her. He always had a smile on his face. Truth was, Alex frightened her, especially these strange feelings he brought out in her. Perhaps his brother would be safer.

"Whatever you wish, my lady." But there was a strange tone in his voice. Could it be disappointment?

Once they had cleared the site and retrieved all their belongings, Maddie waited patiently by Brodie's horse. Alex finally strode over, lifted her as if she were a feather, and placed her in front of his brother.

"Be careful, Brodie," Alex ground out before he turned.

"What did he mean by that, Brodie? I won't break," Maddie

whispered.

Alex barked loud enough to startle her. "It means I am watching my brother, not you, my lady."

They rode hard all day, stopping only to water the horses and to take care of their own needs. Madeline tried her best to sit up straight and not rub her back against Brodie. The frequent jarring up and down in the saddle gave her a sore bottom. While she prided herself as being a good horsewoman, she had never ridden this much or this far. She did not know which hurt more at the end of the day, her back or her bottom.

When darkness started to fall again, Alex found a small clearing where they could spend the night. Madeline was eager to stop— owing to the constant pain, she had been unable to sleep at all in the saddle.

Alex helped her down, holding on to her when her knees buckled. She tried to push him away, but he would not budge.

"Be patient, lass. You have been in the saddle too long. The strength in your legs will return."

His grip loosened eventually. He could not understand how stressful being close to him was for her. It made her think of the other big man she knew, and what they had done to her...and it also frightened her in a different way. In a giddy, strange way that made her feel as if she were in danger of losing what little control she had.

The guardsmen rushed off into the forest while Alex found a place for her to sit. He removed a hunk of cheese and some dried beef from his bag. "This will have to do for tonight," he said to her. "Take care of your needs first and then we will eat."

Alex waited in the center of the clearing until Madeline returned.

He put an extra plaid on the ground for her before passing the beef and cheese around. They ate in silence. Exhaustion caused her head to drop occasionally, but she knew she needed to keep her strength up. She was not sure why he pushed them so much, but she had to believe it was done in an effort to guarantee her safety. Alex probably wouldn't relax until they were on Grant land.

"You need to get some rest, my lady, as we will not be staying here long," Alex said. "We need to keep moving."

Alex settled down on the ground not far from Madeline. He turned his back to her and promptly fell asleep. Brodie was quite a distance away, and the guardsmen were on the other side of the clearing. Madeline settled herself on the soft wool and tried to sleep.

Niles Comming crept into her thoughts. She remembered being tied to the bed, watching as Niles stroked himself, listening as he told her about all the things he would do to her once they were married. Squeezing her eyes together did nothing to forestall the unwelcome images. She jumped up off the plaid in a cold sweat, her breath coming hard, and started pacing. Finally, she picked up the plaid to move it farther away from Alex. She glanced at him.

Alex did not seem to be the type of lad who would attack her in her sleep, but how could she be sure? Weren't all lads the same as Niles? She glanced over to where Brodie slept, wondering which one of the brothers she could trust. Would either one help her if the other groped her in the dark? Probably not—they were family. She finally dropped the plaid about halfway between the Grants. She lay back down and tried to sleep, but found it nearly impossible.

Alex opened his eyes as he sensed movement in the clearing. He watched as Madeline moved her plaid away from him and closer to Brodie. Did she really dislike him that much? But then he saw the raw fear in her eyes. He ached to haul her up against him and soothe her, but he knew that would only make her more afraid. He reminded himself she had a reason to distrust men. Patience was key.

Did she prefer Brodie? He could not bear the thought. He had never wanted a lass more than he had wanted her when she appeared in front of him with her wet gown clinging to her, yellow curls in disarray all around her face. He'd turned away quickly in the hopes that she hadn't noticed his plaid at full attention. Saints above, he needed to get himself under control. He doubted she had noticed. She was probably bewildered from all the stress and trauma of the past few weeks. He closed his eyes and fell asleep with the vision of a golden haired, blue-eyed angel in his mind.

A few hours later, he was awakened by a scream. He jumped up, his dirk in his hand, only to see Madeline thrashing on the ground. "My lady, what is it?" he shouted. Brodie leapt up as well, scanning the clearing for intruders.

Madeline sat up abruptly and frantically looked around. The tension visibly eased from her body, and she let out a deep sigh. Alex decided she must have been dreaming. She stood and hung her head. "I apologize. I must have had a nightmare. Please forgive me."

She was magnificent even in the middle of the night with her hair mussed about her face. His heart went out to the poor lass. She would probably have nightmares for a while. His head ached from the memory of her brother poised behind her with that whip. He glanced around the clearing and said, "Let's take our leave now. We need to get home soon."

She picked up his plaid and handed it to him. After thanking him, she stumbled over to Brodie's horse. She clearly had not slept much in the past few hours.

Alex climbed onto his horse and held his hand out to her. "You will be riding with me the rest of the way, lass." He noticed the dark circles under her eyes and cursed himself for pushing her so hard, for not stopping for the night, but there was no choice. They needed to get away from her brother. He lifted her onto his horse, then placed his soft plaid between them to help cushion her wounds. "This should help." He settled her back against him and pulled on the reins of his horse, whispering in her ear, "Close your eyes, I will not let anything happen to you."

Maddie leaned against Alex and heaved out a sigh that shot straight to his heart. They didn't travel far before he could tell she'd finally relaxed enough to fall asleep. He could feel her even breathing against his chest, a rhythm that settled him for some reason, something that made him incredibly happy to just be sharing this time with her and feel her trust.

He knew she didn't give her trust easily, which made it even more special.

CHAPTER SIX

Maddie gazed over the fields ahead to a huge castle, stunned by the size of it. The stone structure sat atop a small hill, a tower gracing each corner of the main building. Battlements connected the towers, and she could just barely make out warriors pacing the walkway.

There appeared to be both an inner and an outer bailey. Surrounding the outer bailey was another wall to protect the castle's residents. The defenses were strong. She would be safe at Alex's keep, and more to the point, she would *feel* safe, something that hadn't happened for a long time. If Kenneth or the Comming came for her, they would not get to her easily.

The beauty of the land surrounding Alex's home took her breath away. The keep sat in the middle of a large valley, and a small river would its way through the trees that surrounded it. Forests of pine and oak trees flourished in the periphery of the valley. Carefully tended fields were tucked between the forest and the keep walls. A small tranquil loch was nestled beyond the fields to the left, next to a field of heather.

Alex's breath warmed her neck.

"What do you think, my lady?" he whispered.

"Laird, it is beautiful. How pleased you must be to have such a magnificent fortress." She sighed as she turned to gaze into his eyes. "It is not at all like my home."

Alex drew her closer, and without quite understanding why, Maddie rested her hands on his arm. They rode the rest of the way in silence, but the gentle intimacy between her and the laird filled her with a sense of longing. She felt no desire to flinch away from him, and serenity enveloped in her soul for the first time in two years.

There were a number of thatched cottages both inside and outside the keep walls. People came out of their cottages to greet them as they passed, sending curious looks her way. As they approached the outside wall, a horn sounded and the heavy iron portcullis rose for their entrance. Madeline's nerves were rough edged. She was uncertain how she would be received. Would Brenna and Jennie remember her? Would they welcome her?

Dusk descended as they rode their horses into the outer bailey. Alex rode next to Brodie, and he slid off his horse once they were inside. He reached for Madeline and slid her down his body very slowly. Her first instinct was to push him away, but she was beginning to trust this man. *He probably did that to keep from hurting me*, Madeline thought. His hands lingered at her waist, supporting her until her strength returned.

"Careful, lass," Alex whispered. "You have been in the saddle for a while."

"Thank you, but I am fine," she said as she straightened, their closeness lost.

Alex tossed the reins to the stable boy, took Maddie by the elbow, and started toward the keep. Two women raced toward them from the steps of the keep. It could only be Brenna and Jennie.

"Maddie!" shouted the younger of the two as her wee legs carried her straight into Maddie's arms. Alex's little sister Jennie embraced her hard enough to make her legs wobble.

"Be careful, Jennie!" Alex yelled.

Every face in the vicinity turned to stare at him.

Maddie recovered quickly. "It's all right, Laird Grant. She is excited—and so am I. 'Tis wonderful to see my old friends."

Brenna's face broke into a warm smile "What a surprise, Maddie! We were not expecting you."

Maddie turned to look at her with tears in her eyes. "I am very grateful your brothers came for me when they did." She leaned over to embrace her friend.

"You know we are happy to see you, Maddie, but has something happened?" Brenna whispered in her ear. "Is that why you are here?" She lowered a comforting hand on to Maddie's back, causing her to cringe away in pain.

Alex reached over to move his sister's hand. "It has been a long ride for Lady Madeline. She needs tending. Please take her upstairs and see to her wounds while Brodie and I fetch some food."

"Oh dear! Forgive me, Maddie. We will go to my chamber. I think we have much to talk about."

Once they were all inside the great hall, Brenna quickly located her maid. "Fiona, please prepare a bath in my chamber and send a platter of food up with Jennie." She steered Maddie toward the stairs and motioned for her sister to go with Fiona.

Alex's voice followed them. "She is to be in the chamber next to mine, please."

If it were any other man, she would not be happy with the laird's statement, but for some odd reason, this pleased her. She'd be safe with Alex Grant nearby.

But Maddie had to admit, there was more to it than safety.

Alex and Brodie headed for the dais and grabbed tankards of ale. Their brother burst into the room moments later and joined them.

"Well met!" Robbie exclaimed. "I hear you have brought a lass with you. What happened? Was there trouble with the reivers?"

Alex relayed the details to Robbie, ensuring he missed nothing. The brothers were all close in age—Alex was eight and twenty summers, Robbie six and twenty, and Brodie five and twenty—so they shared an especially close relationship. Alex valued both of their opinions, and he considered himself lucky to have his brothers living with him.

Brodie shook his head, "I don't know how a man could treat a woman so, Robbie, when we caught Kenneth MacDonald whipping the lass. Fortunately, he and his guards were called out of the chamber, or it would have been the two of us against the three of them. Alex's thoughts were murderous when he saw what they were doing with the lass."

Brodie and Robbie both turned to Alex for his response. "'Twas their good fortune to be called out of the room, else they would be dead now. Aye, I would like to put my sword through Kenneth's heart, and I will not hesitate to act when I see him again."

The three brothers sat at the table as the serving maids brought in trenchers of stew and dark bread.

"When do you suspect that will be?" asked Robbie. "Were there witnesses? Were you followed?"

"I do not think they saw us," Alex said as he speared the meat in the trencher. "I do not wish to bring danger upon our clan, but that man is a menace. His keep was in a shambles and his servants feared him. I do no' have good feelings about Kenneth MacDonald. I expect he will seek revenge when he discovers we have his sister. 'Twould be a mistake to wait for him to act."

Brodie glanced at Alex, concern etched in his face, "Mayhap if we send a message to the king, he will handle it."

"It will be a fortnight before the king gets the message, and who knows if he will act on it. We must make our own plans," Alex said as he speared another piece of meat. "That bastard will not touch Madeline again as long as I am laird here in Dulnain Valley."

Maids brought a tub to Madeline's chamber and filled it with buckets of steaming water. As the bath was being filled, Brenna helped her remove her torn gown. She wadded up the bloodied clothes and gave them to her maid. "Burn them."

Madeline turned her back to Brenna. The moment she saw the welts and bruises all over her body, Brenna gasped out loud. "By the saints, Maddie, what has happened to you?"

Maddie could not speak. She quickly climbed in the tub in the hopes of preventing Brenna or the maids from seeing all her scars, keeping her body covered with her hands. It felt strange to be unclothed before anyone but Alice. The shame and humiliation she bore from the marks of her stepbrother's ill treatment were almost too much to bear.

The permanent scars he had given her had only been seen by Alice. The old woman had tried to use special herbs and salves to prevent permanent scarring, but to no avail. Kenneth had known what he was doing. Maddie blushed when she thought of the reason Kenneth had given her those scars. It would humiliate her for anyone to notice them.

"Brenna, I have no other gown. We left in a hurry. I was not able to gather my things." Maddie glanced at the confused look on Brenna's face. She sighed and lowered her head. "My stepbrother beats me because I have refused to marry the man he has chosen for me."

"Och, Maddie," Brenna squeezed the water from the linen cloth over her friend's wounds. "I am fortunate my brother is laird here. Alex is a kind and patient man. Many call him harsh, but his heart is soft." Silence descended over the chamber for a few moments. Finally, Brenna spoke again. "Surely my brothers could have let you grab a few things, Maddie."

"Nay, I was in Kenneth's command chamber when they grabbed me, and I am thankful for their timing. In fact, I have not properly expressed my gratitude to your brothers for bringing me here. Niles Comming, the man Kenneth wishes me to marry, is worse even than my brother."

Brenna turned away from her friend, but not before she saw the tears in Maddie's eyes. "Hush now. We shall talk of this later. You are exhausted, poor thing. Fiona, get my salve and some clean linen strips for her wounds. Maddie, I have plenty of gowns you can wear. You are a bit thinner, but I think they will do until we can make you some gowns of your own." Brenna helped her wash her long golden locks and then arranged them atop her head, away from her wounds.

The door creaked open and Jennie proudly carried in a platter of cheese and bread. Maddie jumped instinctively and rose out of the tub, only settling back down when she realized there was no danger. Jennie set the platter down on the chest near the bed, but the moment she saw the bruises and wounds on Maddie's body, she clutched her belly and ran out of the room.

Alex and Robbie turned their heads as they heard the small feet pounding down the stairs. Jennie ran toward them, tears pouring down her cheeks. She threw herself at Alex and wrapped her arms around his neck.

"Oh, Alex," she sobbed as she buried her face in his chest.

"What's wrong, little flower?" he asked, stroking her back.

Jennie picked her head up and managed to squeeze out, "Maddieeee."

Alex continued to rub her back, murmuring to her softly until she was able to catch her breath between sobs. "Alex, someone beat her. Maddie has bruises everywhere. I saw her in the tub for her bath. She is bleeding, too. How could anyone do that to her?

She is so nice. I love her!"

Alex wiped the tears from Jennie's face, "I know, little flower, but I will not let anyone ever beat her again. Do you trust your brothers to protect you and Brenna?"

Jennie nodded emphatically.

"And now we will protect Maddie, too."

"Thank you, Alex and Brodie, for saving my friend." Jennie gave them each a kiss on the cheek.

"What about me, squirrel?" Robbie asked, pointing to his face.

Jennie grinned and leaned over to give him a kiss, too. "And thank you, Robbie, for protecting Brenna and me."

Though he was gentle with Jennie, who settled onto his lap, Alex stared at his brothers over his wee sister's head. The thought of the bruises and welts on Madeline's tender body made his blood boil. He didn't need to explain to his brothers what the storm in his face meant.

They knew.

CHAPTER SEVEN

Kenneth paced the chamber, his arms swinging in every direction. He glared at Egan. "Who could have done it? Madeline never leaves the keep, and who could possibly know what goes on here?"

"I warned you not to beat as you do. The servants love her, and servants talk," Egan explained.

Kenneth continued on in a rage. "Then bring the servants to me again. Mayhap some more beatings will help move their tongues. I will beat them until they talk!" Fury filled Kenneth. Normally, he was fastidious about his fair hair and his clothing. Now everything about him was in disarray. Perhaps venting his anger would help calm him. It was the only thing that ever did.

His mother had taught him at a young age that his blood was noble, and someday he would claim his heritage. In the meantime, she had shown him how to keep the servants in their place, carefully demonstrating the use of various belts and whips. If Kenneth did not beat them enough to satisfy her, she would turn the whip on him. He quickly learned. Servants weren't smart enough to do anything but follow orders, so what difference did it make? The only way to have a well-run castle was to keep the servants in line.

Stupid Madeline! She always treated the servants with respect, and now they were all keeping their mouths shut to protect her. She was always so nice. That stupid maid of hers had to know something. He had whipped her until she could not stand, and yet she had still kept quiet. Somebody must have seen something.

"Do we know anything about the kidnappers, Egan?"

"All we know is that they came through the old tunnels. I

cannot believe the old door still opened. We only tracked two sets of footprints. One of them must have carried her out. The prints were too big for a lass. Then they rode away on two horses."

"Saddle the horses. We leave for the Comming's. Aye, he will know who did this." Kenneth smirked.

"And then we will kill them all!"

CHAPTER EIGHT

Alex paced another circle around the table as Brodie and Robbie proceeded to eat everything in sight. He could not think about eating, not until he found out how Madeline fared. He had been unable to sleep all night. His desire to walk down the corridor and peek inside Maddie's chamber to ensure she was comfortable had been strong enough to chase away any rest.

Alex ran a hand through his hair again and then crossed over to the door to visit with wee Jennie and her dogs for the third time. He had sent the rest of the men outside to the lists so he could enjoy a few minutes of treasured family time.

"Alex, why are you still walking around the great hall? Don't you want to break your fast?" Jennie raised her head to stare at her brother. "You are very nervous today. Why does Maddie upset you so?"

"Upset? I am not upset, and I am certainly not thinking about Lady Madeline. As laird, I have many things to think about." Alex gave a huff to try to convince himself of that fact. In truth, he knew Jennie was right. He had many other things he should be thinking about—he just couldn't remember them at the moment. He scowled at Jennie's dogs before snapping his head around to glare at his brother.

"Aye, Jennie, something else has upset Alex," Brodie offered with a grin. "'Tis the same thing that has stirred him these last few days. If only I could determine what plagues our laird." Brodie glanced at Robbie as he choked on his food.

Alex looked toward his brothers. "Enough, or we will settle this in the lists. I'll take on both of you."

Robbie cackled with laughter and stood abruptly, knocking over his bench. "Come, Alex, what upsets you so?"

Alex ignored his brother, though, for he finally heard footsteps on the stone stairwell. Brenna's face was somber as she descended the steps.

Alex could not wait. "How bad is she, Brenna?" The jesting stopped as soon as his sister reached the bottom of the stairway.

"Och, Alex, it was hard to keep my composure when I helped Maddie with her bath last night." Brenna made her way to the table, wringing her hands. "She has been beaten many, many times. Some of her bruises are quite old. I do not know how the lass manages to walk. She has a few bruised ribs. How did she manage to ride a horse?"

Jennie ran to the table. "I asked you last night to protect Lady Madeline, Alex, you have to promise." She grabbed her brother's hand as she said the words.

Alex whispered to Jennie and Brenna, "Madeline is a strong lass. Her strength of character was evident the moment I saw her. Her brother is a sick man, but she never once cringed from his attack or uttered a cry." Alex squeezed Jennie's hand. "Aye, I will protect her, lassie. I would not forget my pledge." His gaze returned to Brenna's. "How does she fare this morn?"

"I tiptoed into her chamber, and she is still asleep. She has had an exhausting few days. We must allow her time to rest and heal. I need to eat, Alex. May we sit, please? My stomach has churned since last night." Brenna motioned for more food to be brought, then sat down beside Brodie and pulled Jennie to her as she waited for the porridge.

Alex lowered himself to the bench, deep in thought. He needed to focus on training his men for battle. There was no reason for him to share his concerns with them just yet, but preparation was paramount to protecting his clan.

Still, before he did aught, he needed to see Madeline. He covered both eyes with his hands as he tried to calm the turmoil raging through his mind.

Brodie's voice brought him back to reality. "Do you think the MacDonald laird is planning an attack?"

Alex played with his food and answered, "Nay, not yet. Kenneth is a coward. I worry more that Niles Comming will come for the lass. She tells me that she has refused the betrothal

MacDonald arranged for her. Comming's numbers are large enough to be a threat if he decides to come after her."

"I have not even met her. Is she bonnie, Brodie?" Robbie asked. "What is she like? I do not remember her from when she visited here years ago."

Brodie gave Robbie an elbow to the side, then stared at him and said, "Aye, she is very bonnie, indeed. You will meet her soon. She could be your kin someday, Robbie. Mayhap I will marry the lass."

"You will not be marrying her, Brodie, nor will Robbie!"

Brenna turned to her brother, her eyes wide with surprise. "Alex, do you not see that it could be a perfect solution? If she agreed to marry Robbie or Brodie, the Comming would not have any reason to come for her, and she would be out of Kenneth's reach. Or mayhap you would prefer to send her to a convent?"

Alex quickly stood and snarled, "The lass will not be going to a convent, and if there's any marrying to be done, it will be to me. Maddie is mine, brothers! And you both best remember that!"

Not wanting to see their reaction, Alex strode to the door of the keep, only halting at the sound of movement to his left. Madeline was slowly descending the stairs. His heart stopped in his chest as he gazed at the true vision dressed in blue velvet. What was wrong with him of late? Women had never preoccupied him this way before. He was a warrior, a laird, chief of his clan. How could this mere slip of a lass stop him in his tracks each and every time he saw her? He redirected his path toward Madeline and bowed to her. "Good morn to you, my lady. I trust you slept well?"

Madeline took a step back before answering, "Aye, I slept very well, Laird Grant, thank you."

Alex did not miss the way she stepped away from him. *What the devil, why did she always do that?* She acted as a timid little rabbit around him. He leaned forward and whispered, "I trust you know by now that I would not hurt you, my lady. There is no reason to be frightened of me."

"I am not frightened of you, Alex. It is just, well," she stammered, "you are so tall… It hurts my neck at times to look at you."

She gazed up at him with her blue eyes and smiled nervously. Alex lost his ability to reason. How he ached to lean forward and taste her sweet lips. Footsteps interrupted his thoughts as one of his guards entered the hall. He found he could not tolerate the sight of another man so close to her. He glanced around the entire hall. No one appeared to be a threat to her, but he did not like the mere thought of someone else hurting her after all she had been through. His brow furrowed as he considered how he might best protect her.

Before he made a complete fool of himself, he bowed and said, "Your pardon, but I must tend to my men in the yard, my lady." Alex turned, beckoned for his brothers to follow, and left the hall.

Madeline walked to the dais and curtsied as Brodie introduced her to his brother, but she could scarce pay attention. "Did I do something to upset your brother, Brodie?" she finally burst out. "He seemed angry."

Brodie and Robbie chuckled and exchanged glances. "Upset? No, my lady, you have not upset him," Robbie said with a smile. "Why, Brodie and I couldn't be happier with how our brother is feeling today. Is that not right, brother?"

Brodie nodded as he turned to Maddie and his sisters. "My ladies. We must do as our laird bids us."

Brenna's face registered shock, but Maddie had no idea why. Had she missed something?

"Good morning, Maddie," Brenna said, finally recovering from whatever had surprised her. "How do you feel?"

Jennie tore herself away from the dogs she was cuddling and shouted, "Good morn to you, Maddie. I am so glad you are here with us. Would you like to play with my dogs?"

Maddie laughed and said, "I would love to meet your dogs, but for now, I am quite hungry." She sat at the table and turned to Brenna. "Thank you for the use of your beautiful gown. I have not worn anything this lovely in a long time." She had not had a new gown made since her parents had passed away. Kenneth always told her there was not enough money for new cloth. Dressed in this soft velvet gown, she almost felt pretty.

"You are stunning in it, Maddie. I think it was made for you. I hope it is not too tight against your back."

"Nay, Fiona placed extra linen on my back. I am comfortable. Thank you for your concern."

"I will change your bandages later and apply more salve. Why don't you have some porridge and we can talk if you like." Brenna patted Maddie's hand and said, "Mayhap you would like to tell me what has happened to you."

Maddie sighed. "It pains me too much. I would rather not talk about Kenneth yet."

"Can you tell me about Niles Comming? How long have you been betrothed to him? Have you even met him?"

Maddie's gut clenched at the very thought of the man. Would she ever be able to discuss anything about the Comming without feeling ill?

"Aye, we have met, and it was not pleasant. I will not marry the man, no matter what Kenneth says." Maddie's face turned red as she stared at her hands in her lap. She wanted to forget everything that had transpired between them. "I will find my way to a convent if I must." Unable to stop her fidgeting, she whispered, "May we discuss this later?"

"Aye, we will do whate'er you wish today," Brenna offered. "Mayhap you would enjoy a walk outside and I can show you around the bailey."

"I would appreciate that. Thank you." Maddie nodded, forcing a smile. She fought back tears, determined not to cry in front of Brenna. How had she gotten to this point? Now she was dependent on people not of her clan. They would be feeding her, clothing her. She would take up a chamber in a place where she did not really belong. How she hated her stepbrother for putting her in this situation.

What was she to do with her life now? She had no other relatives, at least, not to her knowledge. She had no dowry, and she had lost her maidenhead to the Comming. Who would marry her now? Her life was in a shambles and she had nowhere to turn. She reminded herself of one of her mother's sayings: worry about the little steps, not the big ones.

She decided that would be her goal for today, to focus on the little steps, not the big ones—like Alexander Grant.

CHAPTER NINE

As Brenna and Maddie stepped outside, a warm fall breeze blew their skirts into the air. Maddie giggled, grabbing her skirts before they reached the tops of her knees. Wee Jennie skipped along beside them, the dogs following at her heels. Maddie noted the pride in Brenna's eyes as they made their way through the herb garden. Since Brenna was the clan's healer, naturally she would spend a great deal of time here. She caught the faint aromas of parsley and basil as the wind whipped around them.

They strolled on to the vegetable garden next. Maddie's eyes feasted on the plethora of purples, golds, and oranges in neat rows, but the best part of this garden was the view. Gazing at the rippling surface of the loch, she could almost hear the distant lapping of the water on the banks. Maddie turned her face to the sky to take in the wind, sighing as the sun warmed her cheeks. She smiled and brushed a strand of hair away from her face, reminded of some of the beautiful gifts the Lord offered daily. Perhaps the quiet of a convent would indeed be right for her. Then she could spend her days in the gardens, enjoying the sweet solitude of nature.

She beamed at Brenna. "This must be your favorite place. The view of your lands is beautiful."

"'Tis no' my favorite place, Maddie," Jennie remarked. "My sister makes me work hard in the dirt sometimes. I don't like it. I would prefer to play with my dogs."

Laughing at the child's honesty, Maddie ran her fingers through Jennie's dark curls. "I think you have hair just like your brother's." She furrowed her brow, wondering where that thought had come from. She had not intended to think about Alex.

Brenna guided her to the chapel. Maddie approached the inside carefully, as if opening a special package. Her eyes teared up as she ran her fingers along the smooth carvings with reverence, taking in the details of the lovely woodwork. She was reminded of the chapel Kenneth had turned into another armory. How she missed the beauty of prayerful silence in that place.

"Brenna, do you have a priest that lives here?" She loved how sound resonated in that lovely space.

"Nay, we have a traveling priest, Father MacGregor. He is a wonderful priest, but he has several places in the Highlands he likes to visit. He is due to visit again soon."

"Father MacGregor! Oh, how wonderful!" Maddie could not help but clasp her hands together in excitement. "I have not seen him since my parents' death. He used to visit us as well, but he stopped coming long ago. I thought mayhap it was due to ill health. But he is well?"

"Aye, he was hale the last time we saw him."

"You will not mind if I visit the chapel on my own?"

"Of course not. You may use it whenever you like." Brenna opened the heavy door for Maddie and they headed back out into the sunlight, catching up with Jennie and her dogs who seemed to be living in their own world.

Brenna pointed out many of the buildings as they strolled through the bailey, including the storehouses, the buttery, and the blacksmith. Madeline was introduced to many of the clan. She had to admit she enjoyed meeting them. They were all friendly and helpful, and no one seemed threatening. The hard work of clan Grant was evident in everything she observed. She was reminded of what her own small clan had been like before her da had passed.

As they moved on to the armory, Maddie's discomfort from her ribs and her back grew more acute. She sighed as she realized she would be suffering through another healing challenge. Quietly praying, she begged the Lord for the strength to endure her tribulations without complaint. This, combined with thoughts of her parents, usually helped her to continue suffering in silence.

"Maddie, would you like to return to the castle? Mayhap you should rest a bit? Is your back paining you?"

"Nay, I am fine. I am used to working after my beatings. What about you, do you normally take rest after Alex disciplines you?" Maddie raised her eyes to meet Brenna's.

She jumped at the other woman's sharp intake of breath. Jennie froze in her path.

"Och, nay, Maddie, Alex does not beat us," Brenna said softly. "Jennie, take the dogs to the stables, would you?

Maddie nodded her head after Jennie left and continued on. She tried her best to hide her emotions, but her mind was in turmoil. Alex didn't beat them?

Kenneth beat the servants whenever he had a whim, and she had seen Laird Niles Comming swing at Kenneth's servants as well as his own. Wasn't that what all lairds did? Kenneth had said it was the only way to keep the servants in line. Of course, she could never beat anyone. One time a maid accidentally tore her favorite gown, but she had not even said a cruel word to her. The thought of slapping viciously for something so small did not sit well with her.

Hope rose in her heart. Was Alex truly a laird who didn't beat his people? A laird more like her kind father in temperament than her brother and the Comming?

Maddie had mixed feelings about Alexander Grant. He made her shiver, that much she knew, but she was not afraid of him. And she was so, so grateful to him for having rescued her.

Though she did not know what had brought the Grants to her keep, she was thankful for it. Yet she could not reconcile the confusion this one man was causing her heart. Sometimes her breath caught when she dared peek at him. This morning in the great hall, she had been struck by how devastatingly handsome he was, especially when free of dirt and grime. She wondered why he had not married yet since he could surely have his choice of lasses. Who would reject him?

Surely, Alex would not be interested in someone as plain as Madeline. Kenneth had always delighted in informing her that due to her sour appearance, he was fortunate to find anyone willing to marry her. Madeline knew she wasn't beautiful, and besides, she no longer had the dowry to attract a respectable match.

Saints above, why was she thinking about marriage? She would never get married. If she married a man, he would expect to touch her…and do much more than that. What was Alex doing to her mind? Madeline shook her head to sweep the cobwebs from her brain. She forced herself to focus her attention back on Brenna.

From the inner bailey, they traveled to the stables, where Brenna introduced her to the stable master, Hugh.

"Old Hugh has been with us forever. He really knows our horses," Brenna said with pride. "Hugh, this is Lady Madeline, a dear friend who will be staying with us awhile."

Maddie smiled at the stable master. "It is nice to meet you, Hugh. You remind me of our own stable master, Mac. He is married to my maid, Alice, and I love them both dearly."

"And obviously they love you dearly, too, my lady. My laird told me 'twas the stable master who sent the missive about your stepbrother."

"I am aware, but I worry about them now. Kenneth can be very cruel when he wants to be, especially to servants. He beat all of servants on a regular basis, but he was never allowed to touch Alice because she was my mother's maid. Who knows what will happen now?"

Maddie's mood darkened as they continued with their jaunt around the bailey. Many of the children they passed watched them with fascination, and some even followed behind them.

Madeline rustled the hair on one of the weans and smiled. "If you like, I would be happy to return and tell you a story."

The wee lassie nodded her head and gave Madeline's leg a hug. Maddie glanced over her shoulder as she walked away. "I will be back, I promise." The children waved to them and promised to wait for her to return.

Maddie stopped walking when they reached the lists, gaping at the sea of swords and shields. What an impressive sight to see such a large number of warriors, all following Alex's lead. She had no trouble picking him out. Taller than most, he was training a few of the younger guards at the periphery of the field. Her palms filled with sweat from the nearness of so many men, but she knew it was time to express her gratitude for her rescue. Her mother had taught her to be forthright about expressing appreciation for any hard work that had been done on her behalf. Her manners would not allow her to overlook such a risky deed.

"Brenna, if you don't mind, I would like to speak to your brother for a moment."

Alex turned at the sound of people approaching the lists, and his gaze immediately found Madeline. He noted how she carefully kept her distance from his men as she walked in his direction. The closer she came, the more his throat constricted and his chest tightened. Devil take it, what strange power did this lass have over him?

Maddie tentatively stepped closer to Alex. "My laird, may I have a moment of your time?" She nodded briefly at the guards, who all stared at her with eager smiles on their faces.

Alex removed his helmet and replied, "Of course, my lady." He glared at his guards before he spanned the distance separating him from her. "How may I assist you?"

"Laird Grant," she started, "I fear I have not thanked you and your brother properly for risking your lives to come to my aid. I am truly grateful that you were able to hasten me away from my stepbrother without causing harm to anyone."

"My lady, you do no' need to thank me." He stepped forward, and Madeline stepped a couple of paces back, though her smile did not drop from her face. *Again*, he thought, *she backs away from me.* He did not move again, thinking mayhap he smelled unpleasant after working so hard.

But his thoughts jumped to the situation he had found her in a few nights ago.

"Do not be concerned for your stepbrother. He was hurting you, was he no'? I would have done whatever was necessary in order to stop his cruelty. 'Tis no' right to beat a woman over anything, let alone a betrothal. Lass, you have my apologies for no' getting you away from him sooner. And if he comes for you, rest assured that I will protect you. He will not hurt you again!" Alex's men turned to stare at him as his voice escalated to a shout.

Madeline seemed to be cringing away from him, so he forced himself to calm down to avoid upsetting her more.

"But I do not want anyone hurt because of me," Madeline whispered.

Alex's bluster blew again. Was the woman daft? She could be hurt, but no one else could be?

"If your stepbrother or Niles Comming tries to come to my keep to get you, someone will be hurt." He tried to rein in his anger, but lost the battle.

Maddie stepped back, clutching her hand to her chest.

"No one will touch you again!" Alex's could feel the fire burning in his chest as he spoke, his entire body rigid. The thought of anyone harming Maddie made him clench his hands in rage.

He knew his fervor probably frightened her, but he couldn't help himself. Staring at the ground in frustration, he had to fight the desire to stomp his feet. She had no notion of her own value. Why did she not understand men did not have the right to touch her whenever they wanted? He would have to show her that she was special, but he did not know how. This woman took away his ability to reason. When he lifted his gaze, he found himself drowning in her blue eyes once again.

Her beautiful face and delicate skin were all he could see.

Her voice interrupted his thoughts, "Thank you, Laird, and please convey my thanks to your brother as well." Maddie graced him with a timid smile and fled.

Alex watched her go and sighed. *Great, I have scared her away again. Why does she make me daft?* He reminded himself he was laird with many responsibilities—he could not spend all his time thinking of one woman. He vowed to keep a clear head around Madeline in the future. He would not allow her to interfere with his responsibilities. With that settled in his mind, he turned back to his men.

"Robbie, where are you?" Alex grinned as he bore down on his brother. Robbie was the only lad in his clan who could offer him a challenge with the sword. He definitely needed someone to practice on right now.

Robbie smirked as he peered over Alex's shoulder at Madeline's departing form. "What has addled your mind?"

Alex withdrew his sword, alerting his brother to do the same. He brought the sword down repeatedly, but Robbie expertly deflected his blows, sending the sound of clashing steel ringing through the air.

Robbie danced in a circle, both hands on his sword. "Could the reason you are in this fury have golden hair, brother?"

After a thorough workout, Robbie finally conceded and patted Alex on the back.

"Good to see you befuddled for a change. Everybody loses control once in a while."

Alex stared at his brother. "I do no' know what you are talking about. I do not lose control. Ever!" With that, he stalked away.

His confusing feelings for Maddie had made a liar of him.

CHAPTER TEN

Maddie decided to search out the youngest of the clan, something guaranteed to make her smile. She found Jennie and they headed out to the bailey, searching for anyone interested in listening to one of her stories.

She sat on the ground with Jennie, surrounded by weans of various ages. She had them all enraptured with a tale of fairies in the forest, and she could see the delight in their gazes. How sweet they were. Her pain bothered her a bit, but the bairns made it all tolerable. As Madeline continued her story, Alex appeared out of nowhere and his gaze found hers. She blushed and paused for a moment before continuing with her tale.

Madeline's pulse raced when she caught Alex watching her. She finished her story and waved to him, but he only smiled and moved on to the keep. As she glanced at the wee ones around her, she imagined what it would be like to have a husband like Alex. To have bairns who belonged to them. As she hugged each of the ladies and lassies and promised them another story soon, she sighed and bowed her head. That life sounded wonderful, but it could never be for her. She had experienced a man's touch, and she never wished to do so again. How did other women bear it?

Fortunately, she had already had her courses after that night with Niles. As eager as Maddie was for the terrible marriage to never happen, Alice had actually cried tears of happiness when Maddie started to bleed.

But perhaps coupling with a man like Alex would be more tolerable. He was a much gentler man. But how many times did it take to make a bairn? Maybe Brenna knew. Even though she was most likely still a maid, she was a healer, and thus, maybe had assisted with the birth of a few bairns. Mayhap she had heard talk amongst the women. She would have to find a way to ask her.

Stop your dreaming. It can never be, the cruel voice in her head insisted. *He could have any lass he wants, so why would he want you?*

No, she was going to a convent. She had no choice.

Brenna approached coming from the direction of her gardens, stopping because she apparently noticed the worry on Maddie's face. "Is everything all right, Maddie? There must be something I can do to help you."

"I am fine, Brenna, there is no need to worry about me. May I assist you with your garden?"

"Mayhap tomorrow, Maddie. I think it is time to change your dressing and put more salve on your back."

Alex leaned over the side of the battlements, his favorite vantage point. He drew in a deep breath of the cool night air, hoping to clear his jumbled thoughts. Realizing he was searching for a golden halo in the area beneath him, he shook his head in disgust. Of course, Maddie would not be there. She was probably abed.

"Alex, may I have a word with you?"

He turned as Brenna approached. "Of course, you know I would do anything for you. What is it?"

"Did you really mean what you said about marrying Maddie?"

Alex sighed as he stood and crossed his arms. "Nay, Brenna, I have too many responsibilities to take the time to marry. I doubt Madeline would even consider me, but I am trying to get to know her better. I enjoy having her near me, but she does not appear to return the feeling. Every time I step near the lass, she backs away from me. I try not to frighten her, but it appears I do."

"You know she has a tender heart. I think she is confused right now. I hope you are not planning to send her away."

"Nay, 'twould be too dangerous for her to leave until the situation is settled between her brother and the Comming. I still should not have mentioned marriage, at least no' yet, but you know as well as I do how much Robbie and Brodie love to goad me."

"Aye, they were having a wee bit of fun with you. But 'tis rare for you to notice a lass, Alex. Mayhap if you tried to woo

Madeline slowly, it would work. I think 'twould be a good match, and anyone can see how wonderful she is with bairns. She is a sweet-hearted lass."

"Aye, that I see. The lass does not seem to feel easy around me, but I will not give up yet. Has she talked about the Comming at all, Brenna?"

"Nay, when I ask her, she says she is not ready to talk. She needs time."

"Aye, I know she was in a bad place. I will give her time. She has much healing to do."

The next few days passed quickly. Maddie discovered she was exhausted. She was surprised at how much she slept, but her energy was slowly returning. Brenna fussed over her wounds and continued to apply salve to them daily. Time brought slow relief, as always.

She spent hours sitting outside near the keep, telling stories to the wee ones. Bairns and toddlers had always had a way of putting a smile on her face. Their innocence was precious to her, and it helped her forget her own troubles.

Alex spent most of his time training his men in the lists, and it hurt Maddie to think that it was her fault they needed to be prepared for a possible attack. Still, she could not regret that she was free of her brother. Her days were so much happier here. She sketched drawings to use with her storytelling, and Brenna had given her some needlework to help keep her busy. Everyone at the Grant keep treated her wonderfully, including the maids. She ignored the inevitable. Some day soon she would have to leave. But where did she belong?

One day, after breaking their fast, Brenna convinced Maddie to join her in the garden. Jennie had run off to pick apples with the servants, so they were alone together.

"'Tis peaceful here, Maddie. 'Tis why I like this place so much." Brenna grabbed her friend's hand as they walked toward the small, beautifully appointed plot of land.

"Aye, Brenna, 'tis a wonderful place." Maddie gazed around at the golden flowers lining the outside of the garden. Lavender plants filled the air with their sweet fragrance. She picked a flower and wove it into her waves. "You must teach me about the plants someday."

"We can start today. You can help me transplant some of my herbs." Both of them were dressed in old gowns, fit for working. It was unusual for the chatelaine of a keep to get her hands dirty, but Brenna had told her it relieved her stress.

Together, they worked steadily at weeding and transplanting. Surprised by how much she enjoyed working with the soil, Maddie hoped she would get to see the results of her gardening someday. After they toiled in the sun for a couple of hours, Brenna motioned for Maddie to follow her. "Come join me for some water." They found a stone bench under a shade tree and shared a drink.

They sat quietly for a few moments, enjoying the sound of the birdsong overhead and the sight of the Grant land stretching out in front of them. The fall colors were brilliant at this time of year. Red leaves were her favorite and some trees were starting to turn.

Maddie sighed and glanced at her friend. "Do you know what your brother's plans are for me, Brenna?"

"I am no' sure what you mean. 'Tis no' *his* choice; 'tis yours. What do you want to do?"

"I have no other kin, and I will never marry the Comming, so I do not think there are many choices for me. I cannot impose on you and your family forever. You have done so much for me already. I think maybe it is time to think about entering a convent."

Brenna leaned over and grabbed her friend's hands. "A convent? Maddie, what makes you say such a thing?"

"What other choice do I have, Brenna?" Maddie's voice cracked as she attempted to smile.

"You can stay with us. We have plenty of room. Mayhap Alex and I can find a nice man for you to marry. Or is it your desire to be in a convent?"

"Nay, I cannot say I have the calling. I would welcome the peacefulness, but it would only suit me if there were children about." Maddie's hands played with her skirt.

"Then why no' marry another man? You are so wonderful with the wee ones. You belong with a house full of bairns!" Brenna leaned over and pulled her into her arms. "You have a heart of gold. You deserve a life of happiness. Put your terrible memories behind you."

"I do love little ones, but I am not sure." Maddie's words caught as she struggled to maintain her composure. The time had come to tell her friend the truth.

"Sure of what, Maddie?" Brenna's voice softened as she pulled away enough to look at her.

A tear slowly made its way down Maddie's cheek. She shook her head and put her hands over her face.

"What is it?" Brenna waited patiently before reaching over and hugging her tight.

Maddie slowly lifted her gaze to meet her friend's. "Niles forced himself on me a while ago. I am no longer a maiden. Who would have me as I am?"

"Och, Maddie, is that why Kenneth wants you to marry Niles?" Brenna brushed a lock of hair out of Maddie's eyes.

"Nay. Niles thought he had the right to my maidenhead since we were betrothed. When I refused, he took it. It was horrible, and now I do not know if I could stand the marriage bed. That is when I refused Kenneth, after the Comming brutalized me." Maddie's composure finally broke as sobs wracked her body. "What am I to do now? I am so confused."

"How terrible! Did you tell Kenneth about it?" Brenna whispered.

"Nay, Kenneth has no feelings for me. He would say it was Laird Comming's right as my betrothed. Do you understand my dilemma? What say you now?" She swiped at her tears with her sleeve.

"It answers many questions. But I have no experience with this sort of situation, so I don't know how to help you. Surely there must be someone who can help. Mayhap we should talk to my brother Alex."

"Nay! I would be too embarrassed to discuss this with your brother. Please do not ask me to tell him, Brenna. I will decide on my own what to do. Mayhap when Father MacGregor arrives, I will talk with him about the possibility of entering the convent."

Brenna sighed before biting her lip. "I will agree as long as you promise no' to make up your mind for at least a fortnight. You have been through too much." Brenna rubbed Maddie's arm. "Is there any chance you could be carrying Niles's bairn?"

Maddie could feel her cheeks blushing as she stared at the ground. "Nay, I have had my courses since then."

"Please remember what I said. You are always welcome to stay with us." Brenna helped her up from the bench and gave her another quick hug.

"Thank you, Brenna. I owe you and your family so much."

"You are most welcome. We are here for you, and I hope you believe that. I'll help in any way I can." She glanced up at the sky. "I think we have done enough work out here for today. I will pick some fresh herbs for Cook and return to the keep."

"If you do not mind, I would like to be alone for a bit before returning." Maddie wiped the tears from her face as she straightened her skirts.

"Of course, I will see you back in the hall."

Maddie strolled down the main path away from the keep. She stopped briefly to take in the crisp fall air...and regain her composure. As she glanced around the bailey, she noticed something very different about the Grants' keep. Everyone here was *happy*. Everyone waved or smiled, even the blacksmith, and she could not help but smile back.

Alex must be a very good laird. The people respected him, and it was no wonder. Their crofts and cottages were in good shape, not in need of repair like many of the homesteads in her clan. Food was bountiful—though not rich—at his table, and many of his people were fed in the great hall.

She thought of how things had changed at her own keep since her parents' death. The hall had always been spotless when her mother was alive. Now it was filthy, despite her best efforts. Kenneth even allowed his men to throw their food scraps on the rushes in the hall when they finished eating. He considered it Maddie's job to clean it all up. But with so many dogs pushing around for food, it was an impossible task. Besides, Kenneth had scared away many of the servants, leaving Maddie without the help she needed.

No dogs were allowed in the food area of the great hall at the Grant Castle. Brenna kept her rushes clean by mixing herbs and dried flowers in with them to maintain their freshness. It was an altogether different kind of place.

As she walked down the hill, her gaze wandered to the lists. She sighed when her gaze found Alex, feeling a bit wistful of what could never be. As if on cue, he turned and found her gaze. She wanted to give him a quick wave, but worried he would be angry with her for interrupting his work. She strolled to the stables to visit the horses. They reminded her of Mac. The stables had always been a place of comfort for her at her home. She hoped she would feel the same way here.

Alex was in the middle of instructing one of his soldiers when a flush of heat warmed the back of his neck. Madeline must be nearby, he thought. He had not seen her for days, but only her gaze could have that effect on him. Anger and hurt both crept in. Why did she always turn away from him?

"Chief, is this what you were talking about? I think I know what you mean now." The Grant warrior held his sword in a different stance in front of Alex. "Is this not correct?"

Alex turned and stared at his man. What was he babbling about? He dismissed him with a wave and turned around to look for Maddie. He could not find her anywhere. An unusual tightness built in his chest as he searched for a glimpse of her in the bailey. It was not safe for her to wander about on her own.

He turned toward his brother. "Robbie, I have things to do. You are in charge until I return."

Robbie nodded and returned to what he had been doing. "Brodie, can you believe it? I did not ever think we would see Alex so taken with a woman."

Alex glared back at his brother. "I am not taken with the woman, Robbie. She is currently under my charge and I am just trying to protect her."

"After the farce with Anna Comming, I was no' sure I would ever see it again," Brodie remarked.

Alex stopped dead, spun on his heel, and pointed his finger in Brodie's face. "Do not ever mention that woman's name in my presence again. Do you understand me?"

"Aye, Laird Grant, I do," Brodie ground out as he glared at his brother. "But since we never heard the circumstances, it is difficult for us to understand why you will no' discuss what happened. Anna is a beautiful lass."

"You do not need to know the circumstances. Just never speak her name again." Alex stalked off toward the stables. He probably should have told his brothers about the farce that had been his betrothal, but he did not want to create any more animosity toward their neighboring clan. Some things were better kept quiet.

Now he was barking at his brothers. What was Maddie doing to him?

CHAPTER ELEVEN

Alex stormed into the stables, only to find Maddie feeding an apple to his horse. He froze at the sight of his stallion eating from her hand as she rubbed his head and cooed to him.

"Hugh, what are you thinking?" he bellowed. "You know how nasty my horse gets, or have you lost your senses, old man?"

Maddie stiffened at the chastisement. "Laird Grant, it is not his fault. He did not know what I was about."

Alex's gut clenched at the fear and concern he saw in her eyes. "My lady," he said softly, "I am no' going to hurt old Hugh."

Old Hugh chuckled as he watched Maddie coddle Alex's horse. "As you can see, Chief, there is no need to worry about Maddie. Midnight knows a kind soul when he meets one. Or are you nervous he might like her more than he does you?"

Alex glared at him. "Never mind," he said. "'Tis no' why I came here. My lady, you should not be wandering around the bailey by yourself. I do not want you to leave the hall without an escort. No one knows when your stepbrother might send someone to steal you back. My gates are open during the day. Anyone could sneak in."

Fire lit her eyes before she bowed her head. "I am sorry, Laird. I was in the garden with Brenna, and I thought I would pay a visit old Hugh and your horses. There was no problem when I was in the bailey with the wee ones yesterday, so I did not think there would be any danger."

"Leave us, Hugh," Alex said to his stable master.

After he left, Alex sighed and studied Maddie. Lost in her gaze, her lips, he wanted so badly to kiss her. All he could think of was pulling her into his arms since her sweet scent of lavender and woman was driving him wild. He reached out to touch her, but she pulled back.

He shook his head slightly and glanced at the horses, using the distraction to regain his control.

"My lady, you had a group around you yesterday. Today, you are alone. I would not trust you alone with some of my own clan." The volume of Alex's voice rose as he continued. The sudden vision of another man touching her, hurting her, burst into his head. "And you will need ten escorts whenever you go outside the keep!" He knew he was yelling, but he was desperate to keep her safe and protected. "You will heed my orders, Madeline MacDonald, or I will lock you in your chamber!"

Madeline eyes turned to ice as she stared at him. "Forgive me, I thought to be a guest in your home, not a prisoner." She ran around him and tore up the hill toward the keep.

Alex put his hands on his hips and heaved a big sigh.

Stepping back around the wall, Hugh said, "Well done, laddie. You drove her further away." The old man chuckled as his eyebrows rose. "Laird, I have known you since you were a bairn, and I have ne'er seen a lassie affect you so. Och, 'tis about time." The stable master gave him a warm pat on his shoulder. "From what I know of her, she is as kind as she is fair. Naught like that other lass."

Old Hugh was one of the few men who knew the real reason why Alex had not taken a wife yet.

Years ago, before his parents' death, Alex had been betrothed to Anna Comming, Niles's sister. He had not known her well, but his father had insisted that Alex marry to produce heirs. After much discussion with his mother, Alex had agreed to the plan.

Not long after, the Comming came to Grant land to introduce his sister to Alex. Niles was anxious to commence the wedding, as he always sought ways to expand his wealth and holdings. Anna was a dark-haired beauty, but there was a coldness in her eyes Alex did not trust. Old Hugh was actually the one who had saved Alex from making a disastrous mistake. He had summoned him to the stables one night—just in time to catch his betrothed in the act. Alex found Anna, in all her splendor, being tupped in the hay by her brother's second in command. They knew he was there, but did not stop. Instead, Anna had smiled at him over her lover's shoulder and beckoned him closer. But what had sickened him most was the sight of Niles in the corner, watching with a smile on his face as he brutally twisted the breasts of one of Alex's servants.

Alex had drawn his sword on Niles, but the other man had been unarmed. All he said was, "You and yours will be off my land by dawn." Only respect for his mother had stayed his hand from killing them all on Grant land.

The servant girl had been terrified, but Alex had escorted her home. He had spoken to her parents and made special arrangements for her to guarantee she would be out of harm's way.

He had never told anyone about that horrid night, not even his father. He had merely reported that the betrothal as over, and his father had trusted him enough not to pester him about it.

Madeline was the first woman who had broken through his hard heart since then. She was nothing like Anna, whose eyes were cold and calculating. Maddie's eyes were fathomless, compassionate. She was an innocent, and he was honor bound to protect her. And yet he could not convince himself that he should only be her protector. If only he could hold her and taste her just once, mayhap his desire would be quenched.

"Hugh, it does not matter what I do, 'tis always the wrong thing with Madeline. She runs from me like a deer. I do no' think she cares much about me."

"Aye, mayhap if you stopped bellowing at the gel, she would settle you in closer. You must treat her with kindness, Laird, as I know you are able to do. Stop treating her as you do your men."

"She is so beautiful, she makes me daft."

Hugh chuckled and patted him on the shoulder. "Aye, I can see it. Try some soft words on her, Alex. She is a soft creature."

Alex saddled Midnight and rode out through his gates, followed by a couple of his guards. Maddie was a mystery to him. She drove him to thoughts and feelings he had never experienced before. What did he really want? Was he ready to take a wife? Would allowing himself to feel this strongly about her compromise his leadership? He enjoyed thinking about Madeline, picturing her in his arms. But he also recognized she was not ready yet.

He rode Midnight hard to the loch. It was usually deserted at this time of year, as the water was frigid. After eyeing Maddie in front of that mound of hay, cool water was exactly what he needed.

Did he dare to allow someone else near his heart? He didn't see many similarities between the two women. He hoped he was right about Madeline. She was the only woman able to distract him from his duties as laird. Maybe it wasn't such a good thing, but he couldn't stop himself.

CHAPTER TWELVE

As soon as Maddie reached the great hall, she fled up the stairs to her chamber. Brenna's maid knocked as soon as she closed the door.

"If it would not be too much trouble, Fiona, I would greatly appreciate a hot bath."

"Of course, my lady." Fiona curtsied and left to arrange for a tub and hot water.

Madeline dropped into her chair. She was unable to keep the tears inside any longer. Laird Grant wanted to keep her prisoner. What was she to do? She would lose her wits if he forced her to stay inside. But most men made her anxious, so she did not relish the idea of various strange men escorting her wherever she went. How could she trust them? Being from Clan Grant did not guarantee they would treat her with respect. And even if they did treat her kindly, they would probably stand entirely too close for her comfort.

Kenneth's men had often leered at her, making her uncomfortable, and she expected Alex's men would act the same way. Did she really want to spend her life feeling anxious all the time? She might as well be in a convent. At least then she would not need to fear being groped by the nearest male.

But the surprising thing was that Alex never frightened her. Not even when he was in a tirade. And his touch hadn't bothered her at all as they rode back to the keep on Midnight. In fact, she had loved having his arms around her. She had even rested her hand on his arm without flinching. She did not understand that.

A knock sounded at the door, and two servant lads rushed in with the tub, followed by a few more carrying buckets of steaming water. She turned her head and swiped at her tears. After they left, Madeline reached to bolt the door, but a knock startled her.

She opened the door to see wee Jennie smiling at her. "May I come in, Maddie?"

"Of course, Jennie, I was about to soak in the tub, but you may stay and keep me company."

Jennie entered and Maddie bolted the door behind her. She removed her dirty clothes and linen strips and slipped into the tub. "Oh, this feels so good!"

Jennie washed Maddie's back, using extreme care for one so young.

"Do your wounds still hurt you, Maddie? Is that why you were crying?" Jennie's innocent curiosity was reflected in her eyes.

"Nay, Jennie, they don't hurt enough to make me cry, but they still ache sometimes."

"Then why were you crying? Do you no' like it here?"

"It seems I cry too much of late. I am very happy here, lass, but this is not my home. My feelings are all jumbled. I do not know what goes on inside me anymore. But I am so glad you came to visit me. Why don't you tell me all about your pets?" Uncomfortable discussing her feelings with one so young, Maddie hoped to distract the young lass.

"Alex gave me my first puppy after Mama went to heaven. We named her 'Hope.' Da said Mama would like that name. Then after my da went to heaven, Alex gave me 'Faith' because he said Mama and Da could watch over me through the dogs. He said they would never leave my side. I love Hope and Faith very much. Don't tell Alex, but they sleep with me sometimes. Brenna knows, but she doesn't tell."

Jennie's smile was contagious. What a wonderful thing Alex had done for his sister. She couldn't believe a man would have the foresight to help a wee lass deal with the loss of her parents by filling her time with new puppies. She shook her head at the thought, unable to imagine Kenneth or Niles doing anything with such consideration.

"Jennie, I imagine you miss your mother a great deal. It is difficult to lose your parents anytime, but you are so young," Maddie whispered as she looked at Jennie through tear-stained lashes.

"Aye, I miss my Mama and Da very much. Sometimes I dream of sitting on my da's lap, or hugging Mama. Those are my favorite dreams because I can still feel them after I wake up. But Alex and Brenna and Brodie and Robbie have been so good to me. I know they are spoiling me sometimes, but I like it. Promise me you will not give my secret away, Maddie. I like it when they spoil me. Especially Alex. He is as big as my da was. He always lets me sit on his lap, and sometimes I pretend he is my da even though I know he is not. Some of the servants tell me I am too big to be sitting on his lap, but I don't care. I always feel safe there."

Maddie could not prevent the sigh from escaping her lips. It was undeniable—Alex was so strong and comforting, tender and protective. While riding with him that day, Maddie had experienced a strange feeling that being in Alex's arms was where she belonged. She was safe there, just like Jennie had said. Only she had not admitted it to herself until now. Still, it could never be…

Maddie winked at Jennie's smiling face. "Well, now you have another lap you may sit on, lass. You are always welcome to sit on my lap, and I do not think you are too old."

Jennie helped Maddie out of the tub and handed her the linen. "I hope you like it here, Maddie. I want you to stay with us. You can be part of our family now. Please say you will stay."

Maddie toweled herself dry and stared into Jennie's eyes. She did not want to lie to the lass. "I hope everything will work out for me, lass. You have been a great help, but I think it is time we get ready for the evening meal. I will get dressed and come down to the hall when I am ready. And I thank you for your help."

CHAPTER THIRTEEN

Kenneth arrived at the Comming keep with his men about a day and a half after he left his castle. The guards at the portcullis yelled down, "State your purpose."

"Open the bloody gates now, or I will whip you myself when I get inside!" he bellowed at the belligerent warrior. "I need to see the Comming now. We've problems."

After consulting with the Comming's steward, the guards led Kenneth and his men into the bailey. They left their horses at the stables and headed for the great hall.

"You and your commander only, the rest must wait outside," Comming's steward barked. Kenneth left Iain in charge of the men and motioned for Egan to go with him.

Och, how he hated taking orders from people beneath him. Who did these lowly people think they were? Didn't they know who *he* was?

After all, he was the MacDonald laird. Actually, that was rather amusing to him. He had no more MacDonald blood in him than Niles Comming did. His mother's audacity was entertaining.

His mother's parents had owned a tavern years ago. His grandparents had made their only daughter, Mildred, his mother, work almost every day after she was five summers old. He chuckled about that. His mother was much better at giving orders than she was at working. When she was about ten and five, his mother decided she no longer wanted to work at the tavern. She was tired of scrubbing floors, scouring pots, and washing linens. With all the men coming and going in the tavern, she had learned how much more she could earn on her back.

She had liked the MacDonald laird, James. He was big and handsome, and she believed she could trick him into marrying her. A group of lairds were drinking in the tavern one night, and she plied the MacDonald with her sweetest smiles as she poured her father's strongest whisky into his tankard. When he climbed up to his room, she followed and offered herself to him. Laird MacDonald was totally agreeable, except for one small problem— he passed out.

Even that didn't stop Mildred. When she managed to get herself pregnant soon afterwards, she blamed it on Laird MacDonald.

Kenneth's mother and her da had been smart enough to confront the man in front of his peers. While Clan Chief MacDonald remembered Mildred's face, he did not recall much else. He finally relented and admitted the bairn could be his. And he agreed in front of witnesses that if his wife did not bear him any sons, her son would be the MacDonald heir. Kenneth chuckled to himself. His mother had reminded him every day he was supposed to be of noble blood and he deserved to be one of the ruling classes. And now her plans had come to fruition.

Only Maddie presented a problem. Now that she had left the keep, he was not sure how he would handle Niles Comming.

Moments later, Niles flew down the stairs. "This better be important, MacDonald. What's the problem?"

"Maddie has disappeared. I had to leave the keep the other night after a fire broke out in one of the cottages. When I returned, she was gone. She must have been kidnapped."

"Kidnapped? Have you received a ransom note, you fool? How can you no' keep hold of a mere wench like Maddie? You better find her!" Niles bellowed in Kenneth's face.

"There's been no ransom note yet. But who else would want her? She has no value."

"No value? She is a bonnie wench, and I liked her when I took her. You promised her to me!"

"She probably ran away. You left enough blood on the sheets for five virgins. What in blazes did you do to her? You scared her away. She is refusing to marry you now."

"She is refusing?" The Comming reached out and grabbed Kenneth by the throat. "Well, you had best find her. We have an agreement, and I intend for her to be my wife. I will be able to handle her; I see you cannot." Niles released Kenneth and shoved him across the room. He paced the hall, running his hands through his hair.

"Mayhap another small MacDonald clan has her. They were all loyal to your father. Or mayhap she is trying to return to England. Her maid is English, is she not?"

"We already checked the other MacDonald cottages. No one has seen her," Kenneth said, rubbing his throat. "And I beat her maid senseless. She could not tell me anything. I was hoping you had some ideas. You know the clans in the area better than I do."

"The only one I know who is foolish enough to challenge us is Alexander Grant. He never got over losing my sister, and I heard he was in the area. Perhaps he wants revenge." Niles ran his hand over his chin. "It has to be him. He knows I am the best swordsman of all of the Scots. He would love to be rid of me."

Kenneth raised his eyebrow. "Are you certain of that?"

"Have you been talking about our betrothal? If the Grant chief knows about it, then it could only be him. I told you to keep your mouth shut about it till 'twas done. We should have wed when I was there. 'Twas your idea to wait."

Kenneth jumped quickly to the defensive. "I have no' told anyone, but servants gossip, you ken. And we could have done the wedding if the bride had been capable of standing, you fool." Niles did not need to know he'd mentioned the betrothal to Alex Grant.

Niles stared at Kenneth, then smirked. "Ah, perhaps I was a bit rough on her for her first time. She'll learn to do my bidding." Niles smiled as he stared off into the distance. He shook his head before turning back to face Kenneth. "Mayhap we should search the area tomorrow, see what we can discover. But if Maddie ran away, she will live to regret it."

Kenneth's brow furrowed. The very thought of her running away made him furious. When they found her, he would make her scream. Blazes, but it buggered him when she was silent. She withstood blow after blow without a sound. Just unnatural.

Kenneth turned to Egan. "Tell Iain we leave in the morning. The men can settle in for the night."

He had to admit—Maddie had toughened. Or had he weakened? He would fix that.

CHAPTER FOURTEEN

Maddie arrived in the great hall and found Brenna and Jennie already seated at the table. The hall was filled with Grant warriors and other families from the clan, but instead of feeling crowded, it was welcoming. Grant hall was quite beautiful, very warm and inviting. The rushes on the floor were clean and fresh. Several thick, colorful tapestries hung on the walls. She recognized one that her mother had worked on with Brenna's mother. They were all spectacular, and many of them depicted Grant land in the different seasons. The one featuring the snow-covered valley was her favorite. She glanced over at the hearth. Several chairs were grouped near the fire, all with soft cushions.

No one at the dining tables shouted their discontent as they waited for the meal. The large, boisterous group patiently awaited food while chatting with friends and family. So many things differed from her home—there were no loud vulgarities ringing through the hall, no lewd words or touches forced upon the serving women, and no spitting in the rushes.

Maddie seated herself across from Brenna, and Jennie quickly moved to sit with them. The Grant men sat drinking ale by the fire, conversing with some of the guards, but Alex's gaze locked with hers from across the room. He immediately headed for the table, his brothers following him. Making a polite bow, he looked into her eyes. "My lady, you are lovely this evening."

Maddie nodded her head and murmured, "Thank you, Laird Grant." She wore one of Brenna's pale green gowns. Green usually was a good color for her, and the gown flattered her curves. Blushing at the compliment, she found herself hoping Alex was not just making polite conversation.

She chastised herself. Why did it matter? Despite how safe he made her feel, he was a controlling brute, and she ought not forget it. She glanced at the other men in the room, feeling suddenly overwhelmed, and then stared down at her hands.

It mattered because it had been a long time since she cared how she looked. No one at Kenneth's keep cared about her except for her maid, so her appearance had ceased to matter to her. Besides, Kenneth would not spend a coin on a dress for her if he could spend it on himself. Now she found herself dressing with Alex in mind. Of course, she knew it was foolish of her. He had no interest in her—except, perhaps, as a target for his bellowing.

But she wanted to matter to someone.

Alex sat to her right, brushing against her briefly, and she pulled her arms close to her body, her skin burning from the contact. The thought of all the strong guards seated around the hall invaded again, but the scent of Alex and his soap wafted toward her. *You are safe. He would not allow anyone to hurt you.* Breathing in deep, she focused on the man next to her, letting his calming presence wash over her. She boldly peeked through her lashes at his profile as he spoke to his sister. How could one man compose her and shatter her all at once? What spell had he cast on her? An overpowering urge to brush a lock of hair back from his face coursed through her. She stifled a gasp at the thoughts running through her mind. Did she actually want to touch him?

The memory of how his warm arms had felt around her waist washed over her. Even then, his presence had comforted her—his touch had made her feel protected, not threatened.

Yet he wanted to make her his prisoner. She could not bear that, however pure his intentions.

Alex noticed that Maddie pulled away from him the moment he sat down next to her. She could not be more obvious, although at least she could not walk away from him at the table. Hugh was right. He had certainly made a mess of things in the stables today. He vowed to do better.

The lady was a vision of loveliness. The green gown, her long golden tresses, and her blue eyes almost stole his wits. He was determined to try harder. Sweet words for a sweet creature, old Hugh had said. He scratched his head as he tried to recall the old man's advice. Or was it soft words, soft creature? Blast it. How was he to remember such drivel? He had more important things to do than fuss over words. Couldn't the lass understand his priorities?

Catching her gaze again, he decided to try to get through to her. But it was so hard to think with her sweet scent filling his nostrils.

The rest of the men took their seats, and Brenna motioned for the servants to bring out the food—a feast of stew, platters of brown crusty breads, and baked apples.

Robbie spoke first. "So, my lady, how do you like our home? We are all hoping you will stay with us. Or do you have other plans?"

Alex cut in quickly, "She is staying with us." He abruptly turned and smiled at Maddie. *Soft words, soft creature.*

Jennie jumped up from her seat and clapped her hands. "Aye, I am so happy, Maddie. I so want you to stay!"

Maddie cleared her throat quietly before addressing them. "You have all been so wonderful to me. But I am afraid I cannot impose on your kindness forever. Once I am sure Kenneth will not cause me any more trouble, I will find a place for myself somewhere." She gave them a weak smile and started to nibble at her food.

Alex waited to see if anyone else would respond to her. Didn't they all see that she belonged here? She belonged with him. He searched his family's faces. Silence greeted him, along with expectant gazes from his brothers and sisters.

They thought *he* should be the one to say it.

After a few minutes, he sighed and turned to Maddie. "My lady, you belong here. I will not hear of you going elsewhere."

That should take care of everything. She will have no doubts about where she belongs. Hugh would surely agree with him that his comments had been soft enough for her. Why, he had almost whispered them. He was certain Maddie would accept his decree and agree to stay without argument. He smiled with satisfaction, confident his reasoning was sound.

Four faces darted to look at Maddie. Alex's brow furrowed as he stared at his family. What was bothering them now? They were incredibly rude and their fixed stares irritated him. He watched as Maddie ate a few more bites. Her skin flushed, but why? *She must be excited to know she has a new home.* He grinned at his success, barely managing to stop himself from wrapping his arm around her shoulder and pulling her in tight.

"I am sorry, Laird Grant, but I will not stay where I am treated as a prisoner."

Dead silence fell on the table. Alex's jaw dropped open. Prisoner? Where had that come from? He stared at Maddie, then at the faces of those gathered around the table. Jennie's expression stopped him cold. He recognized it—tears were soon to follow.

Wee Jennie looked back and forth from Alex to Maddie several times before blurting out, "Alex, you made Maddie cry today. It must have been you. Why are you so mean to her?" Tears welled in her eyes as she pinned him with a fierce glare.

Alex froze in astonishment. *What in blazes are they talking about?*

"If you will excuse me, I do not feel well," Maddie said as she slowly stood.

Alex was on his feet in a second, but when he reached for her arm, he poured all the gentleness he was capable of into his touch.

Maddie jerked back from him nonetheless. She stared up at him with some unnamable emotion in her eyes.

"My lady, I am sorry. Would you favor me with a stroll outside, please?"

Madeline's chin rose as she averted her eyes. "Are you sure it is safe enough for me to go outside with only one man?"

He could only blame himself that she was able to throw his own hasty words back at him. It only made him more eager for the chance to explain himself. "Please, my lady, we must talk."

Maddie nodded and proceeded toward the door. The entire hall fell silent as Alex followed her and linked his arm with hers. She flinched a little, but then settled into his touch. He squeezed her hand slightly—his way of acknowledging that he knew this was not easy for her—and led her out of the hall

They strolled in silence for a few minutes toward the gardens, listening to the hoot of an owl in the distance. A full moon brightened the night. Shivering a bit, Maddie leaned against him. He was stunned, but he wrapped his arm around her, cursing himself for not realizing it was probably too cold for her tender skin. He rubbed his hand up and down her arm in an attempt to warm her.

"I must apologize for my brusque manner earlier today." Alex fumbled with his words. He was desperate not to make any more mistakes.

She halted and turned to face him. "There is no need to apologize, but I think perhaps it would be best if I went to a convent. When is your priest due to visit? I am hoping he can help me."

He could not believe what he was hearing. He experienced a strange and painful tug on his heart when he thought of her leaving him—for a convent of all places.

"First of all, Maddie, I think we are past formalities. Call me Alex. Secondly, how could you possibly ask such a thing?"

"As you wish, Alex. I cannot stay here forever. You know I appreciate all that you have done for me, but it is not right for me to continue taking advantage of your family."

He searched his mind frantically for a sound argument for why she needed to stay with him, but he could not think of one. His mind was too addled by the thought of losing her.

"You do not belong in a convent."

"How can you make that statement? You do not know me." She stopped and gazed up at him, her eyes searching his.

Again, he had no answer for her. This connection he felt was not something he could explain. It was in his heart and he had never before given much thought to matters of the heart. But perhaps there was another way of explaining what he felt.

He leaned down and brushed his lips softly across her mouth. She did not pull away, so he cupped her face tenderly with his hands and lightly touched his lips to hers again. This time she stepped back for a moment, but he did not have time to react before she leaned into him. His heart soared as he kissed her again, groaning as he tasted her sweetness, angling his mouth to deepen the kiss. He touched his fingers to her chin to get her to open her mouth for him, and she wrapped her arms around his neck. His tongue mated with hers briefly.

Alex knew he should stop—she was an innocent, and this might well be her first kiss—but she felt so good in his arms. His hands found their way down her back. He reached for her and pulled her in tight to his body. As soon as he did, he knew it was a mistake. Her entire body stiffened and her arms pushed against his chest.

"Nay!" she screamed. Both of her arms swung at Alex's chest. "Leave me alone!" Tears ran down her cheeks as she flailed away from him.

Alex grabbed both of her wrists gently and whispered, "Maddie, stop. I will stop." He searched her face and his gut wrenched at the crazed, raw fear in her eyes—fear *he* had put there. "Maddie, please, I will not hurt you."

Maddie gazed up at Alex and realized what had happened. Her memory had flown to Niles Comming. Her eyes closed with humiliation. Alex must think she was addled. She fell against his chest and sobbed, losing all control. His arms pulled her closer and he spoke soothing words as he caressed her hair. Wrapping her arms around him, she buried her face in his warmth. She did not think she would ever be able to stop the sobs wrenching from her body.

Yet when she stopped to think about what just happened, she should be ecstatic. Alex had kissed her, and she had liked it, more than she ever would have guessed.

A commotion erupted down by the gate. A shout interrupted their embrace.

"Fetch the laird!"

Madeline pulled away from Alex and started to race back toward the castle.

Alex caught her arm. "Nay, you will stay with me."

"I cannot, Alex, I just cannot!" She pushed against him, anxious to get away. How could she make him understand?

"Nay, you have to learn to trust me, Maddie."

She contemplated that for a second, then shook her head.

Alex's voice softened as he caressed her cheek. "Always, Maddie, I will always protect you. You belong with me."

He headed toward the gate, drawing her behind him. She came willingly, but she prayed it was neither Kenneth nor the Comming. She noticed Alex's right hand was on his claymore as they approached the gate.

"Chief, there are two peasants outside requesting to see you. They refuse to leave. One says he goes by the name Mac Dumfrey."

"Mac?" Maddie screamed. She attempted to wrestle free of

Alex, but his grip was strong.

"Maddie." He wrapped his left arm around her waist and whispered in her ear. "Nay, it is not safe. It could be a trick."

Robbie and Brodie ran down the path with several guards, joining them in front of the gate. Alex released Maddie and nodded to his brothers. They immediately surrounded Maddie with several other guards, all with their weapons drawn.

Alex stepped outside the gate with five of his men. After a few moments, he returned with a slow-moving, disheveled peasant woman. "My lady, do you recognize this woman?"

"Alice! Yes, yes, she is my maid, Alice!" she cried, as she tried unsuccessfully to squeeze out from between the guardsmen. Mac followed Alex in through the gate, and his face lit up with a smile when he saw Maddie.

"I told you he would take care of our gel, Alice."

Alex nodded and his brothers stepped aside.

"Seal the gate!" Alex yelled.

Maddie ran and threw her arms around Alice, but her maid cringed when she touched her.

"What is wrong, Alice, Mac?" Maddie asked in terror, searching her stable master's face.

"Och, lass." He gripped her hand tight. "Her wounds need tending. We have much to tell you."

Alex stepped forward, picked up the filthy woman without pausing to consider it, and headed toward the keep.

"My sister, Brenna, will take care of your wounds, my lady," he said as he carried her through the courtyard. Madeline trailed behind him, trying to keep up with his long strides.

"Not 'my lady,' I am Madeline's maid, Laird," she heard Alice explain in a thin voice.

"Did you take care of Madeline?" Alex asked.

"Why, yes, I have since she was a bairn."

"Did you no' get her away from her cruel stepbrother? Did you no' tend her wounds when that bastard beat her?" Alex continued to stride forward quickly without acknowledging anyone except for the maid.

"Why, yes, Laird Grant, my husband and I did our best." Alice was barely able to nod her head.

"Well, then," Alex said, "if you have taken care of my

Madeline, then you will be 'my lady' to me."

Madeline stopped in her tracks when she heard Alex's reasoning. She gaped at him as Alice nodded her head and said, "Thank you, Laird Grant."

CHAPTER FIFTEEN

Brenna settled Mac and Alice into the chamber next to Maddie's. Servants brought up hot water and a tub for the older woman. Maddie convinced Mac to entrust her and Brenna with his wife's care and sent him down to the great hall.

Maddie sank onto a stool near the tub. "Oh, Alice, what happened?"

"It is my job to tend you, Madeline. This is not right." The older woman swiped tears from her eyes.

"Nay, this *is* right. I am guessing you took the brunt of Kenneth's anger after I left. It is my fault you were beaten." Maddie washed Alice's face of the dirt and grime she had acquired in her travels.

"He is angry you are gone, but he has no idea where you are. I did not tell him anything." Alice winced as Brenna carefully washed the lash marks on her back. "Tell me, child, how have you withstood so many lashings? The pain is most unbearable."

Rather than answer the question, Maddie took Alice's hand and squeezed it. "How did you get away?"

"Kenneth left for the Comming keep, so Mac hustled me away. We hoped to find you here. It is so good to see you safe." Alice reached up and pulled Maddie down into her embrace. "Forgive me. I have soaked you, my dear. But I am so thankful you have escaped your stepbrother. I know your parents are at peace right now."

After soaking the filth away and rinsing her hair, Madeline and Brenna helped Alice stand. Her weakness was frightening, but Maddie did not let on—her maid had been through enough. She held her as Brenna applied salve and clean linen to her wounds.

Once Alice was clothed in a clean night rail, they sat her in front of the fire so Maddie could brush her long locks. The soothing motion worked as she had hoped, and Alice's eyes soon drifted closed. The younger women helped settle her in the bed. Before exhaustion claimed her, she reached up, cupped Madeline's cheek and said, "Thank goodness Laird Grant rescued you."

Brenna stepped outside to check on Jennie. Maddie finally broke down and started sobbing, unable to stop the torrent of tears on her cheeks. How many others had suffered because of her? She could not bear the thought of her people being punished because she would not do her stepbrother's bidding. How could she apologize to Alice? Mac must hate her for what had happened. What was she to do?

Her head ached as she considered her options, each as seemingly as bad as the last. Tomorrow, she would spend time in the chapel and pray for guidance about her future path.

Lord, please help me. I know not what to do.

Brenna found Maddie like that in the hall—crying and lost and deep in thought. Wrapping her arm across Maddie's shoulder, she gave her a swift hug.

"Alice is very special to you, is she no'?"

Maddie wiped her tears away with a strip of linen. "Aye, after I lost my parents, she was the only one I trusted in the keep. I knew very few other people when I was a child. My parents were a bit overprotective, I am beginning to realize." She gave Brenna a weak smile as they headed down the stairway.

Mac jumped out of his chair at the sight of Maddie. "How is she, lass?"

"She is sleeping, Mac. What happened?"

Alex stood and ushered Madeline to a bench. Mac had informed them of the numerous beatings Kenneth had inflicted on his servants in an attempt to get information about Maddie. Wanting to protect her, Alex had implored Mac to keep silent about the travesties committed by their laird. The lass had already experienced too much guilt and pain in her life. She did not need any more.

However, one glance at the guilt in Maddie's face was enough to tell him she *already* felt responsible. Alex's need to wreak vengeance on the MacDonald was growing daily.

Alex cut in before Mac could answer. "My lady, we must take care, Laird MacDonald is anxious to find you."

"He doesn't suspect that I am here, does he?" Maddie's face crumpled, etched with concern and fear.

"Nay, no' yet," Mac answered. "He searched for you in the MacDonald lands, but has no' learned anything. All we know is that he rode to the Comming for assistance and we know the Comming is no friend of Alex's."

Maddie stood and paced in front of the table for a while before turning to face Alex. "Laird Grant, what will you do? They could be on their way here with guardsmen from both clans. They may attack your keep. Surely, I must leave." She wrung her hands together and glanced about as if searching for an easy escape. "I could not bear to see your clan attacked because of me. What if people get hurt? It would be my fault. Perhaps I will just go with the Comming if he comes for me."

Alex strode directly in front of her and searched her clear blue eyes. "If they do decide to come, we are ready for them. I train my men every day for that very reason. I will protect you as I promised. And you will *not* be leaving with the Comming." Alex's voice turned harsh when he mentioned Niles's name.

Maddie peered at him through tear-stained lashes. She did not trust him yet—he could see that in her eyes—but what could he do to gain her trust? Because after their embrace outside, he knew better than ever that he would do anything to gain her confidence. To protect her from anyone and anything. His eyes never left hers, though his mind drifted back to the memory of her luscious lips, her taste.

Maddie finally nodded her head. "Thank you, Laird. I feel I am exhausted by this day. I think it would be best for me to retire to my chamber now."

Alex reached out to touch her cheek. When he remembered their audience, he quickly changed his movement from a caress to a brush, as if to erase her worry. She blushed a deep red nonetheless.

Stumbling away from him, she gave Mac another hug. "Thank you for bringing Alice back to me."

Without a glance at Alex, she fled to her chamber.

Maddie bolted upright the next morning, her hand touching the spot where Alex had caressed her in front of everyone. Her cheeks turned pink as she recalled how soft and warm his touch had been—the warm and tender force of it spreading through her body instantly, heating her in places she had never expected. How was it possible she could still feel that small touch today? She forced herself out of bed, finished her ablutions, and dressed in a hurry— hoping it would be enough to put a stop to the carnal thoughts dancing through her mind.

She rushed through the corridor to Alice's chamber. Alice bade her to enter when she knocked. Mac had already descended to the great hall to speak with Laird Grant. It warmed Maddie's heart to see Alice was alert and sitting up in bed.

"Alice, are you better today?" Maddie asked as she sat down next to her maid and grabbed her hand.

"Aye, lass, I am fine now that I am away from that mad man. His cruelty knows no bounds." Maddie sat and plaited Alice's long gray tresses as the older woman told her about the other incidents that had taken place after her disappearance. Maddie cringed at this further evidence of Kenneth's brutality.

"Alice, I hope some of the servants will leave and find other places to live. I am sure Alex and Brenna could find places for them here. I do not want them to stay there with Kenneth. Not when he is in such a murderous rage."

"You must stop taking the burden of your stepbrother's ruthlessness onto your shoulders. It is not your fault. Kenneth's mother was a spiteful woman, and it was a sickness she passed on to her son. It has nothing to do with you. If you remember, even your father had trouble controlling the lad's behavior after he moved in with us." Alice repositioned herself to ease her pain.

Maddie thought back to that time. Kenneth and his mother had moved in with them once they had settled the fact that Kenneth was heir to the land, and it had been a disaster from the first. On numerous occasions, she had seen Kenneth's mother beat the servants for trivial matters. Maddie's mother often interfered to stop the viciousness. The servants worshipped her, for she was a true genteel lady who believed there to be something special in everyone, no matter their station.

After Maddie's parents died, Kenneth started to find fault in everything she did. It was Alice and Mac who supported her and reminded her of her innate goodness. They believed Kenneth's tirade would come to an end someday. But someday never came, and her beatings began over her betrothal.

Now Maddie was numb to most of her stepbrothers' beatings. Whenever he started in on her, she retreated inside her mind and listened to her mother singing to her in a spring meadow. Focusing on the words of the song and the beautiful tone of her mother's voice always helped her ignore the pain. Lately, however, the resonating lilt of her mother's voice had started to elude her. Maddie still remembered the words, but too much time had passed since she had heard her mother sing.

Alice's voice brought her back to reality. "Madeline, you must tell me about Laird Grant. What did he mean when he called you 'my Madeline' last night?"

"Oh, Alice, he is such a confusing man. He is so handsome, strong, and honorable...but he can also be very loud and commanding." Madeline's face blushed at the memory of Alex's hand brushing her cheek, his lips on hers. After twisting the fabric of her gown with her fingers, she peeked at her maid to gauge her reaction.

"The man has serious responsibilities," Alice said. "He is laird of a large clan, so it is his duty to train his warriors and protect his people. Mac and I have taken note of how many people depend on him for their very existence," Alice explained.

"You are right. He takes his responsibilities very seriously. He has so much to do that I fear I am a bother to him and am imposing on his hospitality. I do not know what to do."

Alice cupped her cheek softly. "Even serious honorable men need a personal life, Maddie. Has he ever been married?"

"Nay, I do no' think so. Jennie or Brenna would have told me."

"My angel, has this man shown interest in you?" A smile crept across Alice's face.

Maddie stared at her hands and bit her lower lip. "Well, he did kiss me last night."

Alice reached for her. "And, how do you feel about that?"

Maddie glanced up sharply, her gaze connecting with Alice's keen eyes. "I am so torn! He is a gentle, kind man, and his touch feels…good. It feels right. But when he kissed me last night, I started remembering Niles and what he did to me." Madeline hung her head again. "And I hit him, Alice. The man must think there is something wrong with me."

Alice pulled Madeline's hands into her warm ones. "Mayhap you should try telling him about what happened to you. He is a good man. I am sure he would understand your fears and tread more carefully with you."

"I am no longer a maiden, so what could he possibly want with me?" Maddie started pacing before the hearth. "I have no dowry. He could do much better."

"You are a wonderful young lady who would do any man proud," Alice said fiercely. "You have noble blood in you, and if your father were still alive, this is exactly the sort of match he would be arranging for you. And if Alexander Grant is half the man I think he is, he will not care about your maidenhood under the circumstances. You are a beautiful, kind-hearted woman who can give him many strong sons. But you must be honest with him. No good will come of it if you try to deceive him."

"Alice, may I ask you a female question?" Maddie sat beside her again.

"Of course you may. I hope I can answer it for you."

Maddie sighed in frustration as she looked down at her lap. "How do you tolerate the marriage bed?"

Alice reached over and tipped her chin up, "Look at me, child. The marriage bed can be a wonderful expression of love. Most men treat their wives with gentleness and respect. That is not at all what Niles forced on you. Alexander Grant is not that kind of man. I believe he will be a gentle, caring husband. Look how caring he was with me."

There was a knock on the door, and then Mac entered the room. Maddie leaned down and kissed Alice's cheek. "Thank you, Alice. I have been greedy with your time, and I think your husband needs to see you now. We will talk later."

Maddie smiled as she witnessed the genuine affection between Mac and Alice. They still gazed at each other with such love after all these years. Could she hope to find such a relationship?

She could not stop thinking about everything Alice had said to her as she walked down the corridor and the stairs. Would it be possible for her to tell Alex the truth? When she reached the great hall, she noticed very few people were there. Sitting down to break her fast, she beckoned to Brenna, who was sewing in front of the hearth.

"Good morning, Brenna. Where is everyone?" She broke off a piece of bread and bit into it.

"Alex has taken a group of men to scout the area for signs of your stepbrother. He wants to be ready in case there is an attack."

"Oh, no." Madeline put down her bread and wrung her hands in her lap. "I hope no one is hurt."

"Well, I hope something happens to your stepbrother. The man is a menace. If he isn't stopped now, he will only get worse. My brother has pledged to the king to keep peace in this land, and your stepbrother is a threat to everyone in the area. Alex is no' worried. His men are better trained than either the Comming's or your stepbrother's, and besides, there are more of them. When your father was chief, he had a mighty guard, but many of his loyal men left to join other clans. We have taken some of them in and Robbie says they all have tales to tell. I know he is your kin, Maddie, but I am sorry. He is naught but trouble."

A servant brought Maddie a bowl of porridge covered in honey. "Do not apologize," she said softly. "I know my stepbrother's harsh ways."

What could be done with her stepbrother? He should not be laird. Now his maliciousness was spreading outside his own keep. He did need to be stopped. But how?

It was dark before the men returned. Alex strode into the keep with his brothers at his side, followed by many of his guardsmen. Maddie marveled at what an impressive sight he made, so massive with all his chainmail and gear, his dark hair curled slightly at his collar, his finely chiseled jaw darkened with the day's stubble. When he was focused, his gray eyes turned dark and deadly. According to Mac, he had a reputation for making men cringe just from the serious way he looked at them.

Maddie's breath caught at the sight of this fierce, proud man. She could not take her gaze off him as he advanced toward her.

Alex and his brothers bowed slightly to her before sitting and then Alex said, "My lady, you are a vision of loveliness this evening."

"A true vision!" Brodie added with a smile.

"A pleasure never known to me before!" cried Robbie, his eyes twinkling with mischief.

Madeline beamed at the brothers. "Why, thank you, you are too kind."

Suddenly she felt Alex's scrutiny—his gaze was so powerful, she sensed it down to her toes. For a moment, she daydreamed what it would be like to have Alex come home to her every day. How would it feel to be held in his arms at night, to hold his bairns on her lap? Could she hope for such happiness? She caught Alice's gaze from across the room. Her maid was smiling at her and nodding in encouragement. She turned back to look at Alex again. Was it possible?

Then she reminded herself that she was no longer a maiden. Alice had insisted he would understand, but what if he didn't? She wasn't sure she could stand to tell him. It would be better to focus on the threat posed by her stepbrother.

"Laird Grant, were you able to find evidence of my stepbrother today?" she forced herself to ask.

Alex was vexed at what this one slight woman did to him. With one glance, her innocence and trust undid all his training as laird, forcing him to soften everything he said, everything he did, and all for one golden-haired lass. No wonder his brothers teased him. Alex thought carefully before responding. He did not want to worry Maddie needlessly, but they found evidence of horses in the area. They knew they had been watched at some point, but the invaders could have been Kenneth or Comming. It was impossible to know for sure.

"We found nothing substantial, though we plan to continue tomorrow."

Alex stared at her. What he wouldn't give to see that warm smile bestowed on him alone. He let himself savor the memory of holding her in his arms. Maddie belonged with him. She had been so passionate, but he had made the mistake of going too far. He reminded himself that he would need to move slowly with her after all she had been through, but even though he reminded himself of this repeatedly, whenever she was near, he forgot everything.

He caught a whiff of her lavender scent and sighed like a laddie.

Curse it, the woman drives me over the edge! How long would he have to wait to get her in his arms again?

Her skin was absolute perfection. He wanted the privilege of being able to stroke her tenderly whenever and wherever he wanted. The thought of anyone else doing so burned his insides.

He held his hand out for her and escorted her to the dais, then signaled for the servants to bring food for his men.

"How is your maid faring today?" Alex asked as he sat by her.

Maddie pointed to the hearth where Alice sat with her husband, Mac, and wee Jennie. "As you can see, my laird, she is doing much better. Thank you for helping her. She has a heart of gold and is very special to me."

The sound of little feet pounding up to them interrupted their conversation. Alex turned to see Jennie flying toward him. He pushed his chair back just in time to catch her in midair before she landed in his lap. She threw her arms around his neck and gave him a kiss on the cheek.

"Alex, I like our new friends. Mac tells the best stories."

"Is that so?" Alex retorted. "I have been replaced that easily, my wee one?"

Jennie wrinkled her face. "Nay, Alex, but sometimes you are very busy."

"Never too busy for you, little squirrel," he said, brushing a kiss on her nose.

Alex caught Maddie watching him. The sadness in her eyes broke his heart. How would it feel to have no family to love?

If only he could make it right for her.

CHAPTER SIXTEEN

The relentless activity in Maddie's mind kept her awake for much of the night. Intent on getting some air, she climbed out of bed, slipped on her robe, and tiptoed out of the room. When she reached the end of the passageway, she opened the heavy door. The rush of fresh, cool night air blew across her face, making her smile.

She carefully wound her way up the stairs. After stepping out onto the battlements, she glanced around, hoping she was alone. Once she was satisfied that she had no unanticipated company, she gazed out at Alex's lands. What a magnificent sight. From this vantage point, she could see the treetops in the forest and the fields filled with row after row of neat crops yet to be harvested. Wrapping her robe tighter around her body, she made her way down the walkway to find a place to sit. Soon she found the perfect spot—a flat stone encased in the wall.

Maddie sat and pulled her knees up to her chin, carefully tucking her robe around her. The chaotic thoughts all rushed back to her. Time was what she needed to decide what her next step should be, but she did not have it. Who knew when Kenneth would arrive? She'd escaped from him for the time being, but he wouldn't give up easily.

She shuddered as she thought back on the beatings and injustices she'd endured at her stepbrother's hands. She would never go back, she just could not. Kenneth had destroyed her home, and it was time for her to move on with her life.

Marrying Niles Comming was certainly not the answer. Maddie's eyes closed as the painful memories assailed her. She had tried fighting him, but her struggles had only excited him more. He'd eventually tied her to the bed and taken her over and over.

She had been bruised for a sennight afterwards, but she had tried to be strong around her servants and her maid, always aware of the pitying looks they gave her.

Maddie rested her chin on her knees and thought of how different Alex was from Niles and Kenneth. He was so powerful and strong, yet when he touched her, she sensed only gentleness. Firm but fair, he commanded the respect of his people, and he often put their welfare ahead of his own. Kenneth would never do that. His needs had always come first.

Her thoughts turned to the marriage bed. She believed that it would be different with Alex. But even so, the marriage act was the same for everyone, was it not? How could she bear that pain again?

Alice had said that the act should be done between two people in love. Was she in love with Alex? Nay, it couldn't be love she felt for him. He still made her anxious at times. He was so quick to anger. But then she thought of the many good things she knew about Alex. He was a wonderful brother to wee Jennie. He always had a smile for the lassie—a smile that made Maddie's knees go weak. And then there was the way he had comforted his sister by buying her new puppies. Kenneth liked to beat animals.

Maddie felt a smile stretch across her face as she thought of the quick, decisive way Alex had picked up Alice. She had been filthy, but that hadn't stopped him. And then there was the way he'd called Alice 'my lady' and Maddie as 'my Madeline.' Did he really think of her that way?

She remembered how good it had felt to be in his arms last night. And his kiss…she had never imagined it could feel so wonderful.

The distant sound of footsteps registered in her ears, making her flinch. She hoped it was only a guard, but cold fear crept down her spine. A booming, "What say you?" caused her to jump up from her spot. Alex's dark eyes locked with hers. He towered over her, his hand on his sword.

"Maddie?" he asked. "What the devil are you doing up here?" He studied her slowly and then tugged at the robe around her. "Especially at this time of night?"

"I could not sleep. I thought fresh air might help. Alex, do you have a moment for us to talk?" she asked as she gazed into his steel gray eyes. She needed to apologize for hitting him, and besides, they needed to talk about Kenneth. His eyes almost looked silver in the moonlight. She shivered as his stare raked over her.

"Aye, but you need to keep yourself warm. The nights are cool." He sat on the stone, pulled her onto his lap, and wrapped his plaid around her. "Now what has you so upset this eve?"

Maddie sighed, relaxing into his warm embrace. She forced herself to focus on her words. "I do not know what to do to stop Kenneth from hurting people. I fear I have endangered your family and your clan, and that is not right. You know I would not do anything to hurt any of you. If he attacks, lives may be lost, and it will be completely my fault. What can I do to stop this from happening?"

He rested his chin in the hollow of her neck. She loved the feeling of his warm breath fanning across her skin. "Maddie, 'tis not your fault. Your stepbrother is a danger to us all. If we do not stop him now, he will continue on his rampage. Our king wants peace, and I gave my word to keep it. I'll not allow Kenneth to threaten my people or anyone else. 'Tis my job to stop him."

"Maybe it would be better for everyone if I go back." Maddie twisted her hands back and forth in her lap repeatedly. It was unthinkable, but she would do it if it was the only way to protect Alex and his family.

Alex's voice turned gravelly. "He will never touch you again. I gave you my word that I would protect you, and so help me, I will." Alex's jaw clenched. "Nay, Maddie, you will never go back to him."

Maddie feared she had made him angry again. "Then maybe it would be better for everyone concerned if I were to join a convent. Neither my brother nor the Comming would be able to reach me." She turned to Alex with pleading eyes.

"Maddie, do you no' trust me to keep you safe? I train my warriors every day to protect my people—and you are one of us now. Why would you want to go to a convent?"

"Alex, you do not understand. Things are sometimes not what they seem." Maddie cringed at the thought of revealing her past to Alex, but Alice was right. She could not deceive him. It probably would make him hate her, but it would be best for him to know the truth.

"I understand what I need to understand." As he spoke, he brought his thumb up and grazed it lightly across her cheek, then brought it down to rub her bottom lip. Her heart pounded against her chest. "You are mine. You belong with me. I know you are no' ready for it yet, but I can wait. I will wait as long as you need me to wait."

He brought his lips down to hers and kissed her lightly. He increased the pressure slightly and ran his tongue across her lips to get her to open to him. She whimpered and leaned into him, wrapping her arms around him. He ran his hand up and down her arm and lightly brushed her breast. She thought it must have been by accident, and to her surprise, she did not want to pull away.

She moved closer to him, wanting more, though not knowing exactly *what* it was she wanted. But was it right to satisfy her needs when his feelings would certainly change after he learned her secret?

She slowly withdrew from him and whispered, "Alex, you don't understand. Niles…"

"What is it, Maddie? Whatever it is, it does not matter to me."

She gazed into his eyes and realized that she *did* love this man. The feeling had crept up on her, unexpectedly, over her time at the Grant keep. He was looking at her with such care and concern that the thought of leaving his arms made her want to weep. But she had to be honest.

She placed her hand in his and mumbled, her head down, "I am sorry I hit you when you kissed me, Alex. But when a man touches me, I jump, I cringe."

She couldn't bring herself to look him in his eyes. She did not want to see the revulsion in them.

"Niles raped me, Alex. Kenneth gave me to him when we were betrothed." Tears rolled down her cheeks. "I tried to fight him, but I was not strong enough. I am not a maiden anymore. No one will want me. You especially deserve better."

And she prepared for him to push away from her.

Alex pulled her closer, caressing her back. He was so angry he could not speak. Sighing softly into her hair, he noticed the tears dotting her eyelashes. She was clinging to him and crying softly into his neck. Neither of them spoke. Everything made sense to him now. How had this mere slip of a lass survived so much pain? No wonder she was timid around him. He now understood so much more about her. He kissed her hair, her forehead, and pulled her tightly to him. She belonged with him—they belonged *together*. Forever. He was surprised at how strong his feelings of protectiveness were toward her. But first he had something else to attend to.

Kenneth MacDonald and Niles Comming were both dead men.

CHAPTER SEVENTEEN

Maddie stretched to ease the kinks in her back from a restless sleep and swung her legs over the side of the bed. Late morning light filtered in through a slit in the closed shutter. She bit her lip, dreading the day ahead.

Alex had quietly walked her back to her door last night, kissed her briefly, and bade her good night. She'd lain awake for another couple of hours, worrying about the effect her confession would have on him.

He had said very little, but he had held her tight through her deluge of tears, softly caressing her hair. Still, she had felt the rigidity of his body. Did he think it was her fault? Or maybe he was angry with Niles? Or Kenneth? She was uncertain. How she wished she could talk to her mother. Deciphering Alex was a challenge at times. The man gave no clues as to his thoughts or emotions.

Hopefully, she would have the opportunity to talk to him today. Of course, now that he knew the truth about her, he might choose to avoid her. Maybe he thought her wanton, especially after the way she had acted in his arms last night. He probably would not want her influencing wee Jennie. She closed her eyes, remembering how wonderful it had felt to be held by him. How safe and special and warm. He had told her she belonged with him, but he probably felt differently now that he knew she was not a maiden.

Fiona had left hot water for her, still warm enough to use. She washed and donned a clean gown before heading to the hall to break her fast. When she arrived, the hall was empty. She made her way to the kitchen, where Brenna was busy planning meals with

Cook. Not wanting to disrupt their work, she filled a bowl with porridge and headed back into the hall. Where was everyone?

Brenna followed her after a few minutes. "Good day to you, Maddie. May I sit with you?"

"Of course. You know I cherish your company. Where is everyone this morn?" Maddie glanced around the quiet hall again.

"Alice is still recovering, so she returned to her chamber to rest. Old Hugh was very busy this morning, so Mac has gone to the stables to help him."

"Why was Old Hugh so busy?" Maddie asked, trying to pay attention to Brenna. What she really wanted to know was how to find Alex.

"Alex came into the hall this morning in a fierce mood. He gathered near to two hundred of his guard and left straightaway. He barked at everyone he encountered." Brenna raised her eyebrows as she stared at Madeline.

Madeline chewed her lip with worry. "Where were they going?"

"He said he was going after Niles and your stepbrother. He told the men they would not return until they were found."

Madeline gasped and stared at Brenna. "Oh, nay!"

"I don't know what rankled my brother so. I haven't seen him like this in a long time. Most of us know not to cross him when he is in such a bleak mood, so only a couple of lads had to find out the hard way. Mayhap you might have an idea about what put my brother into this mood?"

Maddie cringed under her friend's gaze. "What do you mean?"

"Those who were foolish enough to question their laird are presently cleaning out the garderobes. They were not allowed to join the jaunt. My brother does not tolerate anyone questioning his decisions. Alex, of course, had to leave some men behind to protect the keep."

Maddie's belly collapsed. She stopped eating and fought to keep her porridge down.

"What's wrong?" Brenna asked quietly.

"Oh, Brenna, I told Alex about the rape. He seemed very upset when I told him, but I thought he was upset with me."

Brenna rubbed Maddie's arm. "That explains much about his mood this morning. But you must know that Alex would not be upset with you. He has a strong sense of honor, and my brothers were taught to respect women. He is probably furious that Kenneth allowed such a thing to happen. I know my brother—when he says something, he means it. They will not return before they find Kenneth and Niles. I have faith in my brother to do the right thing. You must, too." Brenna gave a fierce nod and left the room.

For the rest of the day, Maddie forced herself to stay busy to avoid focusing on her anxiety, but the worried thoughts did not leave her. The men could be back in a day or in a month. Who knew how long it would take them to find Niles or Kenneth? What if Alex lost and was taken captive? What if they killed him? She could not bear to think about losing him now.

Could she possibly hope he still wanted her after learning she was no longer a maiden? She found herself lost in all that was Alex. She remembered his gentleness, the way his skin felt against hers, the way his lips tasted. The way he gazed at her made her heart melt. Conjuring up his scent, his warmth, his essence, she realized her heart was totally captured by the fierce highlander.

Though she was sure it was too soon for Alex to be in love with her, maybe that would change some day. Could she be happy being his mistress if that was the only way she could have him?

Two days later, there was still no word of the men. Maddie searched outside for her little ones, hoping to occupy her time with telling them stories. As she strolled down the hill, she spotted a small group of children in the middle of the courtyard on the grass. She waved and several of them ran up to greet her. Wee Emma was just learning to walk, so she struggled to keep up with the others. Maddie greeted them all and then swept by to scoop Emma in her arms.

"Oh, what a big lass you are, Emma! You are walking about like an expert. I am so proud of you." Maddie glanced at Emma's mother, who beamed back at her.

"She has been waiting to show you, my lady. She is quite proud of her new talent."

"As she should be." Maddie hugged the little girl tight and set her down with the others. "What is everyone doing this morning?" she asked as she looked at her little group of darlings.

Jennie came tearing out of the keep, running right up to them. "We have been waiting for you, Maddie," she said eagerly. "We were hoping you would tell us another story."

"Please, my lady, please!" A loud cacophony of little voices greeted her. How could she refuse them?

Maddie eased herself down on the grassy knoll. "I would be happy to tell you a story, but be sure to sit close to me so you can hear me well." Emma toddled over and plopped herself into Maddie's lap.

Several stories later, a low rumbling noise interrupted her words.

Tommy jumped up, screaming, "They're back! The guardsmen are back! I can't wait to see my da. My lady, you must come and look with me."

Maddie handed wee Emma to her mother and then followed Tommy to the staircase to the battlements. What Maddie saw in the valley beneath them made her freeze in place.

Horses—so many she couldn't count. They filled her vision, moving swiftly toward the keep. Shouts from the clan guardsmen reverberated as they drew near. She saw horses with men, horses without them, and she thought she saw some men tied to horses. What had she done?

She grabbed the stone wall to steady herself. Alex? Where was Alex? Her eyes searched for him, but the guards were still too far away for her to find him in the crowd. Blood pounded through her temples as she scanned the horizon.

"Someday I will ride as a guardsman for Laird Grant!" Tommy pulled on her hand to get her attention. "My da said I could if I work real hard. I will, won't I?"

Maddie glanced at Tommy, but could not focus on his words. Her hand went to her mouth as she continued to search the sea of Highlanders for one man. As they drew closer, she was finally able to pick him out, riding in the front with a grim look on his face. Was that blood running down his arm? Was he seriously injured? Maddie's eyes blurred as she turned to race back down the stone steps.

She fought for control, for focus, but she was not sure she could deal with this situation. What if Alex had come back with both Kenneth and Niles? Saints above, the possibility of seeing them both again was more terrible than she could bear. She rushed so fast toward the steps of the keep, she tripped over a stone in the courtyard. Jennie's voice called out to her as she caught her fall, but as soon as she was steady, she continued on toward the steps. She had to get inside. She had to get to the safety of her room.

Please, Papa. Don't make me have to face them again.

Her skirts crinkled in her hand, she charged forward blindly. The grate of the portcullis raising broke into her thoughts, unleashing panic within her.

Lord, please help me.

Total chaos erupted as mothers shoved their little ones into their cottages and everyone else ran toward the gates. The thundering of horses' hooves came closer and closer. The air filled with clouds of dirt and angry shouts.

Maddie grabbed wee Jennie as the lassie approached the steps. Jennie's eyes were huge as she watched Alex lead the men into the bailey.

"What is happening, Maddie?" she cried out. "I don't understand. My brother looks so mean and mad. What has happened to him! Maddie, please, make this stop!"

Maddie held Jennie tight as Alex and his brothers approached on horseback. "I am not sure, Jennie," she whispered. She wound her trembling arms around the lassie and buried her face in her hair.

Alex's black destrier stopped in front of them, prancing with excitement. Madeline stared wide-eyed at Alex. He sat tall, his sword at his waist, blood weaving a current down his left arm. His dark eyes wrenched her gut as they connected with hers. After a long moment, she tore her eyes from Alex and searched behind him.

Two men were bound and gagged on their horses, thrashing to get free. Robbie punched one of the men in his belly as he yanked him from the horse. Another guard did the same with the other.

Niles and Kenneth!

Madeline's vision blurred as she watched as the men were roughly toppled from their horses. She shrank back and closed her eyes, shuddering, and reminded herself they were both tied up and could not hurt her now. Alex would never allow it.

Madeline vaguely heard Alex shout to Jennie, "Inside!" His wee sister took off toward the keep without question. Maddie turned around in confusion, unsure of what to do or where to go.

Alex dismounted, strode toward her, and briefly bowed his head before returning to the center of the courtyard, bringing her with him. He strode with conviction, his muscles bulging down his forearms, rippling in his legs. The other guards followed, and stable boys rushed forward to remove the horses in the melee. Madeline stood to Alex's right, slightly behind him, while Niles and Kenneth still stood bound and gagged amidst a circle of soldiers, their faces twisted in anger and indignation.

Alex's people gathered in close, seemingly in awe of what was happening. More and more streamed in through the gates, anxious to see the laird and his men. Once the horses had all been removed, a dead silence hung in the air as everyone waited to hear what their laird had to say. What would Alex do next?

Madeline's insides turned to water. Anger was written all over Alex's face. Tension was evident in his every muscle, and she could almost feel the rage coursing through his body. She glanced at Niles and Kenneth, hoping they had not noticed her yet, then quietly moved away from Alex, hoping she could slip inside without being noticed. She was not sure she could face Niles and Kenneth together.

"Madeline!" Alex hollered. "Stop where you are and be still!" He turned to face the crowd.

Madeline froze in her path and turned toward the courtyard. "Yes, Laird Grant," she whispered with her head down. She slowly raised her eyes to meet Kenneth's. He sneered at her, despite the gag in his mouth, but he wasn't so overbearing in his present state. Maddie inched her chin up and stood tall. She scanned all the people gathered in the courtyard, noting their bewildered looks. Well, they would probably hear all now. She was determined to keep her head up. Alex would want her to be strong.

Alex pointed to Maddie's stepbrother with his sword. "Remove the prisoner's gag!"

Kenneth shouted obscenities and accusations as soon as his mouth was freed. "How dare you touch me, Grant! You have no right, you bastard! Return my sister to me. I am her guardian. The law says she is mine to do with as I wish."

"And does the law include beating the lass with a horsewhip? I witnessed the effects of your cruelty, MacDonald. You will never get the chance to hurt her again. Madeline stays here with me. I will take the matter to the king if I must. He won't side with you. You are my prisoner until he decides otherwise."

As the two men battled with words, Madeline listened and subconsciously took a small step toward Alex. She realized what she was doing and inched a little closer yet. She trusted him to protect her. Who knew if Niles could possibly break his bindings? Mayhap Kenneth would break free and lunge for her. She rubbed the underside of her arms without thinking, tears blurring her vision. She inched a little closer to Alex. *Alex, I know you told me to stay still, but you are moving too far away. Please stay. Don't let either of them touch me again.* She brushed at the invisible tears that threatened to roll down her cheeks. Certainly he would not be upset by a little movement.

Alex pointed to the Comming next, ordering for his gag to be removed, too. Niles spat on the ground in front of Alex. "You will pay for this, Grant. First, you back out of the contract with my sister, now you interfere with my betrothed. Madeline is mine. MacDonald betrothed her to me, and I want her back!"

"You are released from your betrothal to this lady. She does not want you, Comming. She never did," Alex stated. "She is under my protection now, and you will no' touch her again."

"At whose orders is she under your protection, Grant?" Kenneth yelled out.

"At the lady's request. She does not want anything to do with you or your friend."

"And since when does a wench have any say about her future?" asked Kenneth.

Alex strode up to Kenneth and positioned the point of his sword at his throat. Madeline could not hold back a gasp.

"Since she came to my keep, MacDonald." A small trickle of blood slid down Kenneth's throat. The man's face instantly went white and his knees buckled. One of Alex's guards caught him before he went down.

Alex chuckled and turned to smirk at the Comming.

"She is mine, Grant!" Niles glanced around at the gathered crowd. "And she will tell you the very same. She begged me to take her maidenhead! Who could possibly want her now?" he yelled out for all the crowd to hear.

Madeline cringed as a collective gasp range out from the

spectators. The crowd quieted as they waited to hear their laird's response to the accusation. What would his people think of her? Her secret was out. She took two more steps toward Alex. He might be the only one willing to help her now. Her stomach churned from the sight and smell of so many male bodies. They could reach her in a moment if they decided to make her suffer for the Comming's accusation. Her eyes snapped shut.

She loved so many of Alex's clan. They had welcomed her with open arms, but how would they feel about her now? Who would allow someone so wanton to tell stories to their children? Her world crumbled in front of her, what was left of it, anyway. She opened her eyes and took another tentative step toward Alex. Toward safety.

Alex strode over to Niles and placed his sword at his belly. Madeline stared at the ground, her breath hitching in sheer fright. Her legs wobbled as she fought to regain control.

Alex! Don't you recognize how much I need you right now?

She took another tentative step toward him. The men appeared to be closing in around her. She coughed to try to draw in more air, tugging at her bodice to loosen it.

I can't breathe!

Angry eyes stared at her from the crowd. Tightness clawed at her chest. Would anyone dare reach for her in front of Alex? She shivered and rubbed her hands up and down her arms.

Just one more step closer. Alex, please don't leave me.

Alex's voice echoed deep but powerful. "How dare you tell such lies about the lady! You are fortunate that I am a laird of the king, else I would gut you right here. Or make certain you will never rape again. Perhaps some time in the dungeon will help to clear your thoughts for now, Comming."

Alex caught movement out of the corner of his eye. He turned and gaped when he realized how close Madeline was to him. She took another step toward him, her eyes locked directly onto his, fear radiating from every ounce of her being. Toward him? She was finally moving toward him? He immediately felt a little tug in his chest, but he fought the urge to let a smile steal over his face. By the saints, he would banish that fear from her eyes forever. He knew what he had to do. He pointed to Madeline, and in an instant, his brothers and three of his soldiers had circled around her.

He then turned to Niles Comming, raised his sword, and shouted, "The lass marries me!"

Out of the corner of his eye, he saw Madeline jump in surprise.

Kenneth hopped up and down as if possessed and shouted, "She'll never agree, Grant. She is a dead woman if she marries you." He lurched toward Madeline, but was restrained by several soldiers. "I will kill her with my bare hands if she agrees. Madeline, do you hear me? I will kill you, but not until I beat you near to death first! If you think the last time was bad, wait until you see what happens this time. You will never be able to walk again."

The angry roar of the crowd practically masked the conversation.

"I have not heard it from her, Grant!" Niles bellowed. "She would not dare to marry you when she knows she is mine."

"She *will* agree to marry me. Will you not, my lady?" He turned to Madeline, who was still surrounded by his men.

Madeline blanched and said, "May I have a word with you, Laird?"

Lowering his voice, he said, "Just say 'aye' Maddie and your troubles are over."

"But could I please have a word first?" she asked beseechingly.

"Are you jesting with me, Maddie?"

The Comming chuckled. "She's daft, Grant. Have you not learned that yet?"

Alex waited patiently for a moment. What was the lass thinking? He knew she was upset by the presence of her two tormentors. But were not lasses supposed to be thrilled by proposals of marriage?

"She does not sound so agreeable to me, Grant!" Niles taunted.

"Please!" she cried.

Alex gazed into her big blue eyes and recognized the fear in them. He sighed, sheathed his sword, and stepped inside the protective circle his warriors had formed around Madeline. They had to step apart to make room for his broad shoulders.

"What is it, Maddie?"

"I think it should be in private, Alex."

Close to losing his patience, Alex ground out, "Niles and

Kenneth cannot hear you. We do no' have time, Maddie, you must ask me in front of my men."

Madeline leaned toward him and whispered, "All right. If you give me your word that you will not tie me to the marriage bed, I will agree to marry you."

The guardsmen shuffled their feet and stared off into the distance.

Alex's brow furrowed, "What did you say?"

"If you promise not to tie me to the marriage bed, I will agree to marry you," she said as she gazed into his eyes. "Please, Alex, I need your word on this." He noticed her wringing her hands as she spoke. He raised his eyes to hers, but could not bring himself to say a word.

That bastard had tied her to the bed? Raping her had not been enough for him? No wonder the lass was afraid of him. He studied her in amazement. In telling him this, she had confirmed two things. One, this woman would give him the strongest lads in the land. Two, Niles would never make it to the dungeon.

Alex squeezed her hand, then stepped out of the group of warriors surrounding Madeline. He heard Brodie whisper to Robbie. "This will not be good."

Then Madeline's sweet voice said, "I do not understand."

"Oh, you will understand in a minute, my lady!"

Alex did the only thing he was capable of doing at that moment. Roaring, he unsheathed his sword, swung it over his head in a circle, and rushed toward Niles Comming. In his mind, all he could see was his Maddie tied to a bed as Niles Comming grinned and grunted over her.

"Untie him and get him a weapon! This is between you and me, Comming. I fight you for my betrothed's honor. We fight to the death!"

"Gladly, Grant. I have waited for the moment to use a sword on you. But know that I will be the last man standing!" Niles snickered. "First, you die, Grant, then I will have my fun with the lass again."

Madeline grabbed Brodie's shoulder to keep from swooning.

CHAPTER EIGHTEEN

A guardsman untied Niles and led him to the center of the courtyard while another tossed him a sword. He spent several minutes stretching his muscles, showing off his strength. He paced and paced, bellowing and shouting occasionally. Alex just stood there quietly, ignoring the bluster, and focused on his enemy's face.

He would have to summon all of his strength and focus to do this right. The vision of his Madeline at the Comming's mercy was something he had to remove from his mind. It would cause him to act emotionally instead of instinctively, which he could not afford right now. His goal was to let the Comming tire himself out. All of his yelling and pacing was costing him energy, energy he would need to stay in the ring with Alexander Grant. Finally, he stepped toward him.

The two men circled each other, measuring the other's strengths and weaknesses, and the crowd moved back to make room for the upcoming battle. Even though he had fought in numerous battles and his reputation as a swordsman was legendary, Alex knew better than to underestimate his enemy. Niles Comming was also an excellent swordsman. But every man had a weakness. He was quite sure he knew the Comming's. But the Comming also knew that Madeline was *his* weakness.

Madeline's gut clenched as she watched the scene unfold. Robbie and Brodie and the other warriors still surrounded her. From the corner of her eye, she saw Brenna making her way down the steps of the keep.

"I do not understand, Robbie. What is happening?" Brenna

asked when she reached them. Her hands flew up to her throat as she surveyed the courtyard.

"The Chief is avenging Madeline's honor. Alex announced that he would take Madeline as his wife, but she insisted on asking him a question before she would accept his proposal," Robbie said, speaking quietly so as not to disturb Alex's concentration.

"But why now? Why here? Why not send both men to the king?" Maddie asked.

"I think that may have been Alex's original plan, but when he heard your question, he did not take kindly to the implications of what you said," Brodie replied.

Brenna gaped at all three of them. "What did you say, Madeline? I was inside with Jennie. I did not hear your question."

Robbie and Brodie both cleared their throats and turned their heads away from the women.

"Madeline?" Brenna prompted.

"I...I..." Maddie swallowed bile. "I needed Alex's word on something before I agreed to the betrothal."

"Word on what, Maddie?" Brenna's tone was becoming more and more insistent.

Too embarrassed to repeat what she had said, Maddie blushed and shook her head.

"Madeline?" Brenna stared at her.

Madeline closed her eyes and whispered, "I asked him to promise me he would not tie me to the marriage bed."

Brenna staggered back in shock. "Oh, saints have mercy! He will kill him," she added, staring at Robbie.

Madeline hung her head and covered her face with her hands. Now she would be hated by everyone, even her few new friends. And what if something happened to Alex? Her gut churned as a vision of Alex bleeding forced its way into her mind. She fought to hold back her tears.

"I am sorry, Brenna. But I cannot tolerate it anymore. With them both here in front of me, their torture is fresh in my mind. Kenneth tied me to chairs, and whatever was closest at the time. Niles tied me to...to a bed. I cannot live my life like that anymore, not even for your brother." She wiped the flowing tears off her cheeks. "I had to know for sure."

Brenna sighed and stepped past her brothers, reaching for

Maddie. Her voice softened, "Maddie, you know my brother. How could you think he would do such a thing to you? He would never treat a woman that way."

"Before I came here, I had started to think all men beat women." Maddie's voice broke as she clung to Brenna. "Kenneth has beaten me for the past two years, and he does the same to most of the servants. They say my da spoiled me, so I thought that was why he never hit me."

Niles's taunts rose above the crowd.

"Alex!" Madeline broke away from Brenna and pushed against her guards in an attempt to get closer to the fight. "Robbie, I need to stop him." Tears flowed unchecked down her face.

"My lady, the laird will have our heads if we let you near him. You will only distract him. He needs to concentrate," Brodie explained.

"Robbie, do something!" Brenna pleaded.

"Brenna, I do not try to stop my laird when he is this focused. This is not a small matter to Alex. It is a matter of honor. From the stories I hear, 'tis about time someone held the Comming accountable for his actions. The king will not retaliate. Alex is acting to keep peace. Now, cease talking!" Robbie glared at her as he turned to watch the action again.

Alex patiently waited for Niles to make the first move. He preferred to get a careful measure of his opponent's strengths and weaknesses. The crowd grew impatient and broke into a chant waiting for their laird to make his move. Niles raised his sword and came at Alex from above. He drove his sword over and over at him. The clash of steel on steel rang out as Alex easily blocked all of Niles's parries.

Niles took a step back. "You will not get her, Grant. She is mine, and she was good, too!"

Alex turned and swung his claymore in a sideways arc at Niles. Niles blocked the blow, just missing having his belly sliced open. Alex parried at him again and again, swinging his powerful arms repeatedly at his adversary. The crowd's chants grew louder. Sparks flew as the sounds of crashing metal continued. The ruthless drive continued, spurred by a power even Alex didn't fully comprehend. Then a shout wrenched from the crowd as Alex slipped on the gravel and took the edge of Niles's sword in his right thigh. The crowd booed at the injury to their laird. First blood had been drawn.

Alex stepped back to reassess. The wound was a small one, but he smiled. It was a reminder to him that he needed to stay in control. Niles would try to anger him with his taunts and lies about Madeline. He had to shut his mind to them if he was to win. He expected the Comming to be a dirty fighter. The man knew nothing of the word "honor" as he expected.

The crowd cheered Alex on. He couldn't see Madeline but preferred it that way. He wanted no distractions. His brothers would take care of her and his sister. He would not have to see the fear in Madeline's eyes anymore because of Niles Comming.

Alex lunged at Niles. Niles anticipated the move and rolled out of the way, but not before Alex sliced into his shoulder. The crowd roared. Niles still got up and was able to block two more blows.

Both men stepped to the outside of their circle. Niles paced as Alex held firm, both changing their strategies. The crowd quieted as they noted the blood dripping on the ground. Alex's thigh was still trickling red, and Niles's shoulder bled profusely. Alex knew he now had a weak spot on Niles. His shoulder had to be paining him and would weaken quickly. He glanced at his thigh. The pain was minimal and the bleeding was already slowing. But not on Niles. His shoulder continued to bleed heavily. He had to force him to swing overhead.

Alex glowered at his enemy. Slowly, Niles smiled. He walked a little closer to Alex and said quietly, "Did your lassie tell you how much I made her bleed? She was such a screamer." Alex's eyes turned dark as coal, but he refused to be baited.

At that, Niles swung his claymore over his head and brought it straight down on Alex, trying to slice him in two. Alex blocked the swing, but stumbled and fell to his left. Niles saw his opening and quickly brought his sword over his head again for the killing blow. Just as he swung in a downward arc, Alex turned back to his right in a flash and forced his blade into Niles's belly and pulled up. Niles looked at him briefly, stunned, before crumpling to the ground, dropping his sword.

A cheer erupted from the crowd as the Comming went down. Alex's men pounded his back as he lowered his sword. He turned to search for Madeline, but couldn't find her in the throng of people. Sweat dripped down his face. He shook his head because his vision blurred, but he couldn't stop. He frantically scanned the area for her. Kenneth was still out there and she was no longer with his brothers.

Madeline screamed as soon as she noticed Alex stumble. Then she saw Niles go down, but it was impossible to tell if his sword had found Alex first. She clawed through her guards in the chaos and ran toward Alex, tears blinding her vision. Robbie yelled at her from behind, but she did not turn back. She had to get to him; he had to be all right. She could not lose him now. Alex was the only man for her—a truth she knew deep in her heart. The crowd surrounded Alex and she could not get through. People were grabbing at her, but she punched, kicked, and scratched at everyone who stood in her way. She kept screaming his name. When she finally found him, she threw herself against him and wrapped her arms around his neck.

He held her tight. She sobbed his name, but he never spoke. His breathing was ragged from the battle. She swore she would never let him go. Drenched in sweat and grime, he ran his hands over her back and swept her into his arms, then started moving slowly toward the keep. Maddie could tell he was weakening. There was too much blood, blood from his thigh and his arm. Exhaustion was overtaking him; she could sense it in his grasp. She tried to pull away from him after he made it up the steps to the great hall, but he would not release her.

"Alex, Alex, are you all right?" Tears blinded her vision as she attempted to assess his wounds.

But as soon as he stepped inside the door, he collapsed.

CHAPTER NINETEEN

The Grant guards dispersed the crowd, and Robbie and Brodie carried their brother to his chamber so Brenna could see to his wounds. To ensure Kenneth did not escape in the chaos, Robbie had one of his warriors throw him into the dungeon. Guards would watch him there. Wee Jennie took one look at Alex and opened her mouth in a wail. Maddie's head spun with confusion. Neither of them were allowed into Alex's room.

Jennie grabbed Maddie's skirts. "Maddie, is he dead? Is my brother dead? What is wrong with him? What happened? Who killed my brother?"

Maddie took Jennie into her arms and sat on the floor. "Hush, child, he is not dead. There was a battle and he fought very bravely. He is injured, and your sister needs to see to his wounds." The fear in the wee lassie's eyes broke her heart.

"Oh, Maddie! I cannot lose my brother, too. Why was he fighting? What happened?" Jennie's gut-wrenching sobs echoed through the stone corridor, wrenching Maddie's heart.

"He was protecting us from a very bad man, Jennie. But that man will never bother us again. We will sit here and wait for your sister."

Jennie sobbed until all that remained were hiccups. Resting the wee lassie's head on her lap, Maddie brushed her hair back and sang a soft ballad she remembered from her mother until all the tension in Jennie's body abated.

Fiona ran by them, carrying hot water, linens, and Brenna's healing box. After a short time, the door opened and Brodie stepped out. Opening his arms wide, he said, "Och, come here, little squirrel."

Jennie jumped into his arms, and he wiped her tear-stained face with a cloth.

"Is Alex going to be all right, Brodie? He is not going to die, is he?" The lassie tugged on Brodie's hair and twisted it as she spoke.

"Nay, lass, your brother is strong. He will be sore for a while, but he will be fine. You know you will have to be extra good to him and help take care of him," Brodie said as he kissed her forehead.

His sister rested her head on his shoulder. "Can I see him? I just want to give him a kiss. I think he will get better faster if I give him a kiss. Papa always said that hurts and cuts need kisses to get better. Alex probably needs a lot of kisses."

Brodie chuckled as he smoothed her hair. "Nay, lass, Brenna has to sew him up first. And he is very tired, so I think he may sleep a bit after Brenna is done. Even I am tired. Alex rode us hard chasing after those bad men. We had quite a battle going before we captured them."

Madeline peered at Brodie expectantly. "Is he talking?"

"Aye, he is in and out, but he has not asked for you yet, my lady."

Fortunately, Brodie's expression was one of sympathy and not of censure. Nonetheless Madeline's shoulders slumped in defeat. Maybe he had changed his mind and he never wanted to see her again. Well, if so, he would not get rid of her that easily. She was not moving from this spot until he either came out of that chamber or talked to her, whichever came first.

After an hour or two, Maddie's legs went numb. How long could she sit on the floor waiting? She chided herself for being so weak, but it did not matter. She would not leave him. Finally, Brenna stepped into the corridor and announced that Alex was dozing off and on. She ushered Brodie into the room with wee Jennie, then turned to Maddie, "Why don't you go down and eat something? It will be a while until he is awake. I slipped him a sleeping draught."

"How bad are his injuries?" Maddie asked, searching her face for clues.

"He will be all right, Maddie. Our biggest worry is fever. His wounds were very dirty. I cleaned them the best I could. I do no' think he has any broken bones. But, as you know, the biggest bone we need to worry about is his head. He will not remain in bed for long. He is much too stubborn."

"Brenna, I wish to stay by his side tonight."

"'Tis not necessary. Brodie has taken Jennie in just to give Alex a kiss. Then he will stay with him tonight. It would be best for you to get some rest before he awakens and asks for you."

"Do you think he will ask for me? After all that has happened, he may never want to see me again," she whispered.

"My brother is pig-headed, but I know he has feelings for you." Brenna patted Maddie's hands. "Give it some time. Much has happened. From the tales I have heard, it is a wonder any of the clansmen are still on their feet. It was not an easy battle."

"I will stay here." She retrieved a stool and posted herself outside Alex's door.

Robbie entered Alex's chamber to speak with Brodie a couple of times, but nothing changed for several hours. Shortly before midnight, when Maddie's head was nodding from exhaustion, Brodie came out and touched her shoulder. "Alex is asking for you, lass. I will go get something to eat."

After smiling at Brody and straightening her skirts, Maddie hurried into Alex's chamber. Once inside, she paused to allow her eyes to adjust to the darkness. One small candle flickered on the table near his bed, providing scant illumination. The chamber was larger than she had expected, and the bed was probably the biggest she had ever seen. There was a hearth on one wall, buttressed by a chair on either side, and there were three chests of various sizes arranged about. Several weapons hung from the walls, and two recessed windows with fur coverings kept in the warmth. Alex stood in front of one with the fur pulled back, donned in nothing but his plaid, staring at the moon. Maddie unconsciously licked her lips as she took in his massive shoulders and the rippling muscles of his back. There was a bandage on his right leg and she thought she saw stitches in his left arm. His hair hung loose and almost reached his shoulders. Maddie waited to be acknowledged.

He turned and stared at her for a few minutes, his eyes so achingly soft, before whispering, "Aye, Maddie, you have my word. I will not tie you to the marriage bed."

Maddie sighed and wrapped her arms around him, burying her

face in the soft hairs of his chest. "Oh, Alex, I was so worried about you. I am so sorry for all the trouble I have caused."

"Maddie, you have not caused any trouble." He rested his chin on her head and sighed. "You have turned my world upside down, but you have not caused me any trouble."

Alex reveled in the rightness of her in his arms. He closed his eyes to take in everything that was his Madeline. He lifted her chin and gazed into her eyes. "You still have not answered my question. Will you do me the honor of becoming my wife?"

A bewitching smile covered her face as she looked back at him. "Aye, Alex, nothing would make me happier. But are you sure you still want me after everything you have learned about me?"

"Lass, you must be the strongest person I have ever met to have survived all the troubles you have suffered. I have always wanted a strong wife."

Alex sensed Maddie's anxiety immediately. "Sit and talk with me," he said, taking her hand and guiding her to one of the large chairs in front of the hearth. He sat there and arranged her on his lap, careful to avoid his bandaged leg.

"Maddie, please listen to me for a few minutes. I understand your fears. What happened with Niles was no' natural. He was an unnaturally cruel man to have treated you that way. I hope you believe me when I say I will never hurt you. What happens between a husband and wife should not be painful after the first time. You know what the act involves. But don't be frightened, lass." Alex massaged her arm as he talked. "Hasn't anyone ever told you that the marriage bed should be enjoyable for both husband and wife?"

Maddie nodded. "My maid, Alice, told me so, but she did not say much. I have heard a few servants talk about it, but I cannot always understand what they mean. I only have my own experience to guide me. And I did not like anything about it. It was very painful and humiliating." Her head dropped to rest on his shoulder.

Alex clenched his jaw and lowered his lips to her forehead so she could not see his eyes. "How many times, Maddie?" He held his breath, not sure what he was about to hear.

"Just one night, but four or five times. I do not remember for sure. But it hurt every time and I bled terribly from it. I am afraid, Alex."

"Do you trust me, Maddie?" He ran his thumb across her cheek.

"Aye, I do."

"Then trust me when I say we will not do anything until you are ready, lass."

She was so beautiful. Her hair was a shambles, but she was as breathtaking as ever. How he longed to feel all of her glorious curves. He longed to trace his tongue over every inch of her body. Someday, he vowed. He believed that just below the surface was a passionate woman; he just needed to be patient.

He ran his knuckles over her cheek. After kissing her forehead, her nose, and her lips, he captured her face in his hands and lowered his mouth to hers. She tasted so sweet and welcoming. He wanted all of her, to possess her. Instead of pushing away, she opened her lips so he could sweep his tongue inside her sweet mouth. She touched her tongue to his briefly and that simple motion stole away what remained of his ability for reason.

Maddie wrapped her arms around his neck and pulled him in closer. She loved the feel of being in his arms. When Alex kissed her, warmth spread throughout her entire body. He ran his hand down the inside of her arm and she shivered as the fluttering sensation in her stomach reached to her core. She was confused by her feelings, unable to comprehend the changes going on inside her body. His hands dropped to her waist and she leaned toward him. She could hear his breathing increase, and her own heart beat faster. His hand swept down her back and across her waist before coming to rest on her thigh.

And then she bolted as if she had been burned. She jumped out of his lap and ran all the way to the far wall. Hiding her face toward the wall, she folded her arms protectively across her breasts. She tried to get her breathing under control, but to no avail. The memory of Niles Comming had ruined their perfect moment. Afraid of the look she would see in his eyes, she darted her gaze everywhere but at him. He was still seated in the chair.

She panted and coughed as her panic escalated.

"I am sorry, Alex. I just cannot do this." She turned her back to the wall and stared at him. What was he thinking? He hadn't moved from the chair. His arms were down, relaxed. A fine tremor rippled through her whole body. Even if he wasn't going to beat her like Kenneth or Niles would have, he probably no longer wanted her. How could he want a wife who would push him or hit him whenever they became intimate? She squeezed her eyes shut again to try to erase the bad memories in her mind. When she opened her eyes, Alex was still sitting in the chair. He had not moved. His eyes searched hers.

"'Tis all right, Maddie. I will wait until you are ready," he said quietly.

"I do not understand. What do you mean?" she cried. "Ready for what?" She swiped at her tears.

"I will help you get past this. When you are ready, I want you to come back and sit with me. I will wait for as long as it takes. I will not touch you again until you desire my touch."

She saw no anger in his face, no condemnation, just a serene sense of control. He turned his head and gazed at the fire burning in the hearth.

Maddie gulped. Was it possible? Was he truly this patient and calm? She glanced at him again, wanting to convince herself that he was not angry or disgusted. She smoothed her gown in place and played with her hair, trying to rearrange it. Her breathing slowly returned to normal. Perhaps he truly did wish to help her, to be there for her. She moved over to the window, folded the fur back, and peeked out over the moonlit fields. Several minutes passed. *I can do this. I would much rather be in his arms than over here by the window alone. He did not hurt me*, she reminded herself. She turned enough to watch him over her shoulder. He still had not moved. Collecting her strength, she closed her eyes and turned to face him, willing herself to trust this man fully and without restraint.

She inched over to the hearth and stood in front of where he sat with his elbows resting on his knees. Leaning back in his chair, he studied her.

Her hands tugged at the folds of her gown, and the fire in the hearth warmed her back as she steeled her reserve. *I can do this.* She sighed as she realized how much she wanted this. A slow blush crept across her face as her eyes met his.

"I would like to come back now if you will still have me, Alex."

There was no threat in his eyes.

"Whenever you are ready, lass." A soft smile crept across his face.

She eased over to him, and he reached up to her. She grasped his hand in hers and settled on his lap again, careful not to disturb his bandage.

"Am I hurting your leg, Alex?"

"Nay, lass, you are not hurting me. Your touch is as light as a feather. You will not hurt my leg." He kissed her forehead and brushed back the soft tendrils of her hair. "You have to learn to trust me. I am not like those despicable men. I may get very loud with my bluster, but I will never raise a hand to you in anger. Can you believe me?"

Maddie's nodded and offered him a tentative smile. In her heart, she knew it was true. She had known it for some time.

"What do you want, Maddie?"

She peered up at him through her lashes. "You, Alex, I want you."

"Then I am yours. Touch me." His eyes darkened, imploring her to move.

She touched his rough beard, then ran her thumb along his lower lip. The way he gazed at her immediately sent another wave of warmth through her body. "Touch me again, Alex. Please?" she whispered.

"I want you to try something, lass. Will you do something for me?" he asked.

She nodded her head.

"Do you trust me not to hurt you?"

She nodded again and chewed on her lower lip.

"Then close your eyes for me. I am going to touch you, and if you want me to stop, just ask me."

She closed her eyes with determination and lifted her chin.

"Maddie, you are so precious to me, do you believe that?"

"Yes," she whispered.

"Let me show you how precious you are to me. I am going to touch your ankle, but I will not hurt you."

She nodded her head, still squeezing her eyes shut. Alex's hand touched her ankle.

"I am going to move my hand up your leg a little." He moved

his fingers up to her calf and rubbed his hand lightly up and down her lower leg. "How does it feel? Does it feel nice? I want my touch to feel nice to you. Tell me how it feels."

She let out a breath she hadn't realized she was holding it. "It feels good, Alex. I like it," she whispered as she wrapped her hands around his neck and rested her head on his shoulder.

She peeked up at him and caught his smile before closing her eyes again. "Good, lass. I am going to move my hand up. Do you still trust me?" He moved his hand up to her knee and caressed the sensitive skin behind it.

Maddie nodded again. She wiggled in his lap a little. Alex groaned but continued to caress her leg. Her breath came a little faster. "Yes, Alex, I like it when you touch me."

He moved his hand up above her knee. "This is the last move I will make, Maddie. I am going a little higher. Do you still trust me?" His hand was nearly at the top of her thigh, but she did not move.

She nodded against his shoulder. His warm skin felt wonderful against hers, but she made a move to push his hand away out of embarrassment. At the last moment, she stopped herself. His hand caressed her leg back and forth, brushing over the top of her thigh. His thumb rubbed a path down the inside of her thigh. Her fingers dug into his shoulder, her eyes still closed.

"Alex," she whispered. What was happening to her? Her belly was full of butterflies again. She kept her eyes closed, rejoicing in the sensation of his caresses. There was a burning at the juncture of her legs that she didn't understand, but she did not want him to stop. She reflexively moved her thighs apart, then gasped when she realized what she had done. Her head jerked up as her eyes flew open in shame.

Alex ran his calloused thumb down her cheek and over her neck. "It's all right, lass. People who are to be married touch each other. It is supposed to be wonderful. You are supposed to enjoy it. Relax." He kissed her lightly on her lips, tugging her lip out before he ran his tongue over it.

"Touch me, lass. I want to feel your touch," he whispered in her ear.

Maddie reached for the hard planes of his chest and ran her fingers down through his coarse hairs to his abdomen and back up again. She brushed his nipples lightly—which made her jump—but she did not hesitate before reaching down to touch him again. She liked the feel of his skin. A dark line trailed down his abdomen and disappeared inside his plaid.

"Precious, look at me," Alex said.

She raised her eyes to gaze at him and saw the desire in his eyes. Blushing to her core, she realized how special she felt at this moment.

"This is how it should be between a husband and wife, Maddie. Touching and caressing should feel wonderful. You should trust me not to hurt you. It is about giving pleasure and receiving pleasure. It is about wanting to take care of the person you care about." He removed his hand from her leg and reached up to brush a lock of hair behind her ear. "We will do this together, sweeting. Do you believe me?"

"Yes." She leaned forward and Alex took possession of her mouth. The kiss was demanding. He angled his mouth over hers, hungrily thrusting his tongue to mate with hers. He stopped abruptly, cradled her head in his hands, and leaned in and touched his forehead to hers, letting out his breath with a sigh.

Wrapping his hands around her waist, he set her apart from him before standing on his good leg. "And now, before you make me completely lose my wits, we must stop." She stared at him with a dazed expression on her face.

"But we still have one more thing we need to decide, my lady," he said as he helped her straighten her skirts and her hair. "We need to decide when our wedding will take place."

"Oh, Alex, I need to make my dress and plan the feast. I don't know how long that will take," she explained.

"You are not going to make me wait too long, are you?" Alex's eyebrows rose.

Maddie blushed when she glanced up at him. "I do not want to wait either," she confessed.

"Alice and Brenna can help you with your dress and the planning, can they no'?"

"Certainly, they will. It is Brenna's kitchen, my lord."

"Soon to be yours," he added with a smile.

Maddie scowled as she thought about it. She had not realized she would be assuming the position of mistress of the keep. "Oh,

Alex, I hope Brenna won't mind."

"I think Brenna will be relieved. Mayhap we can think of Brenna getting betrothed. 'Tis time for her, I think." He paused in thought. "I think a fortnight should be enough time, don't you?"

"Oh, my goodness, that is not much time! Perhaps I should get started."

He pulled her back into an embrace. "Nay, Maddie, to bed with you. It has been a tiring day." He kissed her briefly and opened the door. Brodie was asleep on the floor. They stepped over him so Alex could escort Maddie to her chamber. When they reached her door, she turned back to him and he ravished her mouth again.

She stepped inside with a blush and a smile, rubbing her fingers over her lips, remembering how good Alex tasted. For the first time in a long while, she found herself looking forward to what the future held in store.

CHAPTER TWENTY

Maddie tossed and turned through most of the night, kept awake by the thoughts of all that needed to be done in preparation for her wedding. She found herself torn between fear and elation. Would she be able to be a true wife to Alex? Would he have enough patience for her?

Yet she also rejoiced at the thought of being a true part of his family, of this loving, happy clan who all cherished one another. She hoped her new family would help fill the gap left behind by the loss of her mother and father. Often times, she sensed her mother's loving spirit lingering near her. Intuition told her that both her ma and da approved of her newfound love.

She rushed through her ablutions so she could find Brenna and discuss the big event. It was late, so she guessed Alex was probably already in the lists with his men even though he belonged in bed. What would happen to Kenneth? She cringed at the thought of Alex killing him in cold blood. Even though she hated her brother, she didn't want Alex killing him over her. Now that Niles was dead, would Kenneth be willing to agree to her marriage to Alex? She had never understood the agreement between the Comming and her stepbrother, so she was not sure what Kenneth had hoped to gain from her betrothal.

As she reached for the door of her chamber, a loud bellow from below shook the walls. Was that Alex? She opened her door and rushed to the balcony, cringing as soon as she peeked over the railing. Alex stood toe-to-toe with Robbie, both of them clearly angry, and Brodie was directly behind Robbie.

"What do you mean Kenneth escaped, brother? Why was I not told this when it happened?" Alex raged in his brother's face.

Maddie's knees quaked as she held the railing to keep steady. Had she heard correctly? Kenneth had *escaped*?

"You were a bit incapacitated, Laird!" Robbie retorted.

"I was not incapacitated. You could have told me when it was discovered!" Alex's fury radiated from every pore of his body.

"Since you were flat on your arse with your arms around a lass, I did not think you would answer!"

Robbie and Alex stood nose to nose with their fists clenched. Neither man gave an inch.

A quiet fury emanated from her betrothed. "What exactly are you implying?"

Madeline crept down the stairs silently.

Robbie sighed and lowered his voice. "He escaped around the time Niles was killed. There was a throng of people out of control after the sword fight. By the time Angus got everyone settled down, Kenneth was nowhere to be seen."

"Why did you no' go after him then? You are next in charge if I cannot speak."

"I was busy bringing my bull-headed brother up to his chamber. Next time, I will leave you on the ground," Robbie spat.

Both brothers continued to stare at each other. Neither moved.

"I will have both you and Brodie flogged for losing my prisoner. You were in charge. You should have prevented it from happening."

"My hands were full. My laird didn't give me any warning that he was about to kill a man in front of the entire clan." Robbie gave Alex a scathing look before whispering, "If those are your wishes, Laird, let me locate the whip for you. I would prefer for you to do the task."

Alex nodded. "I would be glad to do the honors."

A high-pitched scream wrenched through the air as wee Jennie tore across the room and latched onto both brothers, wrapping one arm around each brother's knee. "No whipping, no whipping, no whipping!" She screamed and pummeled Alex's legs in a frantic fury that sank right to Maddie's gut.

Alex stepped back and picked up his sister. Maddie's breath caught at the sight of the tiny fist striking her brother's broad shoulders. He grabbed her chin and forced her to look him in the eye. "Jennie, I will not whip your brothers." He sighed as he glanced at Robbie. "I am sorry, little squirrel, to have upset you so."

Jennie was crying, so her words were choked out around sobs. "Say you are sorry to Robbie. Say you are sorry to Brodie. You promised Papa to love and take care of us all. You cannot whip us." Hitching sobs continued to pour out of her. "Alex, you have to love Robbie and Brodie. You have to! You almost died, too, like Mama and Da. No one can leave. Promise me. If you whip them, they will leave. I want them to stay. Promise me!"

Alex turned to his brother. "Robbie knows I love you all. I just lost my temper. I am sorry, Robbie, for my threats. Can we sit down at the table, Jennie? We will sit with Robbie." Alex motioned his brothers over to the table and waved the servants out. He lowered himself carefully, as Jennie's arms were still wrapped tight around his neck, her face buried in his shoulder.

Madeline tiptoed over from the bottom of the stairway to stand beside Alex.

She whispered with her head down, barely audible. "He has escaped?"

"Aye, but we will find him," he answered. Alex ran his hand over his face and sighed. "Robbie, tell me everything."

Madeline attempted to take Jennie from Alex, but she would not budge. She popped her thumb in her mouth for a few seconds, then quickly withdrew it and buried her face in her brother's chest. After her sobbing subsided, Alex motioned to Robbie.

Robbie began his story. "Angus had the grounds searched right away, but nothing turned up. When I found out last night, I took several men with me and searched the area. We found two of Kenneth's guards—" he glanced quickly at Jennie, "—sleeping, but there was no sign of Kenneth. Some of his men must have been waiting for him. So many traveled here on horseback to see the fight that tracking was difficult. Most of Comming's men were released. They chose not to return to his castle, so they all went off to different place. A few requested to swear fealty to you. I have them under guard until you decide what you want to do with them."

"What about the guards who came with Kenneth?" Alex asked.

"I still have some of the MacDonald men under guard awaiting your decision."

Brenna entered the great hall from outside and Jennie immediately hopped down and threw herself at her sister. Gathering the wee one in her arms, Brenna made her way to the table and sat.

"As long as we are all here—" Alex reached for Madeline's hand, "—Maddie and I have an announcement to make, and I hope it will dry your tears, Jennie. Maddie has agreed to be my wife and we plan to marry in a fortnight."

Jennie bounded out of Brenna's lap. "Oh, Maddie, you will be my new sister. I am so happy!" She hugged her tight and then ran over to Alex and hugged him, too. "It does make me very happy, Alex. And can we have new bairns, too?"

"Slow down there, little squirrel, first we must marry. I hope someday we have bairns, but not quite yet." He glanced over at Maddie, who could not help but blush a deep red for everyone.

Brenna stopped short and said, "Did you say a fortnight?"

Alex nodded. "Is that not acceptable, sister?"

"Oh, I think it is possible, but we will be very busy. We need to sew a dress for Maddie and plan a feast. We will also need to notify our neighbors. And what about the priest? We have to get in touch with Father MacGregor to see if he can be here by then."

"Brenna, you and Maddie let me know what you need. I will plan to free up a portion of my men for extra hunting the week before the feast. If you need more lasses from the village to help out, then hire them. I will not have this put off. I have waited long enough for my bride." He glanced at Maddie with yearning, and she blushed again. "I have the blushing bride, now let's get whatever else is necessary." He leaned over and kissed Maddie's cheek before heading out the door.

Halfway to the door, Maddie called out, "Alex, what about Kenneth?"

"Maddie, you take care of the wedding, I will take care of your stepbrother. I will not allow him to interfere with our marriage."

Once outside, Alex said to Robbie, "We need to send a messenger with an escort to the king. Plan on leaving in two days. 'Tis important for him to hear our version of what happened with the Comming and Kenneth, and I must notify him of my plan to wed Madeline. I think he will approve, but I want to do things properly.

"I will have a list from Maddie or Brenna of anything else that is needed for the occasion. Check with me before the messengers leave. They may have invitations to deliver as well. Oh, and we will need to reach Father MacGregor. While you make the arrangements, Brodie and I will ride off in search for Kenneth."

Several hours later, Alex returned to the keep in his chain mail to search for Maddie, but he did not have far to go. She was perched in her chair, diligently working on a project.

"Maddie, I am leaving shortly to search for Kenneth. I don't know when I will return, but we should be gone no more than two days."

She glanced up from her work and gave him a worried look. "I look forward to your safe return, Laird. Please be careful. I fear I will not sleep until you are home safe." She rose and placed a chaste kiss on his cheek.

Lord, but the lass could take his breath away at times. After she returned to her seat, he peeked over her shoulder and asked, "What are you working on?"

"Oh, you know I enjoy the children. I thought I would make some drawings to go along with my stories for the wee ones. I quite enjoy sketching, especially since it relaxes me. Can you guess what I am drawing?" She turned the image toward him.

Alex stared at his betrothed with wonder. How could one person have this much talent? What else would he learn about his new wife-to-be?

"Maddie, the forest you have drawn looks real enough to touch. I cannot believe you did that with just ink and parchment. Unbelievable!"

"Thank you, Alex. I hope the wee ones will enjoy it."

She peered off into the distance and spoke softly. "Kenneth hated my drawings. He tore them to shreds. Even the ones I had done years ago with my father. I have not had the chance to sketch since my parents died." She smiled at her betrothed and said, "Now, I shall try again."

Alex was without words. He bowed to his betrothed and reached for her hand. He placed a soft kiss on her skin and pulled her close. "I will miss you, my lady." He kissed her lips deeply and then turned to leave.

Maddie spent the next two days on wedding plans. Keeping busy while Alex was away was not as challenging a task as she had expected. The first day, Brenna, Alice, Jennie, and Maddie gathered together in the great hall to decide the directions of their plans.

"First is your dress, Maddie. That will take the longest. I will have the maids bring up the bolts of material we have to see what you like," Brenna said.

Alice reached over and held Maddie's hand. "I hope you will do me the honor of allowing me to sew your wedding dress. I owe this to your mother."

Madeline beamed and said, "Thank you, Alice. You do such beautiful work. I would love to have you sew my dress."

"Wonderful!" exclaimed Brenna. "What color do you think you would prefer? I hope we have something you like."

"Oh, I am sure you have many lovely fabrics to choose from. I was hoping for a soft blue. What do you think, Alice?"

"Blue will show off your eyes. Your mother was married in blue as well. But it has to be just the right shade."

"We will check later," Brenna said.

"Can I have a special dress, Brenna? I want to be beautiful, too," Jennie chimed in with a hopeful expression on her face.

"Of course, Jennie. We shall find something special for you to do. Mayhap we could give you a basket of flower petals to toss at the chapel. How does that sound?" Brenna asked.

"Aye, I want to throw petals at Maddie and Alex!" she cried out.

"What else must we do, Brenna?" Maddie asked. "I am afraid I do not have much experience with arranging wedding feasts."

"We must notify some of the smaller clans under Alex's domain. They would like to see their laird and his new bride. We can send notice with the messengers who go to the king.

"'Twill take massive amounts of food, as the warriors and the clan members in the cottages will be feasting as well as the neighboring clans," Brenna said. "We shall hopefully have pheasant, lamb, pigs, and small game, along with some fish. I want to have many meat pies to offer in case we run out of meat. Mayhap if we are lucky, the men will catch a deer or two—perhaps even a wild boar. Alex said he would send them out to hunt. We must obtain extra help from the clan women to prepare the meal. They will love participating in the event. The laird's wedding must show our strength and pride in our clan for all to witness."

"We need a lot of fruit tarts, Brenna. You know I love fruit tarts. Can we have apple and pear tarts? Please?" Jennie begged.

"Do not worry your pretty wee head, there shall be many sweets to choose from," said Brenna. "I think you can help Cook in the kitchen with the pastries, too. We will all have to work together."

"Aye, I would love to help Cook. Mayhap she will let me try one when it is still warm." Jennie's eyes turned blissful at the thought.

"We also need to have the men put up tents in the outer bailey, but that can wait a while. Alex may decide to hold some jousting tournaments for entertainment. I will let him decide what entertainment he wants at the wedding feast. Och, there is much to do! But we will make merry doing it," Brenna declared with a smile on her face.

"Thank you for all your hard work," Maddie said quietly.

Alice turned to her. "We do it gladly, Madeline."

Brenna agreed. "I am so happy that you and my brother have found each other. He needs some happiness in his life, instead of constant stress and worry." Brenna reached out to hug Madeline. "You will make a wonderful wife and sister-in-law."

Much later, the solar was filled with bolts of cloth from the stores, and the four lasses sorted through them in search of just the right fabric for Maddie's dress. Pastels, whites, and ivories tumbled through Maddie's fingers. The abundance of choices made her sigh with pleasure. Could this truly be happening to her? Not long ago, it had seemed like her best and only hope was to join a convent. Soon she would become Alex's bride in front of all his clan. Would they accept her?

"Oh, Maddie, I do not see the right blue, do you?" Alice asked.

Brenna held up a pale green that was beautiful. "Mayhap this?"

"That is very pretty," Maddie said as the soft cloth slid through her fingers.

"I like this pink." Jennie held up a pastel pink that shimmered in the sunlight. "It sparkles—see, Brenna?"

"Aye, Jennie, the shade of pink is lovely. That would be perfect on you," Madeline said with a smile.

Alice held a sky blue silk up to Maddie's face. "Pretty, but not quite right."

They sifted through more bolts and compared and contrasted, but they agreed the right color was missing. The pale blue they had hoped for was not there.

"Oh well," Maddie said quietly. "The beautiful green will be fine. I am happy with that color. It is not all about my dress anyway, now, is it?"

"Oh, but you really do belong in blue. And it is your wedding. I will check the storeroom myself later." Brenna kissed her cheek.

Two days later, Alex had not returned and Maddie's worry grew. If she entertained the wee ones again, it would take her mind away from her anxiety. She tucked her new drawings under her arm and strolled past the courtyard to her favorite tree. A couple of the older boys were playing in the distance, but as soon as they spied her, they sprinted away. Madeline did not think much about it. Just after she located the perfect spot for her storytelling, she noticed a woman strolling down the path with a toddler. She thought it to be Emma's mother, as the woman was wide in the hip like Moira. Maddie shouted to try to gain her attention, but the woman took one look at Maddie and frowned. Scooping Emma in her arms, she stomped off in the opposite direction. Why would Moira be ignoring her?

Maddie ran toward her. "Would Emma like to hear a story today, Moira?" she asked, catching up to her with a smile on her face.

Emma smiled and reached for Maddie, but Moira snatched her daughter's hand back. "Nay," she said. "Emma will not be spending time with your kind."

"What? Moira, what are you talking about?" Maddie exclaimed. But in an instant, her heart broke. She knew her fears were coming true.

"I heard about you and the man our laird killed. Laird Grant deserves better," Moira declared before shuffling down the hill, Emma in her arms.

So at least part of the clan believed the lies Niles had told about her. Maddie had hoped those who knew her already would not be so easily swayed. But that was not to be. She was an embarrassment to Alex, and his people would shun her. He'd probably be forced to send her away. Mayhap life in a convent would be best.

Maddie froze, her eyes roaming around the rest of the bailey. Embarrassment flooded her cheeks as she thought of everything the clan knew about her now. She closed her eyes, willing it all to go away. How could she look any of Alex's clan members in the eye again? Though Alex did not blame her for what had happened, they clearly did. She turned around to see who else was staring at her, a stillness permeating the air.

So her storytelling days were finished then, and there had been no need to complete her drawings after all. Still, she refused to give in to their tactics. Lifting her chin up, she strode back toward the keep.

When she entered the great hall, she almost trampled Brenna.

"Is something wrong?"

"Nay, I am fine, Brenna." Maddie straightened her skirt as she spoke.

"Where are the little ones? No storytelling?"

"There will not be any more stories." Maddie shook her head with a clenched jaw.

Brenna stared hard at Madeline's face. "What happened, Madeline? Did someone say something to you?" Brenna's anger was evident in her face.

Madeline told Brenna the story as briefly as possible. "Promise me you will not tell Alex," she said.

Brenna shook her head, hands on her hips. "Alex should know. He is laird of this clan and he is your betrothed."

"But it is my problem. Promise me, please!" Maddie wrung her hands.

"I will promise for now. But if things get worse, I will break my promise. Moira has no business acting like that. And none of the other clan members should be walking away from you either."

"Thank you, Brenna, but I will be fine handling this on my own."

Maddie would die of embarrassment if she had to discuss the matter with Alex.

CHAPTER TWENTY-ONE

Startled by the yelling in the courtyard, Madeline dropped her sewing needle. Riders were approaching the castle, and she sped up to the battlements to determine if Alex was with them. She surveyed the valley, but the riders were too far to distinguish an individual man. As they grew closer, though, she recognized her betrothed's powerful figure. She could not hide her smile—Alex turned her insides to jelly even from this distance. And he would be her husband in less than a fortnight. She vowed to be a good and dutiful wife to him. Of course, she wanted Alex to be proud of her, but with a twinge, she recalled her meeting with Moira earlier. Perhaps the people would soften in time. Alex had so much on his mind as laird. Burdening him with such a trivial matter seemed wrong.

She rushed down the stairs and into the courtyard to greet her betrothed. Robbie and Brenna were already there, but her attention was all on Alex as he dismounted and crossed over to them. His expression was grim.

"My laird?" she searched his eyes for answers.

Alex bowed and said, "My lady." He took her arm and strode quietly toward the keep. Maddie stared at the dust and grime on his body and the visible exhaustion in his eyes. Robbie followed him into the great hall. Brenna immediately ordered food and ale for the soldiers who now filled the many trestle tables.

Alex lowered himself in his chair after helping Maddie into hers. His expression remained bleak as he searched her eyes and then said, "There is no evidence of Kenneth anywhere. We even inquired at your family's keep, Madeline, but no one has seen him since he left for the Comming's. We searched the entire area and found no sign of him."

"Mayhap he is already dead, Alex," Robbie offered.

"Aye, 'tis a strong possibility," Alex replied. "My men will continue to search and ask questions while on their expedition to the king. Madeline, I am sorry, 'tis the best we can do right now. But I will not give up my search. I stand by my promise to protect you from him." He leaned over and kissed her cheek.

"Thank you for your efforts. You have done more than I could possibly have expected. Mayhap he will turn up when we do not expect him."

Madeline's gut turned somersaults at the thought of Kenneth nearby. Was he out there waiting for her right now? Soon the table was covered in trenchers and the men grabbed at the food as if they had not eaten in days. They ate in silence. Maddie could not bring the food to her mouth. Fear pooled inside her, and she found herself perusing every man at the tables. What if Kenneth had disguised himself and sat among them? What if he had a man inside the keep searching for her? Could one of these men be waiting to grab her to take her to Kenneth?

She jumped as a warm rough hand caressed hers under the table. Her head jerked back to find Alex's eyes on her. He leaned toward her and whispered, "I know all of my men, Madeline." He brushed a kiss against her forehead. "I will protect you."

"I know. I cannot thank you enough," Maddie said as she squeezed his hand. "You are exhausted, Alex."

He nodded his head in agreement. "I am tired. After a bath, I will settle things with Robbie for their journey. Then I plan to sleep." His eyes were filled with some emotion she didn't recognize. "I missed you," he whispered.

"And I missed you as well." She cast her eyes down as the blush spread across her face.

Alex reached over and brushed the back of his hand down her cheek. "Mayhap tomorrow...." He pushed himself away from the table and walked out the door.

The messenger and his escorts left early in the morning. Alex toiled in the lists for several hours training with his guards. His injuries had healed for the most part. But ensuring that his men were braced for an attack was paramount at this point. Being prepared for the wedding was vital, for there would be many strange faces around that day. It would be Kenneth's best opportunity to sneak in.

Searching for Maddie's stepbrother had given him much time to think about his relationship with his betrothed. Mayhap it was time to get to know her better. Perhaps spending time with her would help him be less distracted by constant thoughts of her.

He had gone to Cook early and requested a basket of food to be ready for midday. He had intentionally not forewarned her of the little excursion he had planned. Maddie worried enough, and he did not wish to add to her concerns.

As the sun reached its peak, Alex went off in search of his betrothed. He found her in the solar with Alice, standing for more poking and prodding as she was measured for her gown.

She wore a yellow gown that clung perfectly to her curves. After realizing he was staring at a perfect set of breasts, he forced his gaze back to her face. Her blue eyes enchanted him. Aye, it was the perfect day for a sojourn. He was unlikely to get anything done in the lists anyway, considering how preoccupied he was with Maddie.

"Madeline, may I have the pleasure of your company today? Would you care to ride to the loch with me?"

"Aye, I would like that very much!" she exclaimed.

"Hold still, Maddie," Alice pleaded. She sucked a finger into her mouth, having obviously stabbed herself with the needle. "You must let me finish first, else I will prick your pretty skin."

"Of course, Alice. I am sorry." She gave Alex a sheepish grin.

As soon as Alice finished, Alex caught his betrothed's hand in his, and they strolled to the kitchen to search out Cook. Once they had secured the basket of food, they headed to the stables.

"Oh, Alex, it smells wonderful." Madeline held the basket near her face, grinning as she sniffed at the succulent feast.

Alex vowed to see that expression on her face more often. What a difficult time she had experienced in her short life already. But things would change for his wife-to-be—he had promised himself to make her happiness a priority.

As they strolled to the stables, the warm fall air brushed across his face, carrying the aroma of fall, dried leaves, and apples. Alex helped Maddie onto her horse and then mounted Midnight. As they departed, ten guardsmen fell in behind them.

"You are worried, Alex?"

"Not worried—*careful*. Do no' be concerned. I have ordered them to keep a distance from us, but I want them in the area in case Kenneth is hiding in the woods."

"Shall we race, my laird?" Maddie asked, raising one eyebrow. Without waiting to hear his response, she darted off, her laughter echoing behind her.

Alex smirked as she tore off toward the loch, noting how well she rode. He dismounted before she did when they arrived, and he reached up to help her dismount. He slid Maddie's body down the front of him very slowly, waiting for her reaction. The way her eyes widened with surprise and pleasure made him cup her face and kiss her—not a gentle kiss, but a needy one. Possessing her mouth, his tongue briefly mated with hers. A soft sigh escaped from Madeline when he ended the kiss. That pleased him, but he set her away from him and reached for the basket. His intention was to give his betrothed the time she needed to adjust to his nearness. He did not want to push her away by moving too fast.

Madeline murmured, "Oh my!" She licked her lips and touched her fingers to her mouth as she gazed at Alex.

Chuckling, he spread one of his plaids on the grass near the edge of the water. "Maddie, you are a passionate one, aye?"

Madeline blushed and turned her head away.

"Come, sit with me and eat something."

Maddie helped Alex empty the basket. Cook had packed fresh baked bread, cheese, and wine. There were also apples and ripe pears, and at the bottom, there were two wrapped pastries.

"Maddie, I planned this trip for a special reason."

"What would that be, Laird?"

"Please, Maddie, call me Alex. I would hear my name on your lips."

"Of course, Alex," she replied, her innocent blue eyes gazing into his.

"I do not want you to be uncomfortable on our wedding night. I think it would best if you were to get used to me slowly. I want you to be accustomed to my closeness and my touch, Maddie. I will not have you frightened of me." He brushed a stray hair from her eyes. She nodded her head slowly in agreement.

They ate and drank the wine as they casually talked about the wedding, enjoying the sun, the feast, and each other's company.

"Would you like a pastry, sweeting?" Alex asked.

"Oh, yes, I love pastries," she answered.

Alex unwrapped the pastry and held it to her mouth. She reached for it, but Alex pulled back and shook his head.

"Nay, you must eat it from my fingers. Do you trust me, Maddie?"

"Aye," she whispered. She leaned forward and took a tentative bite from the pastry. She chewed it slowly, savoring the taste in her mouth, never taking her eyes from Alex's.

"More?" he asked.

She nodded and leaned forward for another bite. Sweet juice ran over her lips as she bit into the fat pastry. But when Maddie reached to wipe it off her face, Alex said, "Nay." He leaned in and licked the sweetness off her bottom lip. Madeline gasped, but did not move as Alex continued the gentle assault. He nibbled on her bottom lip and tugged on it to pull her toward him. The pastry crumbled to the ground as he pulled her down on top of him. He groaned as she timidly responded by touching her tongue to his. Eager for more of her, angled his mouth to kiss her deeper.

Alex cradled her face in his hands, enjoying the sweet taste of her. His hands ran down her spine and brushed her buttocks lightly to pull her in close to him. He was hard and did not want to frighten her, but she had to get used to him. He did not want to see any fear in her eyes on their wedding night.

Maddie's senses were on overload. This was not a tender kiss. Alex was hot and demanding. And she liked it. She was a little embarrassed when she realized the high-pitched moans she heard were from her. He didn't let up.

Confusion roiled in Maddie's mind as sheer pleasure coiled in her belly. This was nothing like what had happened with Niles. Did this mean she would actually enjoy the touch of her betrothed? Would she be a good wife to Alex?

Alex rolled over, tucking her beneath him, and leaned his weight on his elbows. He kissed her cheek and trailed a line of kisses down her throat. A light sigh escaped her lips at his tender ministrations. Stopping abruptly, he drew Maddie to her feet with him. Where was he taking her?

"The loch, Maddie. Let's get wet together." He held his hand out to her and she grasped it. As they reached the edge of the loch, he reached down to untie the ribbons on her gown. What was he doing?

He coaxed her toward the lapping water. "Come in with me, the warmth is wonderful." She nodded her head, trusting him completely. Alex drew the fabric of her gown over her head and tossed it to the grass. Then he unhooked the broach on his plaid and pitched them into another pile before removing the rest of his clothes.

Maddie's breath hitched as she realized her betrothed was completely nude. Too stunned to move, she glanced down at herself and realized she was only clothed in a chemise, her taut nipples clearly visible. She glimpsed at Alex's nude body again before gasping. What were they doing?

"Like what you see, sweeting?"

She could not help but giggle as he tugged her into the water.

"Alex, it's cold!" When the water was almost to her shoulders, he stopped and pulled her in close, brushing his arms over hers to warm her.

"Remember that I will never hurt you, Maddie. If you ever want to stop, just tell me. I will accept it. But remember that married people do enjoy each other's bodies. I need you to understand that love and marriage is about giving each other pleasure."

Had she heard him correctly? Did that mean he really loved her? The thought sent waves of eagerness through her. Alex was to be her husband soon. He was right—she needed to get used to touching him and being touched. Their gazes connected and she was amazed at what she found in his eyes: pure desire.

Her courage grew. She ran her hands over his shoulders, loving the way his muscles felt under her fingers. Alex had his own aroma, and she breathed deep to savor it. The sensations he stirred in her were warm and wonderful—and she felt safe. She hoped they would always have these moments together.

Her body started to tingle in places she had never felt before as she stroked every inch of his hard body. It did not frighten her because it was Alex. Why had she always fought this part of their relationship? Exciting possibilities entered her thoughts. She had not expected to want his touch so much. The water was a little cool, yet she was hot. How could that be? He stopped for a moment and gazed into her eyes, and all she could say was, "Alex, don't stop."

He reached up to the front of her chemise and cupped her breasts. He kissed her hard again, and when he rubbed his thumb over her nipple, she groaned and moved into him, trying to get closer. As he continued his assault on her breasts through the chemise, she threaded her fingers through his hair and leaned back and moaned. She let go and floated on the water, letting the unknown sensations send delight radiating through the very pores of her skin.

Alex's hands kneaded her inner thighs, working their way up her body slowly until he kissed her neck and whispered, "Sweeting, you are so soft. I need to feel your skin. I want to feel your skin against mine. Maddie, I want to see the rest of your luscious body." He started to pull on the ribbons of her chemise to free her breasts.

And Kenneth interrupted her thoughts. "Nooooo, Alex! Please do not!"

Shoving against him, she bolted toward shore. Before leaving the water, she realized she was only clothed in the chemise, so she sank back into the loch. Still, she kept far away from Alex. She couldn't let him see what Kenneth had done to her. Perhaps she would never be free of her tormenter. She slapped the top of the loch over and over as she thought of all her stepbrother had done to her.

Alex's fists were clenched at the side of his body. He was still panting and tried to slow his breathing. By the saints, but she had felt so good in his arms. Would they ever work through this problem? Mayhap this was hopeless.

He stared at his betrothed across the water. Her movements erratic, and a moment passed before he realized what she was doing. She had seemed so afraid a moment ago, but now she was angry and swinging at the water. Somehow he knew he was not the focus for her anger. Mayhap it would help her to express her anger at her stepbrother and the Comming. Mayhap that was what she needed. He waited, giving her the time she needed to work through her feelings.

Her breath was still coming out in fast puffs, but she would not look him in the eye yet. She was in a different world, fighting someone. He was going about this completely the wrong way. But who could offer him advice? Who did he trust enough to confide in?

Before he sought advice, however, he needed to understand what she was going through.

"Maddie? Talk to me. I would hear your thoughts. Help me understand. We are to be married in less than a fortnight."

Maddie forced herself to meet the gaze of the man she loved. How could she explain? She was so humiliated. Her arms wrapped tight around her middle. She hated Kenneth for what he had done to her. She knew God did not want her to hate anyone, but she could not help it.

And what would Alex say about this? She was aware there was a possibility he would be so disgusted he would walk out of the water and never return. Then what would she do? Her humiliation would be complete. Maddie buried her face into her arms and reached back with her hands to fist her hair. Everyone would hate her, just like Kenneth had always wanted. He had always been jealous of the affection and respect people gave her, and he had tried to ruin her in every way possible. Mayhap he would have the last laugh.

But if she gave up now, when she was this close to happiness, she would be *letting* him win. Alice had advised her to always be honest with Alex, and this was the time for honesty, even if it hurt.

"I need to tell you something," she said, her arms still crossed in front of her.

Alex's head dropped momentarily, but then rose to look at her. "I am listening."

Madeline fought to keep herself from crying. "My stepbrother was very angry that I refused to marry the Comming."

"I know that, Maddie," he whispered. "I bore witness to his brutality."

"I had refused him two times before the night you rescued me. Kenneth said if I would not marry the Comming, he would make sure and mark me so no other man would want me."

She studied Alex's face, trying to gauge how he was taking the news. He did not react to her words.

"Go on," he said.

"He had a tool that he heated in the fire while he whipped me."

Alex's jaw clench and he closed his eyes for a moment, but she forced herself to continue.

"After he finished whipping me, he turned me around, and while his guards held me, he held the tool to the skin under my breast. He said he would do it each time I refused him, so that my chest would be completely scarred if I never relented." She wrung her hands as she thought carefully.

Alex turned his face to the heavens and let out a deep breath.

"I was not running from your touch, Alex. I was afraid if you saw my scars, you would not want me anymore." A single tear rolled down her cheek. Her hands shook as she reached up to wipe her face.

Alex held his hand out to her. "Come here, Maddie."

She hesitated, but then walked over and placed her hand in his. Alex led her into the shallower water and sat in the pebbles, where the water reached his chest. He settled Maddie onto his lap, wrapped his arms around her tight, and rested her head on his shoulder. Maddie reached her arms around his back and leaned into him. There was nowhere else she would rather be.

Neither one of them spoke. Alex willed himself to rid the anger from his body. He knew Maddie needed him more. They held each other silently.

Alex, totally undone by the unfairness in the world, could not fight the deep sadness that enveloped his body. How could anyone be that cruel to a helpless woman? Although Maddie was not totally helpless, she could not fight the brute strength of three men. In some ways, though, his wee Maddie was stronger than all three men combined. Her strength was an inner strength, a strength of character. He was so proud of her. After all the pain she had been forced to endure, she still had the most beautiful smile he had ever seen. She was wonderful with the bairns, adored by his sister Jennie, and she always held her head high. He knew many strong men who would let such constant torture defeat them. But not his Maddie.

"Maddie," Alex whispered several minutes later.

"Yes, Alex?"

"Is there anything else you have not told me? I would know everything now, please."

"Nay."

"Are you sure?"

"Aye, Alex. They are not things I would ever forget."

Another minute of silence followed. Alex rested his chin on the top of her head.

"Alex?"

"Aye?"

"Are you going to cancel our betrothal?"

"Nay, Maddie, I am no' going to cancel our betrothal. But I must ask you something."

"Anything, Alex."

"I would see the scars under your breasts. I want no surprises on the day of our wedding. I know this is much to ask, but we need to put this behind us."

Maddie pulled back and gazed at him. He knew this would be hard for her, but he was afraid of the anger that might explode inside him when he saw the marks. Even though he prided himself on his strong control, this wee lass could send every ounce of control he possessed out of his body in an instant. He did not want to spend his wedding night in a fury.

She slowly nodded and reached down to untie the ribbons of her chemise. Covering her nipples, she held each breast up so Alex could see the scars. On each side, a small angry curved welt sat just above the fold where her breast met her abdomen. He leaned down and kissed each one with tenderness.

Alex breathed a sigh of relief. He could handle this. He stood, tugging her shivering body with him.

"I think it is time we head back, you are cold." He dressed and helped her into her gown, then secured the basket on his horse. Once he was mounted, he reached down and scooped up Maddie. As soon as she was settled on his lap, he tied her horse's reins to his.

"Alex?"

"Hmm?"

"I feel better now. I do not have any more secrets."

He kissed her forehead and nudged his horse forward. As they moved away from the loch, his men dropped in behind them.

After they dismounted at the keep, they continued to walk hand in hand, much to the surprise of his clan.

"Alex?"

"Aye?"

"I think I would like to stop at the chapel. I have much I need to be thankful for." She gave him a tentative smile.

"I will go with you, Maddie. I will go with you."

CHAPTER TWENTY-TWO

Over the next several days, Alex continued to roam the countryside in search of Kenneth MacDonald. Convinced that finding the man would be the answer to Maddie's troubles, he brutally drove his guardsmen. Each day he returned, he barely had enough time to go over important clan matters with Robbie before eating and heading straight to bed. His exhaustion was so complete he was often asleep before his head hit the pillow. Of course, this prevented him from seeing the disappointment in Maddie's eye.

But he had to find Kenneth MacDonald before the wedding.

After wearing himself—and his men—out with the constant searching, Alex returned to the keep early one day. When he entered the great hall, Maddie was sitting at the hearth with Jennie. As soon as his wee sister saw him, she bounded up from her spot and threw herself into his arms.

"Alex, look at the beautiful book that Maddie made for us. She plans to teach me how to read. Isn't it magnificent?"

Alex glanced over Madeline's shoulder before she snapped the book shut. The splendor of her work stunned him. He couldn't believe she had drawn more sketches on parchment and tied them together to create a book.

He gazed at Maddie as a sharp surge of pure lust shot through him. She was breathtaking even in repose, and he stared at her for a few minutes before he was able to collect his thoughts. Madeline blushed from his perusal.

"Maddie, the book is beautiful. What talent you have! I am sure the wee ones in the village must enjoy your storytelling even more with such vivid pictures to accompany them."

Maddie fussed with the pages, ignoring Alex's comment, but

Jennie whispered in her brother's ear, "There isn't any storytelling anymore."

Alex gaped at Maddie. "What are you talking about? Maddie, you have been weaving tales with the wee ones, have you no'?" he asked.

Madeline refused to make eye contact with him. "I have been busy with the wedding plans." She rearranged her materials around her.

"Nay, Alex, the mothers will no' let their bairns near Maddie. Tommy told me his mama said that Maddie is dirty. She said she isn't good enough for you. I told him that Maddie takes a lot of baths and she isn't dirty at all."

"Maddie, is this true?" he demanded, his gaze boring into her.

Her lack of an answer was almost answer enough.

"Brenna?" he roared.

His sister bolted down the staircase. "What's wrong, Alex?"

"Is this true, Brenna? Is Maddie being shunned by members of our clan?"

Brenna glanced at Maddie. "I think you best direct your questions to Maddie."

He turned again to look at his betrothed. "Maddie?"

"Alex, I can handle my own problems," she said quietly.

"Nay, Maddie. This is my clan, you are to be my wife. I will not allow them to speak of you in such a way. Has anyone spoken to you directly?"

"This is my affair," she insisted, staring at her hands.

Alex's patience came to an end. "Maddie, I want names!" he bellowed.

"So you can whip them like Kenneth whipped me? Nay, Alex, I will not give you any names." Maddie glared at him.

His voice softened when he spoke next. "I do not whip women and children, Madeline."

Alex reached for her. His instinct was to pull her close to him to protect her. But she flinched. Her reaction horrified him. Was his betrothed truly still afraid of him?

Madeline turned and tore up the stairs.

"You know I would never hurt you?" he called out after her. Shocked by his own behavior, he paced in front of the stairway.

"Alex, it's instinctual," Brenna said. "She knows you would

never hurt her. The sad truth is that flinching is habitual for her. You have to help her heal."

"I know that, but I want to touch her. I want to hold her and help her. I cannot stop myself. I wish she would not stop me."

Jennie tugged on her brother's plaid. "Alex, you are very loud sometimes, but when you yell at me, I know you don't mean it because you love me. Mayhap Maddie does not know you love her yet."

Startled, Alex turned to wee Jennie and hollered, "Jennie, you don't know what you are talking about!"

Jennie smiled up at her huge brother, "I know you love me, so I don't mind if you have to shout at me to feel better about loving Maddie."

Alex stared off over his sister's head, befuddled. What was happening to him? Did his wee sister know his mind better than he did?

Skipping off to play with her dogs, Jennie said, "Just tell her, Alex. Then she won't think you are mad at her when you yell so."

Brenna raised her eyebrows at him and smiled.

By the time Madeline came down the stairs to break her fast the next morning, Alex and his men had already left on horseback. Perhaps he did not want to be around her. She had hardly seen him since the day at the loch. Maybe her disfigurement was more than he was willing to accept. But then why had he kissed the marks on her breasts so tenderly? Confusion muddled her thoughts.

Of course, they had also argued last night. She had defied him, which was no small thing since he was now her laird. Had one of his guardsmen refused to give him information, she could not imagine the consequences. She was still eager to improve her relationship with the clan, but as the wedding grew closer, the animosity toward her only worsened. Yesterday, a small stone had grazed her back as she strolled to the gardens. Wee Tommy had been in the area, but she had decided not to confront him. She realized now that it might have been a mistake. What if the stone was larger the next time? Too late to rethink it now.

Maddie spent most of the day embroidering fabric to dress the tables for the wedding feast. The busy work kept her from thinking about her problems with Alex and his clan. Who would have thought a betrothal would cause this much trouble? And this much work? Alice hemmed Maddie's dress in the solar while Brenna stitched Jennie's. Jennie was off playing with friends so she would not be put to work. Thankful for the quiet time, Maddie tried to sort out her thoughts.

Her thoughts were interrupted by shouting in the courtyard. She ran to the door to seek the cause of the yelling, praying it had nothing to do with Alex. Several lads were hollering in the middle of the inner bailey. Something about a bairn. She rushed outside for a better look, and Brenna did the same. Both of them gasped at the next word they heard: "Jennie."

Maddie charged into the middle of the group. "Where is Jennie, Tommy?"

"Out there, my mama told me to come get the laird. Something's happened. They are hurt!"

Brenna shouted orders to several of the guards, instructing them to go after Alex.

Madeline's head reeled with the possibilities. She grabbed Tommy by the shoulders. "What happened?"

"Jennie," he cried. "Jennie and wee Emma. They disappeared into a hole!" He pointed out the gates.

Madeline's heart lurched. Her stomach was in her throat, but she scrambled after the lads, rushing through the gates.

"What happened?" Brenna shouted out after them. "Where are they?"

"In a hole! A sinkhole just opened up in the ground where they were playing and they both fell into it."

Madeline found Emma's mother sobbing in the middle of the meadow. Several clan members were ushering everyone away from the site.

"Stay back, stay back or you will collapse it on top of them!"

"They both fell in the hole," someone else said, "but only Emma is crying. We cannot see them, and Jennie doesn't answer."

Maddie's heart stopped beating. How could they just stand around while the lasses' lives were clearly in jeopardy? Jennie could have hit her head. Emma may have broken her leg. Both of them could be bleeding profusely. When she glanced back at Brenna, she saw the raw fear in her friend's eyes.

"Go in after them!" Brenna shouted as Robbie arrived and

assessed the situation.

"We can't do that, my lady," said one of the men Madeline recognized from the armory. "The hole is too small for any of us and I will not send another child down there. It is in danger of collapsing as it is."

"We need to wait for the laird!" someone shouted. "He will know what to do."

"We sent the guards to fetch him, but we cannot wait for him. It could be too late by then," yelled another.

Emma's mother, Moira, collapsed to the ground sobbing. "Oh, my bairn, my wee bairn. Someone help her!"

Robbie walked up to get a better look at the scene of the accident, then made his way over to Brenna. "It is small, Brenna, too small for any of us. I heard faint crying, but I think it is Emma. She sounds far away, so it must be deep. I called out to Jennie, but there was no response."

He turned to one of his men and sent him back to the keep to retrieve ropes.

"I will go down," Maddie said. "I am sure I will fit."

"You may fit. You are slimmer in the hip than many, but it is no' safe. We must find a solution that does not jeopardize any more lives."

Maddie's hands fisted at her sides. "Robbie, either one of the girls could be bleeding to death. We cannot risk the wait. I can handle it. Lower me down. You can help me."

"Nay, Maddie, Alex would have my hide. We will wait for the rope." Robbie's stern look forced Madeline to turn away in frustration. Clearly, he would not listen to reason—there was no choice but for her to act on her own.

In the confusion, Robbie would have to turn away at some point—and in so doing, he would give her the time she needed. She could not stand idly by. She would make her way down the hole as soon as she had the chance. Perhaps she could help the girls climb up. Determined her plan was sound, she waited impatiently. The instant Robbie turned toward his guard, she darted forward, ignoring the yelling. Judging the fit, she lowered herself into the opening and let go.

As she plummeted into a world of darkness, her body curled into a ball, she roughly rebounded off the dirt and stones on the side of the hole. She finally landed an eternity later, and a loud snap reverberated through the chamber as she braced her landing with her left arm. Sharp pain ripped through her, so she drew her left hand in close to her chest.

She lay unmoving for a few minutes to get her bearings. When she finally pushed herself upright, her chest heaved from exertion and pain. Drawing on her inner strength to overpower the pain, as she had done so often with Kenneth's beatings, she maneuvered around the bottom to feel for soft bodies. There was nothing but dirt. Soot and grime covered her face, but she brushed it away with her right hand to improve her vision. Her breathing slowed enough to allow her to listen for sounds. Finally, wee Emma's hiccupping sobs broke through her concentration. As her eyes adjusted to the darkness, she realized the hole was much wider at the bottom than it was at the top, and they were so far down there was barely any light.

Once she finally found Emma, she held her right arm out to the lass. "It is all right, Emma, come here," she said softly. Emma waddled toward her and fell in her lap, wrapping her arms tightly around Maddie. Hugging and soothing her as best she could, she continued to search the shadows for Jennie.

Emma appeared to be only shaken from her fall. There was no warm liquid indicating fresh blood, and Emma did not react with pain to any of Maddie's touches.

Scooting along with Emma on her lap proved difficult, but Maddie persisted—she knew the wee one needed the comfort of her touch. As she moved to the right, she noticed a small mound. Sliding over to the mound, she reached out carefully to see if it was Jennie. Her hand met with the lassie's soft hair. Maddie brushed the hair back from her face and leaned forward. She sighed with relief as Jennie's breath warmed her face.

"Jennie? It is Maddie, I am here with you. Can you answer me, Jennie?"

Maddie nudged her arm, but received no response. Tears welled in her eyes. The lassie's body pulsed with life, but she would not awaken. Running her hand around Jennie's head she discovered a large bump on her temple. She must have been knocked out after the fall.

Maddie gave Emma a little squeeze, thankful both lasses were alive, but head injuries could be very serious. Jennie was not out of danger. She glanced up toward the opening. There was no way she could get them out without a rope. It was too steep to climb, and there was nothing she could use for traction. Her arm was broken and probably useless. There really was nothing she could do but wait for help. Had Robbie's men returned with the rope yet? She hoped they would hurry.

Bits and pieces of conversations drifted down to her, but she couldn't discern one voice from another. She yelled, but it was impossible to tell if they could hear her. Emma continued to cry on and off, latching onto Maddie.

Maddie picked the lass up with her right arm, shifting her so that her head was cradled against her shoulder. She tried to soothe her with soft words and a back rub. After a few minutes, she quieted.

When all was quiet from above, she covered Emma's ears as best she could and shouted, "Hurry with the rope!"

She knew there was nothing she could do now but wait.

As soon as he saw the Grant guards riding toward him, a strange foreboding hit Alex square in the gut. He rode out to greet them.

"Laird, there has been an accident," the guard shouted.

Alex's insides lurched. "Who?" he shouted. "Who?"

"Jennie and wee Emma. They fell into a sink hole and their injuries are unknown."

Alex did not hear the rest of the explanation, for he spurred his horse on, riding frantically for his keep.

He had never driven his horse so hard and so fast. Fortunately, Midnight could handle what Alex demanded of him. As he approached the keep, he made his way to the small crowd of people gathered on the grounds and dismounted. Brodie was directly behind him. Everyone shouted at once.

"Good thing you are here, Laird."

"We need you, Laird!"

"Help our lasses, Chief. Get them out."

"Your lass sure is a brave one, Chief."

"Never seen anything like it, Laird. Your lass just ran up and jumped right in!"

Maddie? Alex's heart slammed into panic mode. He never went

into panic mode. What was happening to him? He always remained calm, regardless of the circumstances.

His gaze found his brother in the crowd. "Robbie?"

"The wee ones were playing and a hole opened up in the meadow. It seems to be deep. We can hear Emma, but Jennie has not answered. The opening is very narrow. I turned my back and your betrothed jumped into the hole. She had told me she planned to go down there, but I wouldn't allow it. Obviously, she did no' listen to me. A few minutes ago, we thought we heard Maddie yell, but we could not understand her clearly. There are too many conflicting sounds."

Alex rushed over to the hole to make his own assessment. Falling in at his side, Robbie added, "I sent a man back to the keep for rope. I think it best if we throw it down and pull them out. If Maddie is all right, she can hold each bairn as we pull them up."

Alex turned to the crowd and bellowed. "Quiet!" His clan members hushed instantly. He shouted into the hole, "Maddie!"

He listened. He motioned for everyone to be quiet again. He listened again. Nothing. He yelled again. Nothing.

"MADDIE!" he roared.

"Alex?"

Alex twisted his massive body as far into the hole as it would go, but he did not get far.

"Maddie, are you all right?"

"Emma and I are all right. But Jennie won't wake up. She needs tending, Alex."

Alex turned around and motioned to his sister. "I think she said Emma is all right, but Jennie needs tending."

Gasping, Brenna turned and sent Fiona back to the keep to prepare Jennie's chamber with the necessary supplies. "Alex, what about Maddie? Is she all right?"

Just then a man rushed up with the ropes.

"I think so. Now let's bring them up."

The rope was finally dangling above them. Emma, still awake, silently sucked her thumb as she clung to Maddie. Standing without much difficulty, Maddie grabbed for the rope above her head, but she could not reach it with Emma.

"More, Alex," she shouted. "I cannot reach it."

He let more of it down.

"More!" she shouted. Finally, it reached her. "All right, I have it now."

"Tie it around your waist, Maddie."

Maddie tugged it a little more and set Emma down. "Just for a moment, sweeting. We are going to get you to your mama." She clumsily tied it around her waist and picked Emma back up with her right arm, holding her tight. There was no other way. Her left arm was dangling at an odd angle.

She tugged on the rope and yelled to Alex. "Ready, Alex!"

As soon as Maddie's feet left the ground, her entire body swayed. The movement made Emma wail and Maddie was forced to grab the rope with her left hand to help steady them. Stabbing pain gripped her, but she refused to let go. *Just a little pain*, she chanted in her mind. She could bear it until Emma was safe. They continued to move up slowly, the pain in her arm relentless.

An image of her mother singing helped her focus, but it was blurry. She switched to Alex, recalling the warm comfort of being in his arms. She pictured his face and thought of everything she loved about him. Hearing her name again, she snapped to attention—they were almost at the top.

"Stop, Alex, stop!" she yelled. "We will not be able to fit through together."

"Hand her up and I will grab her," he shouted.

She found a wedge for her foot and pushed with all her strength. Alex reached in and plucked the bairn from her. He handed her out as the crowd cheered. Moira rushed over and grabbed the lassie, sobbing as she rocked Emma back and forth.

When Alex turned to Maddie, his eyes landed on her arm.

"Maddie, your arm," he whispered.

"I know, Alex. I think 'tis broken."

"It must pain you. How will you hold Jennie? She is much heavier."

"I know, but I can do it. We have no choice."

He turned to Robbie. "Pull her out!"

"Nay," she yelled. She wedged her foot solidly into the side of the hole.

Alex held his hand up to motion for the men to stop.

"Maddie, I cannot allow you to do this. We will dig the hole wider."

"And the dirt could bury Jennie. We have no choice. You clearly cannot fit in here. If you do not agree, I will let go of the rope and jump down again, but then I would risk breaking my other arm. I have to get Jennie out. She needs to see Brenna!"

They glared at each other until Alex turned and motioned for the men to lower her down.

"What is it, Alex?" Maddie recognized Robbie's voice.

"Maddie's arm is broken."

"How can she carry Jennie out then?" Brenna asked. "Jennie is much heavier than Emma."

"You are about to witness just how strong my Maddie is. She can do it." The words sent more strength through Maddie. He believed in her, and it made her believe more keenly in herself.

When Maddie reached the bottom again, she adjusted her arm to relieve the numbness. She attempted to awaken Jennie, but the lass did not budge. The bump on her forehead was no larger, so that was good—or so she thought. She retied the rope around her waist as tight as possible. Her left hand did not want to cooperate, but she did the best she could. Losing control and falling while she carried Jennie was not an option. She gathered Jennie up in her right arm, fighting the lass's dead weight. It took her a few moments to regain her balance with the extra weight. If Jennie had been any bigger, she would not have been able to manage it.

Finally settled, she shouted up to Alex.

"We are ready, but please go very slow to start. I have to balance her. She is very heavy for me."

Alex shouted for the men to pull. She swayed and almost lost her grip on the wee one, but she managed to hold tight. As they ascended, the tie around her waist began to slip.

Halfway up, Maddie yelled, "Hurry, Alex, the rope has loosened!"

Alex hollered at his men to go faster. Brodie's face appeared next to Alex's at the top of the hole.

"Brodie, be ready to grab Jennie when they get close," Alex barked. "I will grab Maddie. Her arm will not hold out for long."

The tie gave way and the full force of their combined weight fell on Maddie's left arm. She groaned in response to the vicious surge of the pain, but managed to wrap the rope around her upper arm and shoulder for extra support, though her whole body screamed at the added stress. Clutching Jennie tighter, she realized she was losing control. "Alex!" she shrieked.

Alex could see the strain in Maddie's face. Bracing her feet on the walls of the narrow hole, she was just barely managing to keep herself and Jennie from falling.

"Hold on, a few feet more and we will have you both. Hang on, Maddie!"

Moments later, Brodie reached into the opening, grabbed Jennie, and yanked her out. He fell backwards on the ground with Jennie on top of him, yet the lass still didn't awaken. The moment Brodie was out of the way, Alex reached in the hole and attempted to grab Maddie's shoulders. Her left hand was no longer able to hold her weight, so he had no choice but to grab her upper right arm, which was still tightly gripping the rope. Maddie twisted away from him as the rope, still partially wrapped around her damaged left arm, held it at an odd angle. Maddie flailed and sobbed at the same time, fighting for her life.

"Alex, Alex!" she sobbed.

"Maddie, look at me! Hold still, I have you."

Madeline's gaze locked with Alex's. There was fear in her eyes and something else. Pain. He glanced at her broken arm and realized the men were still pulling the rope, grotesquely twisting it.

"Alex, help me!" she sobbed in a whisper.

"Stop the rope!" Alex roared. All sanity and calmness left him, and he knew they would not return until his betrothed was safe. He heaved with all his strength and tugged her up through the small opening. Maddie fell across Alex weeping, clinging to him with her right arm.

"Alex, do not let go, please hold me," she whispered into his neck.

Alex carefully cut the rope from her left arm and straightened it as best he could. He held her as gingerly as he could while she continued to weep into his chest.

The crowd fell into a dead silence as they gaped at the odd shape of her arm.

"Look at her arm," someone whispered.

"Her arm is broken!"

"How could she hold on to the bairns with her arm like that?"

"She never screamed or anything."

Slowly, as word passed, everyone started to applaud and cheer Alex's betrothed. He stood cautiously, and—unwilling to cause her any more pain—he cradled her into Brodie's arms and jumped on to Midnight. As soon as Maddie was safely in his lap, he headed back to the keep. Robbie rode some distance ahead of him with Jennie on his lap, Brenna directly behind them with Brodie.

Maddie clung to Alex with her right arm. He kissed her forehead but said nothing.

For Alex, this event had brought clarity to his life. He chastised himself for the doubts he had entertained for the past several days. Maddie belonged in his arms. How could he have doubted it for an instant? The woman had just jeopardized everything for his sister and another wee bairn. She had never questioned whether it was the right thing to do—she had simply done it. The needs of others always came first for Maddie. Long ago, he had thought her timid—a frightened rabbit. Well, timid, frightened rabbits didn't put themselves in danger jumping down deep sinkholes in the ground.

Somehow, he would have to help her bring the same courage to their lovemaking. He probably would still have to be very patient, but they would find a way to make it work.

She would be his wife and he vowed to make her happiness a priority.

Maddie had just grabbed another portion of his heart.

CHAPTER TWENTY-THREE

When they reached the stables, Old Hugh grabbed the reins while Mac took Maddie gently from Alex. The instant he got off Midnight, he took her back into his arms. She never made a sound when she moved, but the look in her eyes told Alex everything.

As he carried her to the keep, he whispered, "I will take care of you. Brenna will help with your arm, but I promise not to leave you." He leaned over and kissed her mouth.

"Jennie? Emma?" she choked out.

"Emma appears fine. Jennie is with Brenna right now. Once you are settled, I will check on Jennie. You are a brave woman, Maddie."

He glanced down at Maddie and noticed the way she clung to him with white knuckles. The pain she bore showed in subtle ways. Unfortunately, he knew the arm would need to be straightened, so her pain would worsen before it improved.

When Alex reached the door, Alice offered her assistance to him. As she followed him upstairs, she said, "I have her chamber ready, my laird. Brenna is with wee Jennie. I will assist Maddie and then send for Brenna once she is settled."

At the top of the stairs, Alex turned to the right.

"Laird, I am sure you have forgotten in the confusion, but Maddie's chamber is to the left."

Alex ignored her and strode onward.

"Ah, excuse me, but Maddie's chamber is the other way."

When Alex glanced over his shoulder, Alice was standing there glaring at him, her hands on her hips.

He reached his door and pushed it open with his foot. "I am not confused, my lady. Maddie will be in my chamber." He proceeded to his bed and carefully set her down.

Alice jumped. "But this is not proper," she fretted. She stood outside his door as if afraid to venture inside.

"I don't know if it is proper or no', but she stays with me. This is where she belongs. I will take care of her," Alex finished. His glare told Alice his decision was not open for discussion.

"Alex, I already have enough difficulties with your clan. Please do not do this," Maddie begged in a soft, strained voice.

"Stay with her for a minute please, Alice." He turned to Maddie and said, "I need to check in with Brenna. No one will know, Maddie. Do you no' know yet where you belong?" Alex carefully propped Maddie's left arm on a pillow, tucked her into bed, kissed her cheek, and turned toward the door.

"My lord, but what will your people think? They will assume terrible things about her," Alice implored, her cheeks turning red.

"And if they dare to speak it, they will find themselves living elsewhere. She is my betrothed, and she stays here. I promise you, Alice, I will not ravish your charge until after we are wed. But she will stay here where she belongs." Alex nodded his head to Alice and left the room. At the last moment, he stuck his head back around the open door, "But I will allow you bathe her, if you do no' mind. I am sure she will feel better with all that dirt washed away. And I know it would upset you if I did it." He winked and smiled, then shut the door behind him.

Alex found Robbie and Brenna at Jennie's bedside. He leaned over and kissed his wee sister's forehead. "Is there any change, Brenna? Have you found anything else?"

"Nay, Alex. I think 'tis the head wound that makes her sleep. She did talk some nonsense a bit, which I take to be a good sign. Her body needs rest. She knows she is safe now, so hopefully she will relax enough to start healing. Robbie, you stay with her while I tend to Maddie's arm."

As they headed down the passageway together, she turned to her brother. "Alex, I will need you and Brodie to hold her down. Can you handle it when she screams? I can bring someone else in to hold her if it would be too much for you. It is a bad break. I will need to probe it first before I can set it."

"Aye, I will hold her. She will not scream. But I want to be there to help her deal with the pain. Brodie won't be needed."

Brenna shook her head. "Alex, I want another to be there. As you know, I have been kicked and swung at by men who have suffered less painful breaks. I cannot risk any injuries. I need to be strong for both of them."

"Aye, if 'tis what you want, we will do it. I will get Brodie."

"I want to give Maddie something to help ease the pain. Then I will return after I check on Jennie once more. I need to give the pain mixture a little time to work."

As soon as Alex found Brodie, he sent him to Jennie's chamber to check on their wee sister and fetch Brenna. When he entered his own chamber, he found Alice primping Maddie. She had cleaned most of the dirt off her charge, but was still fussing over her.

"Maddie, the rest of your bath will have to wait until tomorrow. We cannot stress your arm any more today. My lord, may I move a few of her things here?" Alice asked.

"You may move all of them here if you would like. This is where she stays." He sat on the bed on Maddie's right side, leaning his back against the wall so he could prop her against his chest and guard her arm. Alice left to retrieve Maddie's things.

Rubbing her uninjured right arm, he whispered, "Jennie is still sleeping, but Brenna thinks she may just need extra rest. She will come and straighten your arm out soon. I promise to stay with you." He brushed his lips across her silky hair. "You know it will hurt, aye?"

Maddie slowly nodded. Whatever Brenna had given her had started to work. He could tell she was fighting to stay awake.

"Alex, are you angry about the loch?" she whispered.

"Nay, love, just foolish."

"No more secrets…" she mumbled as her eyes closed.

Alex caressed her right arm to help lull her to sleep.

"Alex?" Her eyes opened for a second before closing again.

"Hmm?"

"I love you. You are my dream." Her breathing shifted into a more rhythmic pattern as she fell sound asleep.

Alex didn't move—he *could* not move. Had he heard her correctly? She loved him? His heart soared and did a funny little flip. Those three little words had warmed his heart. He wished she would say it again, but she was asleep. He still was not sure he loved her, but he certainly had stronger feelings for Maddie than he had ever felt for any lass. He hadn't realized how strong those feelings were until the accident.

Brodie and Brenna came into the room not long after.

"She is a strong lass for her size, is she no', Alex?" Brenna asked. "I shudder to think what would have happened if Maddie had not been able to pull both lasses up. Is she sleeping?"

Alex nodded. "Aye, though I know you will wake her when you do what you must. Do it quickly, please."

"Brodie, be ready to grab her in case she starts thrashing. I have to probe the broken bone first. I'm afraid it will be very painful." Brenna arranged her supplies, a board to hold the arm straight, linen strips to wrap around it and a piece of linen to fashion into a sling.

Brenna lifted the injured arm and asked Brodie to hold it still for her. That simple action was enough to jolt Maddie awake.

"Maddie," Brenna said softly but firmly, "I have to feel your bones to see exactly where it is broken. I hope there is only one break, but I must check for more. It will hurt, so scream if you must." She leaned in to kiss Maddie's cheek. "Thank you, lass, for saving our wee ones."

Then, without waiting any longer, Brenna started to probe Maddie's left hand, working her way upward. They waited for the screaming to start, but it never started. Maddie's breathing was erratic and she nuzzled her face into Alex's chest, but she kept her arm completely still for Brenna.

"How does she do it? I have never seen a lass who can bear so much," Brodie asked in wonder. "How would you ever know she was in pain?"

Alex smoothed a hand over her hair. "I am starting to learn more about my betrothed. I know when she is in pain. I could see it in her eyes when she was in that hole, and I can see it in the sweat on her brow now. You are all right, sweeting?" he whispered.

Maddie nodded, but kept her eyes closed.

Alex pointed to her right hand. It was clenched into a tight fist.

Having finished her probing, Brenna sat back a little and said, "I think there is only one break in your forearm, Maddie. That is the good news. But I am going to have to pull and twist it to get it back in place. That is the bad news. Can you wiggle your fingers for me?"

Maddie wiggled all her fingers slowly, but it clearly took effort.

"Good. Now, I will do this as fast as I can, but it will be painful." Brenna showed Brodie what she wanted him to do.

Maddie grabbed Alex's hand with her right one. She took a deep breath and nodded at Brenna. After nodding back, Brenna tugged on Madeline's arm, pushing and twisting the bone back into place. Maddie's body arched off the bed, but while her body trembled all over, she never made a sound. Tears flowed down her cheeks as Alex held her in place.

"There, I am done. I think it will heal straight. I just want to get it wrapped. You will not be able to use it at all for at least a fortnight." Brenna wrapped her linen strips around the board, then motioned for the brothers to give Maddie the rest of the sleeping potion.

As she drank the mixture, Madeline smiled weakly. "Thank you, Brenna. That was not so bad. You are very gentle."

Brenna raised her eyebrows and glanced at both brothers before she left the room.

CHAPTER TWENTY-FOUR

When Maddie opened her eyes, she stared at everything in confusion. Darkness enveloped the room. She attempted to push herself up, but pain immediately shot through her left arm. Memories of her fall into the hole came back to her slowly. The contraption on her arm must have been created by Brenna. Another sensation slowly registered, and she looked down to see a muscular arm across her waist and a long hairy leg draped over hers.

She could not stop herself from disturbing Alex. "What are you doing?"

"I was trying to sleep, sweeting, what are you doing?" he retorted.

"Alex, you are in my bed! 'Tis not proper!"

"Nay, you are in my bed, and I know 'tis no' proper, but you are staying." He peeked at her out of the corner of one eye with a slight grin on his face. "How is your arm?"

"My arm is fine. But I am not trying to be amusing. This is not proper. I am going back to my chamber. What have you done?" Maddie sat up quickly and then groaned as her body responded. She fell back against the pillows.

"Maddie, we are to be married in a sennight. I promised your maid that I would not ravish you. But you cannot sleep alone. 'Tis no' safe for you."

"But your clan already thinks I am a whore because of the Comming. What will they think now?"

"What are you talking about? My clan does not think of you as a whore!" His voice grew to a dull roar.

"Aye, they do, Alex. You know 'tis why the storytelling stopped," Maddie said, turning from him.

"I do no' think my clan will be treating you like that anymore. If they do, I will take care of it. I will take care of you," he whispered, turning her face back so he could kiss her brow.

Maddie sighed and nestled her head against Alex's shoulder. "I am too tired to argue now." She promptly fell back asleep.

The next time she awakened, she was being carried down the passageway to her own chamber.

"Thank you, Alex," she whispered.

"This is just for the day. I will return you to my chamber tonight. 'Tis where you belong. But I will give in to your tender sensibilities during the day." He deposited her on the bed and then propped her arm with a pillow. "Brenna said to keep your arm supported for a while. I will send her up to check on you while I see Cook about some food. Are you hungry, sweeting?"

"Aye, I could eat a little something, thank you." Her eyes rested on her betrothed's mouth as the memories of his kisses at the loch rocked through her.

"Please don't look at me like that, or my intentions will no longer be honorable." After a quick kiss on her lips, he turned and left the chamber. Maddie sighed, wishing they were already married so she could stop worrying about her reputation and conduct herself as she wished—which would be to stay as close to him as possible. She supposed she needed to focus on healing first. That thought brought another—she hoped Jennie would awaken soon.

As if summoned by her thoughts, Alex burst into her chamber a few minutes later. There was a huge smile on his face, and wee Jennie was cradled in his arms. Maddie was so pleased to see her awake she sat straight up in her bed. "Jennie? You are better?"

"Hi, Maddie," Jennie said weakly.

Alex set her on the bed in front of Madeline.

"Jennie, are you all right?" Maddie asked as she cupped the lassie's face with her right hand.

"I am fine, but my big brother will not let me walk yet. He does not believe me. I am a little tired though. And my head does hurt sometimes. And I think I have some bruises, but I will get better. Alex said I could have pastries to break my fast. Cook made me the biggest pastry I have ever seen, and it is covered with icing! I wanted to come and see you before eating it, but I did lick some icing off already." Jennie's words flew out of her, as if she hadn't talked in days.

"Is your arm all right, Maddie? What is that thing on your arm? Does it hurt very much? How can you take a bath with that?"

"Och, little flower, slow down or you will give Madeline a headache, too," Alex said with a smile. "Give her a kiss so I can return you to your room to eat your pastry. Maddie needs to rest."

Jennie leaned over and gave Madeline a big kiss. "Thank you for saving me, Maddie."

"Jennie, thank the saints above you have improved. We worried so."

Alex picked her up and left. Her excited chatter continued and he shook his head, chuckling as he walked. "I think she is feeling better," he shouted back to Madeline.

The next few hours flew by. Brenna and Alice helped Maddie bathe and then Alice clucked her way around the room, fixing everything. She ate in her chamber, as she was still in a bit of pain and not quite ready to face everyone. Robbie and Brodie stopped in briefly to see how she was doing, and they filled her in on wee Jennie and how much the lassie enjoyed being the center of attention.

She awoke several hours later to find Alex seated at her bedside.

"How long have I been asleep, Alex?" she asked.

"Quite a while, but your body needs it. What you did yesterday was no small feat for a lass your size. Your body needs to heal itself, especially your arm. Is it paining you much, lass?"

"Nay, only when I move it certain ways. I think I am ready to walk a bit. I cannot sit here forever." Maddie moved herself to the edge of the bed.

"I think you could come down to the hall for supper. There are some people there who are anxious to see that you are all right."

"Well, I do not know who could be interested in my welfare. I have seen all of your family and most of the servants today. But I would like to go to the hall and eat with your family. Can you send Alice in to help me get dressed into something more appropriate?"

"I will help you." He walked over to her chest. "What gown do you want?"

"Alex, you cannot help me. It would be improper for you to see me naked." Maddie blushed under his scrutiny.

"Maddie, in a sennight I plan to see you naked every day. Every inch of your body that I have seen is beautiful, so do no' be shy. But today, I promise just to help you into your gown. You have a chemise on underneath, aye?" Alex asked.

Maddie glanced at the determination on her betrothed's face. His arms were crossed in front of him, and she probably could not sway him. She finally conceded by standing up. After all, he had already seen her in a chemise.

"All right, but do not dawdle!" she said with a firm set to her jaw.

Alex turned his back to her and reached into the chest, emerging with a lavender gown. "How is this?"

"That will be fine," she said, clenching her teeth. She turned her back to Alex and tried to remove her night rail, but she only managed to tangle it.

"How am I supposed to dress and undress with my arm like this?" she sighed in frustration.

"Let someone help you," he whispered near her ear. He stood behind her and helped untangle her arms and remove the night rail.

He stood so close to her she could feel his heat, even through the material of her chemise. His scent of horse and pine washed through her senses, reminding her of the day he had rescued her. She remembered the gentleness with which he had pulled her chemise from the dried blood on her back in the woods. She gave in to him, letting him control her movements. His hands ran down her body as he helped her put the gown on. She leaned back into him and felt his hardness against her back. She shivered at the sensation.

"Are you cold, lass?" Alex asked as he turned her and pulled her into his arms.

She shook her head as his mouth descended on hers. His tongue pressed against her lips, and she opened her mouth for him. Maddie wrapped one arm around his neck and pushed him closer. She couldn't stop the little moan in the back of her throat as he deepened the kiss, begging for more.

Alex heard her moan and pulled her closer. He ran his hands over her soft bottom. He had wanted her for so long that he was sure he would embarrass himself and lose his seed the instant his hardness touched her flesh. He set her away from him as soon as he heard footsteps in the hallway. The door flung open and Alice marched into the room.

Alice stopped her advance and gasped, her hand going immediately to her mouth as she took in Maddie's dazed look and drew her own conclusions. Only then did Alex notice how red and swollen Maddie's lips looked. The maid picked up one of Maddie's storybooks made of parchment and promptly swatted him across the back of his head.

"Just as I thought, you swine. This is not proper. You will not treat her like this. You are not to be alone with her until after you are wed. Why, her mother is probably rolling in her grave as we speak!"

Maddie's eyes were big as saucers. "Alice, you hit Laird Grant. That is not your place!"

Alice's chin jutted forward. "Perhaps not, but I won't take it back. I promised your mother that I would take care of you, Madeline, and I will not let this man, laird or not, take advantage of you."

Alex squelched the grin on his face, and before he knew it, he was shoved out of the door by the petite commander. From the quick look he got of Maddie before he was ousted, she was fighting a smile, too. He was propelled right into Robbie.

"Huh!" Robbie said. "What do you suppose that is all about? Any ideas, brother?" His eyes sparkled as he ducked Alex's swing and turned and ran down the stairs, laughing all the way.

Eventually, Alex returned to carry Madeline downstairs to the great hall. He sat her at the main dais, but he moved her chair away from the table, tuning it to face the door. Robbie, Brodie, Brenna, Alice, and Mac were all present, and it felt as if they were waiting for something. They were acting in a peculiar manner, but she could not fathom their intent. Jennie positioned herself at Maddie's side, a big smile lighting up her face.

"What is this about?" Madeline asked as she searched everyone's faces.

Alex motioned for Brodie to go to the door, then turned to Maddie and said, "There are some members of my clan who have been asking to speak to you."

The door opened and Moira rushed in with Emma in her arms. She marched up to the dais and curtsied to Maddie. "My lady, I came to thank you for saving my wee Emma." She set the bairn down and tucked a package into her tiny hands. Emma waddled over and offered the package to Maddie with a big smile.

As Emma walked back to her mama, Moira continued. "I also wish to apologize for the way I treated you. I was wrong, and I hope you will find it in your heart to forgive me. You are truly a fine lady."

Tears welled in Maddie's eyes as she opened the package. Inside, she found a bar of lavender-scented soap.

"I made it with me own hands, my lady. I hope you like it."

Madeline held the soap up to her face to take in the sweet scent. "It is lovely, Moira. Thank you, I will treasure it." She lifted herself up and walked over to give the other woman a one-armed hug. "Of course I forgive you." Emma reached up to kiss Maddie's cheek and then Moira curtsied and left the hall.

Maddie turned to Alex, only managing to say, "Oh, Alex!"

The door opened again, and this time wee Tommy scrambled up the steps to Maddie, followed by his mother. He bowed to Maddie and handed her a glorious bouquet of dried flowers. "Me Ma and I picked them and dried them ourselves a while ago, but we want you to have them, my lady."

Tommy's mother curtsied and said, "Forgive me, my lady, for the wrongs I have done you. The laird could not find a better lady to take as his wife." She turned and curtsied to Alex. "We will be proud to have her as our lady, my laird." Alex nodded before they turned and left.

Maddie stared at the two gifts in her lap. How long had it been since anyone had given her a gift? Brushing the moistness from her lashes, she jerked as the door opened again. The blacksmith and his family crossed the room to Alex and bowed. "Forgive me, Laird, for my behavior. I should no' have shunned your betrothed for something that was no' her fault. She is a brave lady who will make you a fine wife." He stepped forward, bowed to Madeline, and placed a long, thick rabbit pelt on her lap. "To keep your hands warm on the cold winter nights." He bowed again as he and his family turned to leave.

Maddie forced a weak, "Thank you, sir," as she fought back tears.

Jennie clapped as she looked at the gifts. "You see, Maddie, I knew they would like you once they got to know you better!"

And the line continued...

Another pelt from the tanner.

A sleek jeweled dagger from the man in the armory.

Maddie's tears were flowing freely at that point. But she always managed a smile and a polite "thank you" for each of her visitors. There were so many, she lost track. Some were there just to thank her for saving the wee ones. Others apologized for misjudging her. Her gifts filled the table.

A bouquet of fresh flowers.

Embroidered cloths for the tables.

Scented candles.

A jar of honey.

Pastries.

Apple tarts.

Apple bread.

A beautiful shawl.

A pair of beaded slippers.

Embroidered chair cushions.

Embroidered linen squares.

But the last gift was for wee Jennie.

"A new puppy?"

It was from Emma's father. "For always watching over the wee ones, Jennie."

Jennie jumped up and down as she cuddled her new puppy in her arms.

"I had no idea. All these gifts are beautiful!" Maddie exclaimed.

"My clan is full of good people. They do get confused at times, but they are honest, hard-working people." Alex's eyes shone with pride as he gazed at her.

"Alex, did you tell them they had to apologize to me?"

"No." He kissed her cheek. "Had I thought of it, I would have. But I was too busy worrying about you and Jennie."

CHAPTER TWENTY-FIVE

In just a few days, Maddie would be Alex's wife. Despite Alice's ranting and raving, Alex went to Maddie's chamber every night and hauled her down to his own, returning her before dawn. Maddie found she did not mind at all. Actually, she had grown accustomed to falling asleep in his arms since he was very warm and she knew it was the safest place for her.

At first, she was afraid he would try something improper, but other than a few kisses, he behaved like a perfect gentleman. Truth be known, she was becoming quite fond of his kisses and actually ached for them at times. But she never let him know. At least now she did not feel panicked over the thought of their wedding night. She knew the bedding would take place, but she trusted Alex. Even though it might hurt, she knew in her heart he would never humiliate or hurt her.

Maddie and Brenna were laboring in the vegetable garden together one afternoon, harvesting what they could for the wedding, when they heard a commotion at the gates. They strolled down in time to see Father MacGregor dismounting from his horse.

"Father, is it really you?" Maddie cried.

"Och, my child, are you no' a beautiful lass!" he shouted in his usual boisterous way. "How long since I have seen you, lass? And what has happened to your arm?"

"At least two years, Father. I promise to tell you about my arm later. But I must know, why did you leave us?"

Father MacGregor put his arm around Madeline's shoulder. "Maddie, your stepbrother ordered me to stay away. I could not believe he would speak to a man of the cloth as he did, but it did not stop him. I knew your people needed me more than ever after losing your parents, but his threats were quite clear. I did not wish to endanger anyone. But why are you here, lass?"

They turned to make their way toward the steps of the castle.

"Because I am betrothed to Alex—I mean, Laird Grant. He has asked me to be his wife and I have accepted."

"Och, that is wonderful news. I am so glad to hear that you are safe from that cruel man. But were you no' already betrothed?" Father MacGregor asked, giving her a puzzled look.

"Father, let me settle you inside where it is warm and arrange for some food for you. Then I will tell you all that has transpired. But it is so good to see you!" She hugged him and led him up the stairs to the keep.

Alex did not return until dusk. Traipsing into the hall, he immediately welcomed Father MacGregor. Brenna called for food and they enjoyed the meal together with much laughter. Afterwards, Alex took Father MacGregor aside.

"Father, will you walk with me outside for a bit?"

"Why, certainly, Laird, I would enjoy a walk."

As soon as they distanced themselves from the hall, Alex asked the questions he needed answered.

"Father, have you heard anything about Madeline's stepbrother, Kenneth? Do you have any idea where he might be hiding?"

"Nay, Laird, I have neither seen nor heard anything about the man. At least, not since he left his home to visit Niles Comming. I heard about the Comming's death, and I thank you for saving Madeline from *two* horrible men. Her parents would be sick if they knew how poorly her stepbrother treated her. I was at the MacDonald keep for about three months after their death. Eventually, I was told in a threatening manner to leave and never return.

"It broke my heart as I was very fond of Madeline, and I knew Kenneth did not like her. It encouraged me to know that she at least had Mac and Alice to watch over her. Alice would protect her until her death."

"I have already seen the evidence of that, Father." Alex grinned as he thought of the old woman hitting him in the head with the parchment and calling him swine. "But even Mac is no' a match for Kenneth."

Alex then brought up the subject that had been burning inside him. "Father, I need to ask you another question, and mayhap you will not have an answer for me, but I still have to ask. I'm not sure what you know of the cruelty Madeline suffered at the hands of Kenneth and the Comming? I worry that she will have trouble putting such things behind her once we are married."

"Och, you ask difficult questions, Laird. But I will share with you what I know. Kenneth was a very sneaky, deceitful man. While I was still there, he decided to sell some jewels Madeline had inherited from her mother. I recall a pearl necklace that her mother wore often. They were gifts to Madeline, though, and she would not part with them. He finally concocted a scheme of allowing her to visit an aunt in England.

"Madeline was so excited at the prospect of escaping Kenneth, I'm afraid she was not thinking clearly. He hired someone to take her on the journey, loaded her trunks, and sent them on their way. The next day, he set out on their trail, beat up the driver of the wagon and ransacked through Madeline's possessions. He found all the jewels, but 'twas not enough punishment. He beat her and left them both to die."

Alex's rage flew at the image of Madeline lying alone on a dirt road, beaten. How could someone treat an innocent woman in such a way? Kenneth was a madman. Alex clenched his fists, wishing they were wrapped around the MacDonald's throat. He forced his attention back to Father MacGregor. "What happened?"

"Maddie is a fighter, and she was found several days later wandering just outside the keep. Mac found her and brought her back. He and his wife hid her and nursed her back to health. I was actually called to pray over Madeline's body, as they did not think she would survive, but she did. That was when I had my conversation with Kenneth. I reminded him of what the Lord would think of men taking advantage of weaker creatures. Rather than listen to me, he banished me from the keep.

"My guess is that Maddie does not trust easily after all she has suffered. The Comming is another bad story, but I will only tell you that I did hear what happened, and I cannot be sorry that he met his fate. Kenneth is a sick man, and I do not doubt that if he is still alive, he is plotting against Madeline. He truly hated her, but I do no' know why. So I wish you luck, my son. I hope you find him before he finds her.

"As for your question about the marriage, I cannot think of a finer woman for you. Madeline truly has a heart of gold. She is one of God's true gifts in my eyes, and he has finally sent her in the right direction. You may need a little more patience with her, but you will not regret it."

Alex nodded and felt a little weight lift off his shoulders. He relaxed as he thought of all Father MacGregor had said. The man was right. Maddie was special.

As they turned to go back to the keep, he said, "Thank you, Father."

Father MacGregor answered with a smile. "I vow you will not regret your marriage, Laird Grant."

As Alex opened the door for him, he said, "And Father?"

"Aye, my son?"

"Thank you for being there for her when I could not." Alex smiled at him.

Father MacGregor beamed.

CHAPTER TWENTY-SIX

Father MacGregor left the next morning to visit a few of the neighboring clans, but Maddie did not mind. She was so excited he would be performing their ceremony. Only two more days remained before she would become Alex's wife, and she found she was not as nervous as she had expected she would be. Alex and his men left early again, so she spent the morning putting away her wonderful new gifts. The embroidered cloths she saved for the wedding since she would not be able to finish her own with a broken arm. She found very special places for her flowers, both fresh and dried. One arrangement was placed on the hearth in the great hall and another on the main table. Her favorite earned a place in her chamber.

Her lavender-scented soap, however, was special and would be saved until the day of the wedding.

She was holding the beaded slippers in her hands, thinking of where to stow them, when Jennie flew down the stairs toward her.

"Maddie, Alice needs you to come up for another fitting."

"Another one? I thought she'd finished. Are you she sure she needs me now?"

Jennie nodded and spun on her heels, giggling.

"All right, I will be right there." Maddie headed for the stairs, Jennie close at her heels.

"I really do not think she needs your help. You can go play with your new pup," Maddie said as she climbed the stairs.

"Oh, nay, I want to watch."

When Madeline stepped into the solar, she was surprised to see Alice was crying.

"Alice, what is wrong?" Maddie asked.

"Oh, nothing, my dear. I am just so happy for you. I never thought I would see the day of your wedding after all we have been through." Alice wiped her tears and walked around the table.

Alice pulled the dress out from under a cloth and held it for Maddie's inspection.

Maddie gasped. "How did you...where did you...oh! But it is beautiful."

"Your betrothed arranged for the material. It is the perfect shade of blue, don't you think? Will you try it on?"

Brenna entered just in time to help her slip the dress on over her broken arm. Maddie could only stare down at the beautiful dress, unable to speak. Standing in the corner of the room, Jennie smiled and clapped.

"It is perfect. You will make a stunning bride," Brenna said with tears in her eyes. "My brother is truly fortunate. Finding you has been such a blessing for him."

All Maddie could get out was, "How?"

"Alex asked the messenger who brought news of your marriage to the king to bring back bolts of cloth. He actually brought back several different shades of blue fabric, Maddie. Alex must like your blue eyes!" Brenna exclaimed. "And those beaded slippers you were given will match perfectly."

"He loves her, Brenna. I think Alex loves Maddie!" Jennie shouted.

"Do you think so, Jennie?" Brenna asked with a smile on her face.

"Aye, I see him kissing her sometimes," Jennie said, grinning back at them.

Maddie continued admiring Alice's work. The bodice of the pastel gown was decorated with beads and the thin and silky sleeves had been adjusted so they could accommodate the wood and the linen straps on her left arm. Alice had sewn ribbons around the neckline, at the end of the sleeves, and around the hem.

After she removed it, she hugged Alice. "It is the most beautiful gown I have ever seen. Thank you. You even managed to make it fit over my broken arm. How did you do that?"

Alice could not stop crying. "Oh, Maddie, you know I would do anything for you. If only your mother could see you."

"She will be there, Alice. She will be with us in spirit. And so will my father."

Several hours later, Maddie still found herself sighing over Alex's thoughtfulness. He certainly was a man full of surprises. She had thought very hard about how she could repay his generosity, but she could only think of one thing. It would have to wait until he returned, so she asked Robbie to come and get her as soon as the men returned.

A short time later, Robbie stuck his head in the door and yelled to her. Maddie hurried to the door.

"Has he arrived yet, Robbie?" she asked.

"Aye, I hear the horses. They will be arriving soon."

"Robbie, would you mind escorting me to the stables? I would like to be there as soon as he gets back."

"Of course, my lady. I will take you now if you are ready, as I need to see him as well."

Maddie put away her ink and followed him to the stables.

"There are many strangers about, are there not?" Maddie asked.

"Aye, the clan members are starting to arrive for the big event," Robbie said. "The tents are being assembled around the keep and outside as well. Some people are eager to arrive early so they can raise their tents in the outer bailey instead of outside the walls of the keep."

"Won't it be more difficult to protect everyone, Robbie?" she asked nervously as she looked around at the crowds.

"Aye, but we have done it many times before. This is similar to a fair or tournament. I promise you we will be watching for Kenneth. We know most of these people, and I will not allow anyone to stay inside the gates unless I know them well. The guardsmen will continue searching for Kenneth. The laird made it very clear to everyone that your safety is our first priority."

They were almost to the stable when Maddie heard the horses' hooves above the din in the bailey. She quickly headed into Midnight's stall.

"If you do not mind, Robbie, I will wait for Alex here. I hoped to have a private moment with him."

"Aye, my lady, there is no one around. I think it will be safe for you, and Alex is almost here."

A few minutes later, she heard Alex shouting to Old Hugh to

grab the other horses. She knew Alex preferred to rub Midnight down himself if he had the time. Seconds later, he opened the door ahead of Midnight and stopped short at the sight of her. Before he could even drop the reins, Maddie strode over to him, cupped his face with one hand, and gave him a passionate kiss on the mouth. When she ran her tongue across his bottom lip to tease him, he dropped the reins and grabbed her, pulling her tight to his body. He groaned and kissed her exactly the way she needed, desire evident in his strong hold and rigid body.

She stopped and gazed into his eyes. "This pleases you, Laird Grant?"

"Aye. Mayhap you will greet me like that every day after we are married. Or is there a special reason?" His eyebrow quirked as he stared into her eyes.

"Aye, actually there is. I came to thank you for the bolts of cloth. My dress is beautiful."

How fortunate she was to have found Alex. She enjoyed seeing the hungry look in his eyes when he glanced at her body, feeling the tingling she experienced whenever he was near. Hope blossomed in her heart at the prospect of living her life with this man.

He kissed her again gently. "It cannot be as beautiful as you, my lady."

A rustling from the opposite end of the stables interrupted their interlude.

"Leave me alone, please!" A young girl's plea wrenched the air.

They heard a slap, followed by a male voice saying, "Be quiet, wench, you know you want this."

Then another shriek. "Nay!"

Madeline bolted out of the door and ran to the end of the stables. "Unhand her!" she shouted. She felt her face and neck go red from her boiling blood.

"Mind your own business, lady," the lad yelled back.

Alex was directly behind her, but the lad did not notice him until he grabbed him by the neck and lifted him clear off the ground.

"You are her business, lad, and I suggest you start apologizing to my betrothed!" he barked in the lad's face.

The lad scrambled. "Laird Grant, I am sorry, I had no idea she was your betrothed. You know I would never have spoken to her like that if I had known." Strange choking noises erupted from him as he talked.

"Who is your father, lad?" Alex ground out.

The lass in the corner cringed from all of them.

"Uh, Gavin Grant, Laird. I promise. It will never happen again."

"You are right about that. I do not allow rape on my lands. Now get yourself out before I change my mind and decide to take a whip to you. And you are no longer welcome at our wedding feast. Understood?" Alex set him down so fast that he lost his balance and tumbled to the ground directly in front of Madeline's feet.

"My lady, I beg your forgiveness," he cried.

"You need to beg the forgiveness of the lass," she whispered. "You will never mishandle a lass on our lands again, do you hear?"

"Aye, my lady." He turned to the lass and bowed and yelled, "So sorry!" before escaping as fast as he could.

Madeline wrapped her good arm around the lass as the poor girl shivered.

"Come along. Laird Grant and I will escort you home." Alex gave Mac some instructions and then joined them.

"Where do you live?" Maddie asked.

"My father is the tanner," she said in a shaky voice, pointing to a nearby cottage.

"Lass, you know there will be many strangers about. Please be careful who you talk to and don't wander about unescorted," Alex warned her quietly.

"I did not know what he wanted. He was very insistent. Thank you, my laird." She curtsied in front of her house. Silent tears coursed down her cheeks.

Alex knocked on the door and briefly explained the incident to the lass's mother and father. The mother hugged the lass tight and ushered her into the cottage. After Alex had a short conversation with the tanner, he and Maddie left and returned to the hall.

Madeline could no longer hold back her own tears. "Oh, Alex, I am so emotional. I hope it does not scare you away. I just cannot help myself sometimes. It seems I cry at anything and everything lately. I do no' want any lass to be mistreated on our lands…well, when they are *our* lands," she said sheepishly.

Alex turned her to face him. "Nay, Maddie, I do not mind that you are emotional. I have known many cold women, and they are not for me. I will gladly deal with your emotions. Considering all the hardships you have survived, I believe your emotions are natural. I just hope that someday most of your tears will be tears of joy." He wiped the tears from her face, and escorted her into the great hall. "And it pleases me to hear you say 'our' lands. Soon they *will* be ours."

CHAPTER TWENTY-SEVEN

The first thought that crossed Maddie's mind when she awoke was that her wedding day had finally arrived. Her second was that this was the last time she would be in bed alone. Father MacGregor had returned, so Alice had shamed her into sleeping by herself the night before the wedding. She found herself missing Alex's warm, comforting embrace.

She sighed, wistfully thinking of the day ahead. She was a little nervous about the ceremony because there would be so many guests in attendance, but believed she could handle it. The wedding night still caused her anxiety despite the trust she had in Alex. Various excuses had surfaced in her mind over the past few days, but she had decided not to use them. She believed she owed Alex this much after all he had done for her. Besides, she could not deny the feelings Alex stirred in her. Curiosity was starting to win her over, and in a way, she was anxious to finish what they had started many times.

Maddie was surprised by how busy the great hall was when she descended the stairs. Everyone was smiling at her, and she heard the expression "special day" over and over again. Alex was nowhere to be seen, but mayhap it would be better for her not to see him until the ceremony.

After she finished her porridge, she left the great hall, which was being rearranged to fit the tables necessary for the large number of guests, but Cook invited her back into the kitchens to sample some of the fare for the feast. She enjoyed sampling the various dishes with wee Jennie, but decided she would be unable to fit into her dress if she continued. Since she had nothing specific to do other than bathe and dress, she decided to spend some time wandering the battlements. She loved gazing over the land. It was Alex's land, but soon it would be hers as well. She thought about everything that had transpired in the last fortnight or two. It bothered her that Kenneth was still free...and she knew it bothered Alex, too.

In an instant, two hands wrapped around her waist and she jumped. Turning around quickly, she stared into her betrothed's steel gray eyes.

"Alex, you startled me."

"And what were you so deep in thought about, sweeting?"

"You do no' really want to know," Maddie said with a sigh. "I was thinking about Kenneth, wondering if he is still out there."

"Aye, I have failed you, love. I promised to find him and I have no'. But I do no' want you fretting about him today," Alex said as he pulled her to him. Maddie allowed herself the comfort of settling in against him.

"I believe your stepbrother is dead," Alex continued. "If not, he would have come here before today to try to stop the wedding. He will no' bother us, sweeting. I just wish I had managed to bring you proof of his fate." Leaning in closer, he nuzzled her neck. "I missed you last night, lass."

"I missed you, too. I apologize for Alice. She felt she owed it to my mother." She grabbed his arms as she shivered in delight.

"'Tis all right. I will be able to look at Father MacGregor today with a little less guilt, and it will make tonight even more special."

Maddie blushed. "Alex, I am still a little nervous," she admitted.

"I know. But you know I need to make you mine tonight, aye lass? We will go as slow as you need, Maddie. If I have to wait one more day, I think I may explode. I need you desperately," he whispered in her ear.

"Aye, I know. I want us to be a true married couple in all ways. I love you, Alex Grant. I would be lost without you. And you have never failed me. Just know that I am probably different from other women." Turning to face him, Maddie ran her fingers down the side of his face, stroking his cheek. "I am really the most concerned about the bedding ceremony. What is your normal custom here? I do not wish for anyone to see the marks on my body. I fear it would embarrass us both."

"Ah, I see your concern. Don't worry, lass. There will be no bedding ceremony tonight. I will take care of it."

"You would do that for me?"

"Och, lass, I would run through burning embers for you. You have no' realized that yet?"

His smile melted her heart. He leaned down and kissed her softly.

"Thank you," she whispered. "I will be much more relaxed today knowing that I do not have to worry about that tonight." She felt the blood rush to her cheeks.

He reached into his tunic to retrieve a package. "I wanted to give you something special on our wedding day." He handed her the small parcel wrapped in twine. "Why no' open it now, lass? I would know if it meets your approval."

He gazed at her intently, yet seemed a bit nervous.

"But, Alex, I have no gift for you!"

"*You* are my gift, sweeting. Now open yours."

She untied the twine and carefully pulled back the wrapping. Inside the package was a beautiful set of pearls.

"Oh, Alex, they are just like my mother's." As she ran the cool gems across her fingers, her hands trembled and her eyes welled up with tears. "My mother gave me her set of pearls right before she died. They were a gift from my father. I treasured them, but Kenneth sold them."

"I know. I confess that I had Father MacGregor's help in this. He remembered your mother's pearls, so I asked him to search for them when he left a few days ago. I know they are probably not your mother's, but I hope they are similar enough to remind you of her."

She wrapped her arms around his neck. "Oh, Alex, thank you. They are exquisite. I will always treasure them. Will you help me put them on?"

She lifted her hair so Alex could help with the clasp, then turned to face him and said, "How do they look?"

"Almost as lovely as you."

Maddie giggled and threw her arms around his neck. After kissing him thoroughly, she said, "I think they will look perfect with my gown. I promise not to remove them today."

Alex quirked an eyebrow. "I look forward to your promise,

lass." He paused a moment, then said, "You realize what happened to you before was not your fault."

"I know that now. But Kenneth made me feel guilty for just about everything I did. He was extremely critical, and Niles was just cruel." Maddie found herself gazing off into space as she spoke. "But things are different here. People appreciate me. I tried to live my life in a loving way before, but I was always punished for it. But my mother's teachings are still in my heart. I cannot change that."

"Kenneth and Niles were sick, twisted men. I promise you it will never be like that between us. Do you believe me, lass?"

"Aye, I do, Alex." Maddie reached up, cupped his face, and kissed him lightly.

There was the sound of yelling from down below, so Alex brushed her lips with another quick kiss and pulled her back down the stairs. He turned at the bottom of the steps and kissed her knuckles. "Until tonight, my lady."

Maddie was still beaming when she sauntered into her chamber. Alice had her back to the door, so she did not notice her at first, but as soon as the maid turned around, she gasped and burst into tears.

"Oh, Maddie, where did you get them? They are just like your mother's."

"They are a wedding gift from my betrothed. Don't you think they will look lovely with my gown?"

"Oh, they will be perfect," she said as she hugged Maddie. "In fact, I think it is time for you to start getting ready. I want to have plenty of time to do your hair. Have you decided if you want your hair up or down?"

"Oh, I think Alex would like it better long and flowing."

"I think so, too. I would like to see those golden tresses down with some ribbons and maybe some flowers woven through your waves. What do you think?" Alice pulled some of her long strands free.

"I agree. Are you sure it will not be too much work for you, Alice? I am limited with my arm."

"Nay, I think there is time. But we need to get the tub up here quickly so we can wash your hair. Where did you put that bar of soap that Moira gave you?" Alice bustled around the room, searching for the soap. "I cannot find your soap, child."

Maddie smiled at her maid's nickname for her. She wouldn't be able to call her that tomorrow. Alice left the room to find Fiona while Maddie retrieved the soap. There was much for her to do.

Alex searched the bailey for his brothers. The day was getting shorter and there was still much for him to do. He spotted Brodie across the bailey and shouted for him. Robbie was not far away.

He gathered both of his brothers to him. "I need you to help me tonight."

"Aye, you know we will," said Brodie. "What is it?"

"There will be no bedding ceremony tonight and I need you to guard the stairs." His chin jutted out in anticipation of their arguments.

"What?" Brodie yelped. "No bedding ceremony? Have you lost your wits, Alex?"

"Aye, there is always a bedding ceremony. You cannot take away the best part of the night!" Robbie argued.

"Aye, but 'tis my wedding, and I do not want one."

"Och, Alex, you know all the men wait all night for it. Most of 'em are too drunk to see anything anyway. There will be too many guests to stop it from happening tonight. You are asking the impossible."

"As laird, I am telling you there will be no bedding ceremony." Alex's eyes turned dark.

Robbie argued, "You used to love bedding ceremonies. You cannot change Scottish tradition. The clansmen will revolt."

"Now that you are a little more mature, Robbie, do you no' see anything wrong with it?"

"Nay, 'tis always done. Every lass knows it!" Robbie countered.

"I agree," Brodie said.

"Aye, so when it is wee Jennie's turn, do you want to be the ones to hold up the linens so everyone can see your sister's bare body? Robbie, I assign you to help at Jennie's wedding and Brodie, you will do the same at Brenna's wedding."

Brodie's hands went up to his head. "Och, do not put that image in my head!"

Robbie started sputtering, "Alex, that is no' right! You know we will not let it happen to our sisters."

"And it will not happen to my wife, either. 'Tis just a way for some old men to get a thrill. 'Tis a stupid custom. A lass has enough to worry about on her wedding night. And my wife is no' a maiden. So it will no' be happening. And you need to keep the drunken men away. I will not have my wife tortured tonight."

Both of his brothers stared at him, then Robbie scratched his head thoughtfully. Quietly, he asked, "Did the Comming really tie her to the bed and rape her?"

"Aye, he did. And I will not have her reminded of any of it tonight," Alex whispered. "Maddie has been through enough. You especially know it, Brodie. You saw how cruel her stepbrother was to her."

"Aye, you are right. We will stop the bedding ceremony. Maybe Brenna can help us create a diversion. We will need a few more sober guardsmen to help us, too." Robbie hung his head sheepishly.

"Do whatever you must. I am counting on you both. Now I am heading to the loch for a bath." He sniffed the air loudly around him. "You might want to consider it, too, Brodie. That is, if you want to get 'tween some skirts later. The lasses like their men to be sweet smelling." He grinned and headed to the stables.

Brodie threw a stone after him.

CHAPTER TWENTY-EIGHT

Maddie paced in the great hall with Mac, Alice, Jennie, and Brenna. Everyone else had been sent ahead to the chapel. Looking at all the people she loved around her, she realized how fortunate she was to have found the Grants. Mac had done her a true favor the day he sent his missive to the Grant chief. Maddie thanked God every day for her blessings.

Robbie stuck his head in the door and said, "We are ready for you, my lady."

Smiling at her soon-to-be brother, she moved toward the door, hoping Alex would think she was as lovely as she felt in all her finery. Outside, little Tommy was proudly holding the reins of two white palfreys. Their tails were woven with ribbons—pink for one horse, blue for the other. Tommy bowed to Madeline and said, "A gift for you from my laird, my lady." He held out the reins of the horse with the blue ribbons to Maddie and offered the reins of the horse with the pink ribbons to Jennie, who looked angelic in her pink finery. The wee lass jumped up and down excitedly before dashing forward to give her horse a quick hug around the neck. While Mac helped Jennie mount her horse, Robbie seated Maddie on hers.

The sky was blue, there was a light breeze, and the air was warm for fall in Scotland. Tommy led Jennie and Maddie down through the courtyard to the chapel, while Mac, Alice, and Brenna followed on foot. Well-wishers greeted them in the courtyard, cheering as they passed.

Maddie was pleased to see the number of people who were shouting out greetings and pleasantries. When they reached the chapel, Robbie helped her dismount, but she waited in the back while the others found their seats. As soon as her eyes adjusted to the light, her gaze found Alex immediately at the front of the altar.

Maddie's breath hitched at how magnificent her betrothed was in his wedding attire. Alex wore his red and green plaid proudly, secured with a jeweled brooch at his shoulder. Her body tingled at the very sight of him.

Alex heard a few small gasps as soon as Maddie stepped into the chapel. He turned his head to find her. Their gazes locked, and his breath caught at the sight of his beautiful bride-to-be. She turned sideways and he noticed the tiny flowers woven through the golden tresses cascading down her back. The pearls he had given her were draped across her neck, and her blue dress perfectly matched her eyes. The cloth of the dress clung to her curves as she glided toward him, her regal carriage befitting her noble birth. She carried the bouquet of dried flowers Tommy's mother had given her days before, and the beaded slippers on her feet had also been given to her as a gift. Noticing Brodie's stunned expression, he elbowed him, hoping to entice him to close his mouth.

Jennie skipped down the aisle like a little fairy, throwing fistfuls of flower petals as she went. Though he knew he should be watching his wee sister, Alex could not take his eyes off his Maddie. She came toward him on Mac's arm, and when they reached the front, the older man kissed Maddie's cheek and stepped back. Madeline placed her small hand in Alex's large one, and he was humbled by the gesture of trust. Her hands trembled, but when she gazed up at him, there was no fear in her eyes—only excitement. His heart melted.

As one, they turned toward a beaming Father MacGregor. The couple said their vows, and when Alex leaned down to kiss his bride, cheers exploded from outside the chapel.

The time came for the newly married couple to leave the chapel, and they were preceded by Jennie, who rushed out ahead of them so she could throw more petals. Once they were outside, little Tommy ran forward to hand Alex Midnight's reins.

"Here you are, Chief!" Tommy beamed as he did his part, clearly proud to have been allowed a role in the festivities.

Alex mounted his horse and settled Maddie in front of him.

"Finally, you are mine," he growled into her neck. Maddie

proceeded to give him a kiss as the crowd roared around them.

Normally, they would have ridden around the bailey and even outside the gates. But with Kenneth possibly still at large, Alex had decided not to chance it. They pranced around inside the bailey for a bit and then headed to the great hall for the feast.

As they dismounted at the steps to the great hall, Alex turned to Maddie and said, "I am sorry, sweeting. This will take a while, but it must be done. You may lean against me if the crowd is too much for you."

Grasping her hand, he guided her up the steps to the keep. At the top, he turned and waited quietly as his guardsmen formed columns in front of them. Once they were in formation, the entire crowd quieted.

Maddie was perplexed, but she let Alex take her hand in his and lift their entwined hands above their heads. Surveying the crowd, he said, "Behold my wife, Lady Madeline. Treat her as you treat me."

He lowered their hands, and they stood there on the steps as Robbie and Brodie marched forward, knelt down before her, and placed their swords on the ground pointing in her direction. After they retrieved their weapons, they bowed to her and strode away. She glanced at Alex in confusion as the next pair of guardsmen came forward and repeated the process.

Leaning down, he whispered, "My men must swear to honor and protect you as they do me. You are my wife. It is a requirement of all my guardsmen."

Since there were many guardsmen, Maddie eventually leaned back against her husband, but she managed a smile and a nod for each of the clansmen. When the last guardsmen stood, the entire area erupted in a cheer. Alex bowed to his men and turned to lead his wife into the great hall.

As soon as they reached the dais, and Brenna called for the food service to start. People filled the hall, anxious to take part in the great feast. When Robbie and Brodie joined them, the family exchanged hugs and well wishes.

Brodie held up his mug of ale and announced, "To many years of happiness!" The yelling in the hall was deafening.

Alex leaned over and whispered in Maddie's ear, "Are you

happy, my lady?"

"Oh, aye, Alex, I have never been happier." She smiled up at her husband's gray eyes.

"And I think you have never been more lovely, lass," he said as he rubbed his hand down her hip.

Maddie blushed and whispered, "You are very handsome, my husband."

Jennie found her way to the table and quickly hugged her brother and Maddie. "Kiss her, Alex. You are supposed to kiss your wife!"

Needing no more prompting than that, Alex kissed Maddie, making his wee sister giggle. "I love weddings!" she declared.

Brenna ushered them all to their seats as the food was served. There were loaves of brown bread, pheasant, roasted pig, lamb, fish, and trenchers of various stews and meat pies. There were also baked apples, squash, cinnamon pears, and turnips.

"Brenna, the food is wonderful," Maddie said as she fussed over the baked apples.

"When do we get the tarts, Brenna? I want an apple tart!" Jennie exclaimed.

"We have plenty of time, little flower," Alex said. "Did I tell you what a pretty lass you are in your pink dress?" Leaning over, he lifted her out of her chair and set her on the floor. "Let me look at it again." He twirled her in the dress until she was dizzy and chuckling. She promptly forgot about the pastries. Tommy rushed over and they twirled about together.

Brenna sighed and shook her head. "It does not take much to distract her, does it, Alex?"

Alex laughed and said, "'Tis good to hear her laughter again. Isn't there any lad here to distract you, Brenna?"

"Nay, I am too busy with my own family, as you know," his sister answered quickly.

"Well, there are plenty of lasses here to distract me," Brodie said wistfully. "I cannot wait for the dancing to start."

A short time later, the hall was cleared of tables, and the dancing began. Maddie danced with Alex, Robbie, Brodie, Mac, and even some people she did not know. After a while, Alex tugged her off the floor, found a chair, and settled her on his lap.

"I do no' want you to get too tired, lass, especially with your arm," he whispered. "We have much ahead of us."

Maddie leaned her head down on his shoulder. "Oh, Alex, I am fine and my arm is fine, although it feels a wee bit heavy when I am dancing. But 'twas such fun! I have not danced in a long time, but I think I have had enough."

"Those words are music to my ears, lass. Are you ready to depart for our chamber yet?" He quirked a brow at her.

As if intuiting their conversation, Alice appeared at his side. "My lord, may I escort Maddie upstairs and help her get ready?"

He sighed. "Aye, you may, Alice. I will be up shortly." He gave Maddie a quick kiss on the cheek and set her off his lap. Hopefully, Alice would offer some advice to Maddie. He chuckled a bit, realizing that even he was feeling apprehensive. Tempering his desire for his wee wife would not be easy, but he did not want to make any mistakes tonight. It was important to him for Maddie to have fond memories of their wedding night.

Maddie and Alice made their way up the steps to the chamber. Maddie's face turned bright red when she heard all the crude comments some of the guests were making. She turned slightly and noticed Alex had posted guards at the bottom of the stairs. Breathing a sigh of relief, she reminded herself she would get through this night. *Give me strength, Lord. Help me, Mama.*

After Alice gave her hand a final squeeze and left the room, Maddie sat in front of the hearth. She twisted her new gown nervously. Alice had made her a night rail of the finest silk. It was completely transparent, and she was a little embarrassed to be wearing it. Of course, Alex was now her husband and he had a right to see her naked. Alice had prodded her to discuss her concerns about coupling, but she just could not talk about certain things. She repeated in her mind the last thing Alice had said to her, "Trust your husband, lass, he is a good man." Maddie believed that statement with all her heart, but it still did not keep some of her old fears from surfacing.

What is keeping Alex anyway? She stood and started pacing. She glanced at the door and the bed, making sure she could make a quick dive for the bed and bury herself under the covers if anyone made it past Alex.

She jumped when the door finally opened, but when Alex

stepped in alone, she breathed a sigh of relief. She could hear some yelling from below, but there was no one behind him. He bolted the door quickly and said, "For them, lass, not for you. I do not want them bothering us."

Alex turned and stared at his wife. His mouth went completely dry and his thoughts were lost. She stood in front of him in a gown that hid nothing. He could see her full breasts, her hardened pink nipples, and the fair patch of curls between her legs.

She still wore her pearls. He walked over and kissed her. He could not take his eyes away from her body. Running his gaze down the length of her, he said, "So beautiful."

Maddie clutched her pearls and said, "I agree, I think the pearls are beautiful as well. They do remind me of my mother. I hope you don't mind if I keep them on."

Alex smiled. "Not the pearls, Maddie, you. I was talking about you. You are absolutely stunning."

Maddie's blush only made her bonnier. After removing his leine, he reached for her hand and said, "Come sit with me by the fire." He poured two glasses of wine from the bottle that had been left in the room, he handed one to her it to her. "I had Father MacGregor bring us back a special wine. I hope you like it."

She sipped the wine and said, "Aye, I do."

Determined not to rush, he sat in the chair and pulled her onto his lap. He wrapped his arms around her. "Are you cold, lass? Is your arm bothering you?"

Maddie was shivering, but she answered, "Nay," and snuggled closer to him.

He kissed her softly on the mouth. She gazed into his eyes and the love and trust he saw there gave them faith that this would work, that they would be able to lay together as husband and wife. He kissed her again, but deeper this time. His tongue swept her mouth, and she leaned into him, driving him mad when she pressed her breasts against his chest. He groaned and kissed her harder on the mouth, possessing her.

Alex thought he would lose control when she touched his chest and started caressing his nipples. He noticed her breathing was increasing at a rate to match his own. He moved his hand up her thighs and over her hips, caressing her luscious curves. Detecting resistance, he stopped to give her more time to adjust to him. Then he slowly moved his hands up her sides until he was cupping her breasts. How was it possible his wee wife had the most perfect body he had ever seen? He would love to kiss every glorious inch of her. Following a path down her neck with his lips, he flicked his thumb across her nipple, causing her to moan and arch her back, bringing her even closer to him. How much more could he take? She squirmed in his arms with a little catch in her throat and he turned rock hard underneath his plaid.

He kissed her shoulder and down her collarbone. Shifting her in his lap, he was able to maneuver her broken arm so the full beauty of her breasts was revealed to him. She gazed at him, panting, licking her full lips, her free hand tangled in his hair. Moving slowly, he made his way down her right breast and stroked her nipple with his tongue. He teased her other nipple before taking it full in his mouth and suckling her. She arched her back, pushing her breast closer to him, and he chuckled low in his throat at his wee wife's passion.

Confusion battled in Madeline's mind. She lost all ability to think when Alex's tongue raked her nipple. She never wanted him to stop; there were too many strange and enjoyable sensations in her core. She didn't understand it, but he was making her body writhe. She reminded herself to trust him.

Nothing hurt. In fact she wanted more—more kisses, more caresses. Shocked at how good it felt for him to suckle her breast through the thin material, she pressed her breast closer to him. She clutched his chest as his hand moved down her side and over her belly, causing her legs to spread wide on their own. He caressed a spot on her woman's part and she groaned. What was he doing? Wiggling in the chair to widen her opening, he used his thumb to brush lightly over that spot, caressing her, and she lost all sense. Was this what the servants were always talking on about? Her hand clenched tight on his arm to spur him on.

She didn't know what she was supposed to do next. His hardness pressed against her, but she did not care. She was shocked to hear herself panting.

Standing her up, Alex unhooked her gown and let it pool on the ground. He lifted her and deposited her on the cool sheets that had already been pulled back, pausing to place a pillow under her broken arm with a tenderness that moved her. Then he dropped his plaid on the floor. He moved in close, gathered her in his arms and kissed her hard, almost desperately. Wandering fingers found her core, and she spread her legs for him without thinking. He moved on top of her, lifted her hips and started to thrust inside of her.

And Maddie fell apart. As soon as his hardness breached her entrance, she panicked. Pummeling his chest, she yelled, "Stop, Alex, stop! Nay!" She clamped her legs together and jumped out of bed, hurtling across the room.

Alex rolled over onto his back and groaned. He stared at the ceiling for a minute to try to regain his control. He glanced at his wife cowering over by the hearth, her entire body trembling.

Alex did not know what to do. "Maddie, did I hurt you?"

"Nay!" She was crying now.

"Do you trust me?" he asked quietly as he stared at the ceiling.

"Aye," she whispered as she tried to cover her body.

"Then, come back to me, wife. I will not hurt you."

It was a long minute before Maddie returned to the side of the bed.

"You will be on top," he said as he lifted her on top of the length of his body. Tears still stained her cheeks, but she did not fight him. She swiped them off her face with determination.

"I want you on top so you know you can leave any time. The choice is yours. Mayhap having you underneath me is what frightens you so. I will never force you, lass. You always have the right to refuse me and take yourself away. You need to believe in me." Alex caressed her neck as he spoke, then ran his hands down the soft skin of her back to her bottom, feathering her soft mounds. His arousal grew in response.

They positioned her arm, and he arranged her as best he could to make her comfortable without hurting his erection.

"Lass, you need to trust me," he said softly as he kissed her brow.

"I know. I am sorry, Alex. I do not know what makes me do such things."

Alex thought hard before he made his next move, but he thought it might be the only way. Taking her nipple in his mouth, he suckled her as he slipped his fingers along her opening, caressing the very heat of her to gauge her response. She was still wet and her soft moan indicated she desired him. Softly grasping her hips, he easily thrust inside her with a shift of his pelvis. He did not think it would hurt her.

"Nay, Alex, nay!" she screamed. She pushed against him hard.

He held her hips gently in place, trying to let her get used to his invasion.

"Maddie, stop! I will not hurt you. I love you. Please, I do not know what else to do. I have tried everything!"

Maddie stopped struggling when she heard his declaration of love.

Shocked at his own confession, he recognized the truth of it. He wanted her more than anything, and he wanted their marriage to work. He considered various paths he could take from here to help her accept him, and he chose the riskiest of all. "Do you trust me, lass?" he whispered. He was still buried deep inside her.

"Aye." She nodded.

"Then stay where you are for five minutes. I promise not to move. If you do not want me at the end of five minutes, we will stop, and I will not touch you again tonight. You need to see that this will not hurt. You are no longer a maiden, sweeting, so there should be no pain. Can you do this for your husband?"

Maddie peered at him and slowly nodded her head. She then lowered her head down to his chest. He stroked her back and she started to relax a little.

Five minutes, she thought. *I only need to do this for five minutes.*

She could feel his hardness inside her. She did not like it. It reminded her of Niles. She wanted him out. Alex was big and hard and as soon as he moved, he would probably hurt her as Niles had done. She tried to slow her breathing, tried to stop her feeling of panic. *Only five minutes.*

She reminded herself that it was Alex, her husband, not Niles. This was the man she loved and trusted. Just as he had promised, he was not forcing himself on her. What if she moved away? With a strange ache, she realized she did not want him to completely stop touching her. She liked to be in his arms, just not this way.

She turned her head to the side and sighed deeply. *I need to focus on something else.* She was twirling her pearls slowly between her thumb and forefinger, so she decided to focus on her mother's pearls. As she rotated them, they grew warm against her body. She closed her eyes for just a moment and thought of her mother. What would her mother tell her to do? She glanced across the room and caught a shadow. *Mother?*

Her vision was blurred from tears, but the woman appeared to be her mother. Was she dreaming? The pearls were still warm. *Mother, what should I do?* She thought hard as she stared at the vision of her mother. Her mother smiled at her. *Help me, Mama,* she thought as she reached for her in her mind.

"We have, child. Your father and I sent this man to you. Now you must help yourself."

"But I cannot do this, Mother. I just cannot."

"Do you love him, Maddie?"

"Aye, I do, with all my heart."

"Maddie, he loves you, too. Love him back, and trust him. You will not regret it. Your father and I are anxious to see your bairns. We will always be near."

Her mother started to fade. *"Wait, Mother!"*

But her mother was gone.

Alex was still inside her, and suddenly she realized there was no pain.

She lifted her head and gazed at her husband.

"Alex?"

"What, love?" He brushed a tear from her cheek.

"It does not hurt. Oh, my goodness, it is not uncomfortable at all!"

"I know it, Maddie, I am shrinking." Alex rolled his eyes in frustration.

She wiggled her bottom and he instantly grew hard again. Then she pulled herself across the length of him and thrust him back inside. Alex groaned. She did it again. Alex groaned again.

"Maddie, you are killing me. If you do that again, we will finish this, I promise," he said to his wife.

"Oh, Alex, I am so happy! I like this! What do you want me to do?" She kept moving up and down, slowly picking up her rhythm.

"Lass, are you sure you are all right?"

"Aye, Alex, this is starting to feel nice." Maddie's face beamed.

Alex groaned again. "Can I roll you over, lass? I am about to explode."

She nodded and Alex rolled them over so he was on top of her.

He moved slowly at first to make sure she could handle him, but then instinct took over and he thrusted hard until he was in agony. He searched his wife's eyes, trying to gauge if she was enjoying it. She was not breathing hard, but she was not screaming in fear either. He kissed her roughly because he did not know if he could hold out much longer. He was sheathed deep inside her wetness and almost lost all control. He forced himself to focus so he could hold out long enough for her to find her pleasure. He took her nipple in his mouth again and sucked hard. She gasped and arched toward him as he drove into her again and again. She was so tight, it was sweet torture. Lifting his head, he caught her blue gaze as she whispered, "I love you, Alex."

That did it. With two more thrusts, he exploded his seed into her with a loud roar. His wee wife had put him over the edge with four words. What was this lass doing to him? He had never experienced an orgasm anywhere close to one this powerful.

Of course, he was upset with himself. He had gone ahead of her when he always pleasured a woman first. No lass had ever made him lose control. Balanced on his elbows, he tried to level his breathing as he looked at her in confusion. She was smiling a glorious smile.

"Oh, Alex, I am so happy. That did not hurt at all."

"Good, I am glad." He played with a curl around her face. Still not capable of thinking clearly, he nuzzled her neck.

"I am ecstatically happy, but, husband, you do not act happy. Is something wrong?"

He sighed. "Maddie, I am not happy because you did not find your pleasure. I will not be happy until you find your pleasure."

"But I did find my pleasure, Alex. It did not hurt me, and it made me happy to make you happy!" she exclaimed.

"Nay, Maddie, you did not find your pleasure."

"Yes, I did. I told you I did."

He groaned. "Sweeting, you did not find the same pleasure that I did. A man and woman should both find pleasure before they are done. I could not hold out for you. You drove me over the edge with those blue eyes."

Maddie bit her lower lip before adding, "I do not understand what you are talking about."

Alex whispered into her ear, "I promise you, you will understand before we leave this chamber."

He rolled onto his back and pulled her into his arms, cradling her head on his shoulder.

She lifted her head briefly to peer down at him. "Alex, did I not please you?"

He kissed her softly. "Aye, you pleased me very much. Go to sleep, sweeting. You have had a long day."

"Alex?"

"What, love?"

"Did you really mean it when you said you loved me?"

"Aye love. How could I no' love you? You drive me to madness!"

She smiled and kissed him on the cheek. "I love you, too."

Maddie fell asleep quickly in her husband's arms. All her fears were gone.

CHAPTER TWENTY-NINE

The new couple awoke to banging on their door. Alex grunted and rolled out of bed, threw on his plaid, and unbolted the door. His two brothers were gaping at him with huge smiles on their faces when he opened the door.

"How goes it, brother?" Robbie said as he and Brodie tried to peek around him at Maddie in the bed.

"Everything is fine. There better be a good reason you interrupted my sleep," Alex growled.

"Sleeping a bit late, are you no'?" Robbie grinned.

"We just came to get you for the feats of strength. Are you no' coming?" Brodie asked.

"Nay, I will not be there. I am busy today. You both can act in my place."

The brothers chuckled as they turned to leave.

"Busy! I like that," Robbie said.

"Wish I was busy today!" Brodie laughed.

"Send Fiona up," Alex yelled at them as they left.

Alex closed the door and turned to his wee wife, all wrapped up in a cocoon in the covers. He leaned over and gave her a gentle kiss. "Good morn to you, wife."

Maddie sat up, the covers dropping from her chest. She quickly grabbed them and covered herself.

"Wife, it would please me if you would stop hiding yourself from me. I like your beautiful body."

Maddie blushed. "Alex, it is daylight. You can see me."

"Och, 'tis the point, Maddie. Your body is glorious. I ache to see it in the daylight."

A knock sounded on the door and Alex opened it to address

Fiona.

"May I bring something to break your fast?"

"Aye, Fiona, we need lots of food, some mead, and a tub for my wife."

"Aye, my laird." Fiona turned to do as she was bid.

"A tub? Where are you going? I thought you told Robbie and Brodie you were not going to the tourneys."

"I am not going anywhere. I am staying here with you all day. We will not leave until you find your pleasure."

"But I told you, Alex, I *did* find my pleasure."

"I will ask you that question again later, lass. Let's not discuss it now." He kissed her again.

"Well, you sent for a tub. I cannot bathe in front of you!" Maddie's eyes searched the room nervously. She stared at him, wondering how he could be so comfortable with blatant nudity.

"Aye, love, you can, but I think I will bathe you."

Maddie gasped and pulled her covers closer. "Alex, 'tis not proper!"

"Och, Maddie, anything is proper between a husband and wife so long as they both agree." He leaned across the bed, yanked the covers down and kissed her nipple. Maddie's eyes grew as big as saucers. Alex was chucking when he opened the door for Fiona.

Along with beverages, Fiona had brought in pastries, fruit, cheese, and bread. She turned to leave and said, "We are heating the water for the tub, my laird."

"No hurry, we have plenty to eat." Fiona left and Alex closed the door behind her. He held his hand out to his wife, "Come, wife, break your fast with me."

Maddie slowly crawled out of bed and looked around for something to wear. The only garment she could see was the transparent gown Alice had made for the wedding night. Grabbing a large linen cloth, she wrapped it tight around her middle.

Alex pulled her down onto his lap and held a pastry up to her lips.

"If I remember correctly, my wife has a taste for sweets. Aye?"

Maddie nodded her head and studied her husband. Though confused by his mood, she was hungry, so she opened her mouth for him. She chewed her food slowly, never taking her eyes off her husband. His eyes turned dark. "Lick my fingers, sweeting, I have more for you."

Maddie looked at the icing all over his fingers. She moaned in anticipation and started to slowly lick his hand. She giggled at all the icing on them.

Alex selected another pastry, this one filled with strawberry jelly. He pulled her cloth down and squeezed the strawberry jelly over her nipples. She gasped as the cold fruit dripped over her tender tips.

"Do you know how much I love strawberries?" He lowered his head to her breast and proceeded to show her. Maddie grabbed his hair and tugged him closer. Leaving her nipple, he took her mouth in a passionate kiss, angling his mouth over hers until she gave a small moan in the back of her throat. Then he pulled away and suckled her nipple again.

A knock sounded at the door. "Just a moment," Maddie croaked out, her voice ragged with pleasure. She pulled up the cloth and ran her hand across her mouth to get rid of the icing. Maddie blushed and turned her head away as her husband bade Fiona to enter with the tub. Her behavior was wanton. He made her forget everything but the sheer pleasure humming through her body.

After the servants filled the tub with hot, steaming water, they left the room and closed the door behind them, Alex cradled her face. "Maddie, do not be ashamed of your passion. Passion for your husband is a wonderful thing. Come, I will wash you now."

Alex urged her to step into the warm water. Deciding to trust him, she reached for his hand and did just that. She attempted to sit once in the bath, but he would not allow it.

"Nay, love, I shall wash you first." He winked at her as he reached into the water.

Grabbing a linen square, he found a slice of her lavender-scented soap. First, he held the square up and trickled water down her body. Starting at her neck, he squeezed it over her front and her back, paying special attention to the round globes of her bottom. Maddie heard a moan and blushed when she realized the sound had come from her.

"Oh my!" was all she could manage.

He rubbed the linen with the soap and slowly massaged her breasts, rubbing the lather over the hard peaks of her nipples.

Opening her eyes, she watched as he trailed his hand down her belly, across her curls. Maddie placed her hand on his shoulder to steady herself. He picked up each long leg, one at a time, and washed from the ankle up, using his bare hand to caress the tender area behind each knee. When he washed her woman's place, Maddie closed her eyes and moaned lightly.

"Alex, this cannot be proper."

He chuckled. "There is nothing wrong with a husband assisting his wife in the bath."

What was happening to her? He eased her legs apart and slipped a finger inside her.

"Ah, Maddie, you will be a passionate one. I see you are enjoying your bath as much as I am." His eyes twinkled as he dropped the linen square in the water and let his plaid fall to the floor.

Maddie gasped as she noticed his arousal. "Oh my!" She slowly slid her eyes back to his face. What would it feel like to touch him there?

"Aye, precious, see what you do to me?" Alex stepped into the tub and sat down, helping her onto his lap. He carefully set her arm outside the tub so it would not be jostled.

Maddie's eyes darted about the room. "Alex, what are we doing?"

"Hush, love, trust me," he whispered into her ear.

He leaned her head back against his shoulder and softly caressed her upper body. "Close your eyes and relax, Maddie. I will not hurt you."

He bent her knees up and caressed her legs slowly, easing them apart. With his one hand, he slowly caressed her breast and rolled her nipple between his thumb and finger. He slipped a finger of his other hand inside her and used his thumb on her nub.

Maddie shifted her position so he could have better access to her core. She did not understand the sensations flowing through her body, but they were both wonderful and torturous at the same time. Without realizing it, she moved her legs apart for him. Her eyes opened and she flushed with embarrassment at her position.

"Och, lass, you are torturing me." Alex stood up, dried her languorously and then helped her onto the bed.

Confusion settled in on her. Why had he stopped? She felt she was hanging over the edge of something, and she didn't want him to end the sweet agony. Desire made her frantic. She finally whispered, "Alex, I need more."

"Aye, sweeting, we are not done. Now we will find our pleasure together."

A slow smile crept across her face as he slid in beside her and kissed her hungrily. She pushed him away.

"Alex, can I touch you?" she whispered. "I want to touch you like you touch me. Show me how."

He pulled her hand down onto his erection. She grasped him carefully and he groaned.

Snatching her hand away, she stared at him with wide eyes. "Did I hurt you?"

"Nay, 'twas a groan of pleasure. Try again," he said through clenched teeth.

She touched him again and ran her finger around the tip of his penis, smiling, enjoying the feel of his soft skin. Moving her hand down, she gently cupped his testicles. He groaned again, but she did not stop this time—she *enjoyed* giving Alex pleasure. He kissed her hard on the mouth, possessing her. As his thumb brushed across her nipple, she squirmed toward him, forcing her body against his. Pulling her hand away, she rubbed her mound against his erection.

How could anything be so soft and yet so hard?

She writhed against him, realizing that she wanted him desperately. She ran her hand up and down his arms and his sides.

"Alex, please, I want you inside me. I need you." She gasped, confused by the fever tearing through her body.

Alex tasted her nipple in his mouth again, curling his tongue over and over the surface until she peaked hard. She wiggled harder against him, feeling the tension build and build. He caressed her long legs and back, cupped her bottom, and slid his penis between her legs. As he rocked the tip back and forth against her nub, he slipped a finger inside her.

"Alex, please!" she rasped out with a moan. "I cannot stand anymore. I want you inside me. Now, please!"

He held her hips and slipped inside her slowly, gazing into her blue eyes all the while. "Are you all right? Does it hurt, love?"

"Nay, it does not hurt. Please don't stop!" Frantically, she rocked against him. "Oh, Alex, you are wonderful inside me."

He moved with slow, gentle thrusts. Rolling her head back, she grabbed his shoulders and raked her nails across his skin. As he increased his pace, she pulled her knees up to make their contact even deeper. He reached in between her legs and found her nub, caressing her.

"Alex, oh, Alex!" Maddie screamed as she careened over the edge. Wild tremors possessed her as she tightened against him, sending wave over wave of pleasure rolling over her. Alex followed her over the abyss.

"Maddie, did I hurt you?" he asked through choppy breaths, cuddling her close.

"Nay, it was wondrous, Alex." As her awareness returned, she peeked at him. "What happened?" she asked, feeling a little shy about her exuberant response.

"You found your pleasure, or so I believe." His eyes twinkled.

"Aye, I believe I did." Her brow furrowed a little. "Alex?"

"Aye, love?"

"I did not find my pleasure last night."

Alex laughed. "You understand now, sweeting?"

"Aye, and please stop laughing at me." She slapped his hand.

"Sorry, but I could no' stop myself. You know I love you."

"I love you, too, Alex." Was it possible to be any happier than she felt at this moment?

She thought about everything that had happened since their wedding as she relaxed in her husband's arms.

"Alex?"

"Aye, Maddie?"

"Can we do this again later? I think I like the marriage bed."

He chuckled.

CHAPTER THIRTY

Approximately three months later.

Alex headed back to the great hall after a long day in the lists. He marveled about how wonderful the first three months of his marriage had been. He chuckled when he thought of his wee wife and her voracious appetite. He had hoped she would become a passionate lover in time, but she could not seem to get enough of him. Nor could he get enough of her. Maddie had certainly turned his life upside down. Though other women had offered him their favors over the months since his marriage, he was not interested. There would only ever be one woman for him—a blonde-haired, blue-eyed enchantress.

He caught sight of his wife's blonde hair out of the corner of his eye in the gardens. She sat on the bench by herself with her head down. As he approached, he saw her tear-stained cheeks.

"What is wrong, sweeting? You know I hate to see you cry," he said softly.

"Oh, Alex, my courses started again today. You know how much I want to give you a son. I had so hoped to be with child this time." Maddie hung her head and played with the linen square in her lap.

"Och, sweeting, we have lots of time. I am not worried about it, and I do no' want you to worry about it."

"But, Alex, what if something happened when Niles raped me and I cannot get with child? You will have no heirs. That would be so wrong. But I know not what to do."

He lifted her onto his lap. "Maddie, I could not be happier than I am with you as my wife. If we do no' have bairns, then Robbie or

Brodie surely will. Our land will stay in the family. That is all I worry about. But I do worry if you are no' happy."

Maddie knew her husband loved her. But what would happen two years from now when she was still barren? How could he love someone who could not give him a son?

But she simply smiled at him and said, "I am happy. I am just eager for us to have a bairn of our own. You would be such a wonderful father."

"It has only been a short time. I know many couples who do not have bairns until their second or third year of marriage. Give it time." He wrapped his arms around her and held her, seeming to sense her continued ill ease.

Then she stood and said, "Aye, you must be right. Let us go back. I am better now." They trudged their way up the hill hand in hand. Perhaps she would speak with Alice to see if there was something else she could do to help her get with child. She loved the wee ones in the clan much. Watching them grow was so fulfilling. Was it too much to want to have her own bairn with Alex? She would love to have a wee laddie who looked just like his father.

Then she remembered the vision she had seen of her mother on her wedding night. Her mother had said that she could not wait to see Maddie's bairns with Alex. Did that mean they would eventually have one—or maybe even more than one? She hoped so.

Maddie vowed to keep saying her prayers.

CHAPTER THIRTY-ONE

A few months later…

Maddie could barely get herself out of bed. It was late. She didn't know why she felt so tired lately. She pulled on a clean gown and made her way down the stairs to the hall. She found Alice eating at a table, so she trudged over and sat down.

"Good morn to you, Alice."

Alice turned to Maddie. "Oh, my dear, you do not look well. In fact, you look a little green. Are you all right this morning? Mayhap you should stay in bed."

Fiona came out and set a bowl of porridge in front of Maddie. "Sorry, my lady, but this porridge has been sitting awhile. Mayhap you would prefer a piece of fruit or an egg?"

Maddie took one look at the porridge and ran for the door, her hand covering her mouth. As soon as she opened the door, she vomited, just missing her husband's boots.

"Maddie," he exclaimed. "What is wrong with you, lass? You slept away yesterday and half of today, and now you are retching. Get yourself back to bed." Alice walked up to them with a smile on her face, and when Alex saw her expression, he started fuming. "Excuse me, Alice, but I do not think my wife's illness is amusing!"

Alice laughed. "I do not think it amusing, Laird, but joyous. My guess is that your wife is with child. Maddie, how long has it been since your courses?"

When Maddie stopped heaving, she stared at Alice first, then Alex. "Oh, my goodness, do you think 'tis possible, Alice? It has been at least a …" Maddie's face lit up as she counted with her fingers.

"Congratulations, Madeline. I think you and your husband will have a bairn in about eight months!"

Maddie threw her arms around her husband. She was so happy, she cried out, "Oh, I love you, Alex Grant!"

Alex was speechless.

CHAPTER THIRTY-TWO

About eight months later…

Madeline waddled over to the hearth. Alex was working in the lists somewhere with his men. It was almost time for the evening meal, but she was worn out. She aimed for their favorite chair, the extra large one that Alex had ordered to accommodate both of them. After all these months, he still preferred to sit with Madeline on his lap. Of course, he preferred to sit with his hands wrapped around her belly, so Madeline thought it was probably just because he liked to feel their bairn kicking.

She sighed deep as she positioned herself in the chair. Alex was always thoughtful, considerate, compassionate—and passionate, although that part of their lives was becoming more and more difficult. A smile crept across her face as she thought of how inventive her husband had become as a lover. He had promised her all along there were other ways to make love, and he had proven to her that he was right. She closed her eyes to rest for a minute.

Much later, Maddie awoke to the noise of the men entering the great hall. A pair of strong arms lifted her and she gazed at her big husband with a smile as he settled her on his lap.

"You are tired today, sweeting?" he asked as he kissed her full on the mouth.

"Just a bit, husband. You know we won't be able to fit on your lap much longer. It is time for your son to come out."

"When our wee lass is ready to come out, she will. Although I understand why you are anxious to hold our bairn in your arms," he said, mindlessly caressing her belly.

Maddie sat up and attempted to lean her head down toward her belly, "Get out, laddie! It is time to come out now. Listen to your Mama and get out. Or your Papa will paddle you!"

Alex chuckled as he caressed her shoulder, but Jennie darted and said, "You will not paddle the laddie, Alex. I will protect him like you protect me."

"You mean you will protect the lassie, Jennie. You know it is a lass in my wife's belly," he teased her.

Maddie leaned back against her husband and closed her eyes. She was so comfortable that she slipped into sleep in a matter of minutes.

"She sleeps much lately, Alex, she must be near her time," Brenna said as she entered the room.

Jennie whispered, "Alex, some of my friends told me it hurts to have a bairn. Is it going to hurt Maddie?"

"It may hurt a wee bit, but my Madeline is a strong lass. She can handle it, little squirrel. She will not make a sound." Alex thought about all the pain Madeline had tolerated in her life. He had no doubt that she could handle this. He knew she would never scream. Good thing, as he would not be able to handle it if his gentle wife did scream.

"Alex, stop calling me 'little squirrel.' I am a big lass now."

Just then, Madeline sat up straight, clutching her belly. "Oh my!" was all she said.

"What's wrong?" asked Jennie.

"Och, it must be nothing," Maddie answered. "It has stopped now." She leaned back against her husband and closed her eyes again.

Several minutes later, Madeline bolted up again with a confused expression on her face. She clutched her belly again but said nothing.

Brenna stared at her, concern evident on her face. She knew her sister-in-law had a very high pain tolerance. "Maddie, are those birthing pains you are having?"

Maddie peered at Brenna. "I do not think so, Brenna, but I am not sure."

Alex jumped out of the chair, still cradling his wife in his arms. "You are having the bairn, Maddie?"

"Set me down, Alex! I am not going to have the bairn right

here. It takes a while to have a bairn."

A warm rush of water ran down her leg as soon as he set her down. She stood back and looked at the clear fluid on the floor. "Mayhap I am ready to have the bairn," she said quietly as she peeked up at all the faces staring at her. Brenna had warned them this would be a sign.

Alex promptly scooped her up and charged up the stairs to their chamber. Brenna followed after sending Jennie to fetch Alice and Fiona. As soon as Alex reached their chamber, he turned around and stared at Brenna with a perplexed expression on his face.

"What do I do now?"

Brenna smiled a little and said, "Set her down here, Alex. We still have to prepare the bed." He did not—he did not wish to be away from her for even a moment.

Fiona and another maid flew into the chamber with hot water and extra linens. Then they hurried down the stairs to get more supplies just as Alice was hurrying them up.

When Madeline clutched her belly again in pain, Alice said, "Alex, take yourself back down to the great hall. A birthing room is no place for a man. We will take care of your wife."

Alex finally set Maddie down and kissed her forehead. He stared at her for a minute, wanting to tell her he loved her, but there were too many people around. He knew now that he had loved Maddie almost from the first moment he had seen her. Only it had taken him a while to figure out what he was feeling. But now he knew how strong his love was for her. She was the center of his life. He could not bear to think about losing her.

"Go, Alex!" Brenna interrupted his thoughts. "Who knows how much time we have? Usually, the first bairn takes a long time, but no one knows for sure."

Alex glanced wistfully at his wife, but he turned around and headed down the stairs. When he reached the great hall, Robbie and Brodie soon joined him there.

"What is the cause of the long face, brother?" asked Brodie.

Alex turned and plopped into his favorite chair. "Maddie's time is here. She is in our chamber having the bairn."

"Time for a celebration, Brodie! Get this man ale," Robbie cried out to a nearby maid.

His brothers then sauntered over to him and slapped him on the back, "Time to be a papa, big brother," Brodie said with a chuckle.

Alex glared at his brothers, then jumped out of the chair and started pacing. "I know my Maddie will be safe; she is a strong lass."

"Absolutely," Robbie said.

"She is the strongest lass I have ever known. She will be fine." Alex turned and paced in the other direction.

"I agree completely, brother," Brodie called out as he downed his ale. Both were in such obvious good spirits, but it did little to dampen his worry. To make matters worse, more people had gathered into the hall.

"Why are all these people here?" Alex scowled at his brothers.

"Word spreads quickly, brother. Everyone has been waiting for your wife to have her bairn. Everyone wants to see if it is a laddie or a lassie."

"Get them out. I do not know all of them. By the saints, how can I hear what is going on in the chamber?" Alex was distraught. "Robbie, go listen outside the door and see if Maddie is safe," he ordered.

"Nay, I think we best stay down here, Alex. Nothing could drag me away from your side right now," Robbie replied.

"Quiet!" Alex yelled out. Dead silence descended. He tried desperately to hear some sounds from his chamber, but all was peaceful. He ran his fingers through his hair, realizing it would be a long night.

Alice and Brenna quickly prepared the bed and helped Madeline into a clean night rail. Though pain rocked her, she bore it quietly.

"'Tis all right, Maddie," Alice said. "Everything is happening as it should be. You will make a great mother for your bairn. It will not be long now."

While Alice continued to coach Madeline, Brenna readied herself for the birth. The cradle was already in place, along with clothes to swaddle the babe in, she had her healing kit in case she needed it. Maddie knew her sister-in-law was a little nervous—she had not yet seen many births—but Alice was experienced enough to help them through it all. Maddie's pains continued without incident, but then they heard the door to the chamber quietly open and close, followed by the sound of a bolt sliding into place.

Madeline's face turned stark white when she recognized their unannounced visitor, and Alice and Brenna twirled in unison.

"Kenneth!" Madeline yelped as she clutched her belly against yet another pain. "We thought you were dead. Why are you here?"

"Leave immediately, Kenneth," Brenna said, her demeanor calm and cold. "You do no' belong here and my brother will kill you when he finds you."

Kenneth reached over and grabbed Brenna by the hair. Yanking her head back, he held a dagger at her throat.

"You will be quiet unless I tell you to speak, or I will kill each of you slowly. Agreed?" he asked. When Brenna nodded her head slowly, Kenneth released her.

Maddie grasped her belly again as another pain shot through her. They were getting worse. She could not think what to do.

Staring at her with disdain, Kenneth said, "You are a disgusting whore, Madeline. Look at you, fat as a pig. I loathe you," he snarled at her. "But I have waited a long time for this moment."

He paced the chamber as he peered at her. His hair was a mess, his clothes were filthy, and his stench was overpowering. What could he possibly want with her now? Maddie willed herself to remain calm for her babe.

He muttered as he paced. "Finally, I will get my revenge on you and yours. I will pay you back for all the pain you and your revolting husband have caused me."

"Kenneth, what have I ever done to you? Why do you want revenge against me?" Madeline asked. She could not believe this was happening now. How had he gotten into the keep? Where was Alex? She had to do something to protect her bairn, but it was a little difficult focusing through her constant pain.

"What have you done to me?" he stopped in front of her to scream at her. "You ruined my life! You and that vile husband of yours ruined everything. You took the only thing I ever cared about away from me."

All three women turned and stared at Kenneth. What was he talking about? Alice shook her head in denial. Maddie was certain he had finally lost his wits.

"Niles! Your husband killed him. He was my best friend. And now, thanks to you, I have lost all my men and my best friend, too. We had so many plans. We were going to conquer the Highlands together. But you ruined all our plans. Now I have nothing. You and the Grant will pay."

Kenneth started pacing again. "Hurry up and push that bairn out so we can be done with this."

Alice peered at Kenneth. "What will you do, my lord?"

"What will I do? Why, of course, I will kill them! I will kill Maddie and her bairn. I will watch them bleed all over the sheets, and then I will call her husband so he can watch them bleed. I want him to watch the life drain out of their eyes just like I had to do with Niles. I want the Grant to know what it feels like to watch someone you care about die in front of your eyes and be powerless to stop it. Then revenge will finally be mine." There was a mad edge to his laughter.

He paced and paced for the next hour. Occasionally, he mumbled about his life. Brenna tried to calm him, even suggested he go for ale, but he refused to listen to anyone, his rambling getting worse.

"Maddie, you are so vile. I don't know why your stupid father liked you so much. He should have liked me better. I am the one who was going to take over his lands. He should have trusted me most. Why did he no' love me more? I deserved it. You don't deserve anything. You were just a stupid lass. But everyone always loved 'dear Maddie' better than me. Och, and that is the best part of it all, Maddie! I am not really related to you. My mother made it all up. She lied to your father just to get me some land. But he was so drunk, he could not even remember what happened." Kenneth shook his head and snorted over it all.

As he laughed and laughed over that revelation, Alice peeked at Maddie and whispered, "I knew it. He is too nasty to be related to you."

Kenneth whipped around to face Alice. "Silence, you stupid cow! Sweet Elizabeth is no longer here to save you from the beatings you deserve, or did you forget that?"

He started pacing again and dragged his fingers through his hair.

Maddie stared at Alice, shocked to have learned that she had suffered so for no reason, that Kenneth had no rights to her father's land. On the other hand, she was relieved to know he was not her family.

"This is taking forever. I cannot wait much longer. But I have waited this long, have I no'? What is a little more time? I have all the time in the world! I need to savor these moments. Take your time, wench!" Kenneth raked his hands through his grizzled hair, tugging on the ends in frustration. "Do you no' see how funny it all is? I am the bastard, but I am the smart one. You are the noble born, but you are so stupid! See how I have finally outsmarted you and the Grant, Maddie? I just had to be patient. Your husband can't see anything right now, he is so worried about you. It was easy to sneak past the men in disguise."

He marched back and forth as he continued to mumble to himself. He was truly mad after all these months alone and in hiding. Maddie tried to think of some way out. Her brain felt like mush.

"You know I had to do it, Maddie. I just could not wait any longer to take control of the clan. My mistake was no' waiting for you. I should have dragged you into that building. But I became so excited, I could not wait. I had to set that fire when I saw both your parents enter that place. The opportunity arrived. I had to take it."

Maddie gasped and stared at Kenneth with wide eyes.

"I could not risk their leaving. My mother told me to hurry up. I kept telling her to 'shut up,' but she would not listen. Nag, nag, nag! That is all she ever did. That is why I had to get rid of her, too. And no one ever suspected me of anything. I got away with three murders!" Kenneth chortled and patted his chest in delight.

"See how smart I am? Three murders! Never got caught. I will get away from here, too. I will escape just like the last time. No one can outsmart me. I am the best."

Brenna whispered, "Kenneth, please allow Alice to let the laird know his wife is doing fine."

"Nay, no one is leaving."

"But I could get ale for you. Are you not hungry? Would you like something to eat?" Alice asked.

"Nay!" he shouted. "Be quiet, all of you. I need to think."

Maddie's pains grew more intense and closer together. Alice and Brenna mopped her brow, worried expressions on both their faces. She wracked her brain, trying to come up with a way to get Kenneth out of the room or summon someone to help, but to no avail. Kenneth denied every request they made. He continued pacing. Every once in a while, Kenneth stopped and stared at Maddie with a smile on his face. At one point, he leaned against the wall and snickered, staring at Maddie's belly.

Finally, Madeline could take no more. She had to protect her bairn somehow. She would not lose this laddie—the bairn and Alex were her whole life. Madeline felt another pain coming, and she instantly knew what she had to do. She roared a blood-curdling scream that could be heard over half the valley.

"Scream all you want, Madeline. Nobody pays any attention to a woman screaming in childbirth." He chuckled.

Alex, Robbie, and Brodie all jumped when they heard Madeline's scream. Alex and Brodie instantly rushed toward the stairs.

Robbie appeared bewildered. "Where are you going? She is having a bairn. All women scream in childbirth."

Brodie looked over his shoulder at Robbie. "No' Madeline, you fool, she never screams."

Alex reached the door first and pushed on it. It was bolted from within.

"Open the door!" he bellowed. There was no response. "Brenna, open this door or I will kick it in!"

Alex and Brodie kicked in the door, and Robbie followed right behind them with several other guardsmen. Alex froze the instant the door fell. There was a dagger at his wee wife's throat. Kenneth. Time stood still for him. He saw the sweat on her brow, the fear in her eyes, and the fine trembling in her fingers. He met her blue eyes and willed her to be strong. He wanted her to know how much he loved her. He tried to tell her with his eyes, but he felt like a failure.

He had failed his wife in more ways than one. How could she ever forgive him? He had promised to protect her from her stepbrother, and now the man had returned to threaten her and their bairn.

Kenneth was a dead man. Alex's focus returned to him and he stared at his enemy. "What do you want, MacDonald?"

"I want to make you pay for what you did, Grant, and my revenge is just moments away. I lost everything because of you. I lost my friend and all my guards. As soon as this whore drops the bairn, I will kill them both while you watch."

Every muscle in his body tensed and fury coursed through his veins. His eyes turned fiercely dark as he stared at his wife. He willed her to give him what he needed. The next moment, Madeline turned her head and let out another blood-curdling scream right into her stepbrother's ear.

Kenneth started for a second, providing Alex with the only opening he needed. Reaching over, he grabbed Kenneth by the shoulders and threw him as hard as he could against the far wall near the window. Kenneth was momentarily stunned, but he quickly stood up. When he did, he saw the three huge Grant brothers all lunging for him simultaneously.

Kenneth turned and jumped out the window.

He screamed all the way down, but then there was only silence. Everyone in the room froze. "Alex, please!" Maddie huffed out, her face red.

Brenna started to shove everyone out the door.

"Robbie, make sure he is dead!" Alex ordered. When Brenna tried to push him out of the room, too, he stood fast. "Nay, Brenna, I stay!" he insisted. "My wife just had a dagger at her throat." Gazing at Maddie, he strode over to the bed and said softly, "I need to tell Maddie that I love her. That I have always loved her." He leaned over the bed and kissed her soundly.

Maddie gaped at her husband and smiled. "I love you, too, Alex. But right now, I have more important things to do. Your son wants out," she ground out through her teeth as she pushed again.

Alex glanced at his sister, then at his wife, and did the unthinkable. He picked up his wife, sat down on the bed, and settled his wife in front of him. He positioned himself so as not to be in the way of the babe. "I am not leaving, and I do not think anyone here can force me out."

"Then help me push, would you please." Maddie shouted as her body heaved again.

Brenna and Alice lifted the sheet and got Maddie in position for the birth. Each time she pushed, Alex could feel the strain on her body. He wished he could assist her. Marveling at the amount of stamina of his wee wife, he whispered his love into her ear whenever she had to push and let her grip his hands.

"One more push, Maddie, I think." Alice cried. "I can see the bairn's head."

With Maddie's next push, the bairn gushed from her body, and she leaned back against her husband in relief. Alex wrapped his arms around her and kissed her cheek as he wiped the sweat from her brow. They both held their breath until they heard the wee one cry.

"You have a son, Alex! He is beautiful, Maddie." Brenna swiped at her tears as she cleaned up the squalling bairn and handed him to his parents.

Tears flowed from Maddie's eyes as she looked at their son. "Oh, Alex, he is so beautiful, isn't he?"

"Aye, he is," the proud father said.

"You do not mind that he is not a lass?" Maddie pleaded.

"Nay, nothing could make me happier than the sight of our wee lad in your arms, my love." He leaned in and kissed them both.

"Oh, Alex, it's starting again! Oh, Alice, I have to push again!" she announced as her body heaved once more.

Brenna shouted, "Twins! Two bairns. Keep pushing, Maddie."

"Two?" Alex couldn't believe what he'd just heard. He glanced at his wee wife as she began to push again. "Another bairn, wife?"

A few minutes later, Alex held their firstborn and Maddie held their second son. "I hope I am done now, Alice," looking at their two boys with eyes full of wonder.

After the afterbirth came out, they sent Alex out with one son in each arm so they could clean the bed and get Maddie washed up. They slipped a fresh night rail on her and allowed her to relax on the bed.

"You did beautifully," Alice said as she kissed Maddie's brow. "How I wish your mother could be here."

"I think my mother *is* here, Alice. I can feel her spirit with me."

Alex beamed with pride as he showed his new sons off to his brothers and Jennie. He let his wee sister hold one bairn with Brodie's guidance.

"I think one looks like you, Alex, and the other looks like Maddie!" Jennie decided. "What are their names?"

"Maddie and I will decide when we get a moment alone. She is quite exhausted right now."

"Amazing," said Robbie. "What a day! I still do not understand it all, but it ended well."

"I will worry about that another day," Alex said. "Today is for my new family."

A little later, Brenna came downstairs and told Alex he could return to his wife. She picked up one bairn, and Alex followed with the other lad, hardly able to take his eyes off his newborn son. He marveled at how he could almost hold the wee babe in one hand. He loved to put his finger in his son's hand so he could squeeze it. *Strong laddie!* Brenna walked in first and gave Maddie their first born. Alex followed with the second bairn. Brenna and Alice took their leave to give the couple some time alone.

Madeline was propped up in bed looking radiant. Alex had never seen his wife look more beautiful. He sat down on the bed next to her and set their other son down between them.

"Maddie, I am so sorry. I did not protect you as I vowed I would." Guilt washed over him as he took his wife's face in his hands and kissed her tenderly.

"Husband, I could not be happier than I am at this moment. You did protect me. It was you who saved me from my evil stepbrother. So many things could have gone wrong, yet here we are with not one, but two healthy lads to love. I would prefer to forget all the bad things that happened today and never mention them again. This day is the day our sons were born and we should rejoice in that."

Alex locked eyes with his wife. "I love you, Maddie. You are the Highlander of my heart. You have the strongest spirit of anyone I know. You were brilliant, love."

Maddie touched her husband's cheek tenderly. "And I will always love you, Alex. You are my heart."

She glanced at the bairns in their arms. "Alex, we have to name our sons. What do you think? We need two names."

"I don't know, love. What do you think? You choose, I cannot."

"What about James after my father, and John after your father?"

"I think that is a splendid idea," he said.

Maddie kissed her husband again, but their firstborn started to fuss. "I think your son is hungry, Alex." She untied her gown and settled her son at her breast. He latched on quickly and was quite happy suckling at his mother's breast.

Alex studied their second son and said, "You will have to learn to share, wee one."

He moved behind his wife again, and after much maneuvering, held his second son to Maddie's other breast.

Maddie giggled, leaned against her husband, and sighed. Life didn't get any better than this.

THE END

ABOUT THE AUTHOR

Keira Montclair is the pen name for an author who lives in Florida with her husband.

Keira loves to hear from her readers. Stop by her website at www.keiramontclair.com to sign up for her newsletter. She also has a Facebook page at Keira Montclair, Author.

See her view of her characters and the settings for this novel at her Pinterest page.
http://www.pinterest.com/KeiraMontclair/

Feel free to contact her at keiramontclair@gmail.com. She promises to respond to all emails.

Made in the USA
Middletown, DE
24 July 2017